Finding Phi

By Abigail Beck

DEDICATION

To my husband, with whom all dreams come true.

ACKNOWLEDGMENTS

The publication of this book may not have come to fruition if it were not for the encouragement of my husband and life partner, Michael. Every moment with you is a blessing. I am so grateful to enjoy the fortune of sharing my life with you.

Many good people helped to make this novel a reality. In particular, I would like to thank Alan Weisman for his kindness in pointing me in the right direction to a great editor and writing coach. I would also like to thank Thom Kephart for enlightening me to the ways of self publishing and my great friend Mark Smith for early draft review and technical suggestions. My long time friend Carl Charpentier graciously lent his aesthetic wizardry to the cover artwork. I will be eternally grateful for his talent and selfless enthusiasm. Last but certainly not least, I would like to thank all of the physicists of the world for helping us understand what makes this world tick and lending us their wisdom and perspective.

Prologue

Beneath phenomena, the world is a seamless whole.

Nick Herbert, *from "Quantum Reality"*

Sarah's constant, quiet observation of the world around her brought into focus the dark-colored sedan following her. It looked out of place—a clean, dark sedan in a town where almost every car still sported studded snow tires from the long winter and a light-colored coating of road salt. A single intersection in Wilmington, Vermont directed cars both in and out of the sleepy historic village. The dark sedan stayed three to four cars behind her as she headed out of town on the two-lane road. Sarah noticed the car again after stopping for gas an hour later once she had descended the mountain.

She slowed down and sped up—the sedan stayed about the same distance behind. The next freeway exit lacked any indication of food or gas. She turned on her blinker and got off of the highway. The crossroad was a minor rural route. The shoulder was large enough that she was able to pull off to the side. She picked up her cell phone, pretending to make a call. She watched the road from the corner of her eye as she leaned over the phone.

A few moments later, the sedan appeared. It coasted slowly past her. The man driving kept his eyes on the road ahead. The sedan continued slowly down the road and Sarah imagined that she saw a pair of eyes quickly look back at her in the rear view mirror. The sedan continued down the road. Sarah made a U-turn to get back onto the freeway.

The timing was cruel. She hoped she was just being paranoid, but a knot began to grow in her stomach. Previously, she had deliberately lived her life without emotional attachment, without someone to miss her if she were to disappear—for this reason. But now everything was different.

"Why now?" She demanded the empty road reflected in the rearview mirror.

Sarah then realized that she must be closer than she had thought to bringing down the corporate giant that her gut told her had tracked her down. But she had also started something far greater. The improbable love that Darin had kindled in her skeptical heart had begun its work on her. She was not the same. The feeling was bigger than even her lifelong obsession with correcting all the wrongs in the world. In a panic-driven moment, she wanted to give up the fight to be with him, to pull over and waive her arms over her head in surrender. But on a lonely stretch of New York highway, she realized that she may not be given the choice.

Sarah caught sight of the dark sedan in the rear view mirror. A hole formed in the pit of her stomach as she made out its familiar shape. It couldn't be too hard to lose the car, but if they knew who she was they must also know where she lived. Her eyes nervously eyed the laptop case sitting in the passenger seat of her car. The information they wanted was on there. She wished she had thought ahead and wiped the laptop clean when she had run her backup before leaving home. But wiping the laptop every time she had to do field work would have been a nuisance throughout the years.

She was in deep. She had not yet made anyone privy to her research—she wasn't ready for this yet. If anything happened to her, all could be lost. She had backed up her files to her external hard drive, as well as a password-locked folder in the cloud. But without her password, the online files would not be accessible. She had written a program to destroy the files if the password was entered incorrectly. There was no safe deposit box at a Swiss bank, whose key location could only be deciphered by the good guys. There was only a simple external hard drive sitting in the bottom drawer of the desk in her home office and data floating about in cyberspace—both easily destroyed. She didn't want to get Darin involved, but the shadow she brought back with her from Wilmington had backed her into a corner.

Sarah gritted her teeth and picked up her cell phone. She chose his name from her recent call log. The line rang a few times and then went to voicemail.

"Dammit." She cursed to an empty car.

"Hello, you have reached Darin Hemming. Please leave a message and I will return your call shortly."

The sound of the voice on the other end caused a wave of emotion that tightened her chest. She had trouble speaking at first as she fumbled over the words that would come at him out of nowhere. Her mind was heavy with the knowledge that could narrowly avert mankind's slow march toward self destruction. Her heart ached as she pulled him, unwitting, onto her path of self-sacrifice.

"Darin, it's Sarah. I really wish you had answered the phone. There's something I need to tell you. It's not that I need to tell you, I just... I need your help. If something were to happen to me, I need you to get my laptop to my boss at the CIA—Greg Walen. Tell him to look at folder 'M10'. Send a copy of that file to Nancy Milcroft of the Organic Consumers Organization. Make sure no one knows that you have sent a copy to Nancy. Even Greg. I also have a hard drive at my house in my desk in case anything happens to my laptop. If anything happens to my hard drive, I keep a copy of that folder in the cloud. Call me as soon as you get this and I will give you the password." Sarah paused and her rapid fire words turned soft. "Darin," she paused again, "I love you."

When Sarah ended the call she was immediately relieved. She had been alone in this fight for over a decade and now there was no going back. She had also been itching to tell him the words that her heart had been murmuring incessantly like some medieval incantation. I love you I love you I love you I love you. She felt her lips forming the words repeatedly, feeling them well up in her as they spilled out into the world. The words were her lifeline. She gripped the steering wheel tighter and wished for more time.

Her eyes were trained on the sedan in the rearview mirror. The glare off the windshield disappeared momentarily as shadows passed over the car and she squinted to make out the features of the person driving the car. When she looked back at the road, she saw the yellow arrows indicative of a hard turn too late. She was going too fast. She hit the brakes. Her rattled nerves caused her foot to slam to the floor. She turned the wheel as the yellow arrows rushed at her too quickly. Her car hit the guardrail—resistance gave way to a sudden drop. Sarah closed her eyes and braced for impact, her fingers clutching the steering wheel.

When the car became airborne she felt her heart reach out toward the mountain that she had just left behind.

Φ

Dr. Stan Cobald thought he could see the woman glancing in her rearview mirror too frequently—that made him nervous. He was no professional private investigator. He cursed himself for not hiring out this part of the work. He knew who she was on paper but he didn't know what kind of a woman she was. If pushed into a corner would the petite former Greenpeace member suddenly grow claws? He wondered to himself.

The woman pulled off on a rural exit. Stan followed, and then noticed her car pulled off to the side of the road. He coasted coolly past her with the sinking feeling that she was on to him. He should have put some kind of tracking device on her car to avoid having to be this close, like they do in the movies. He felt hugely inept at this.

"Why couldn't I have hired someone to do this?" Stan asked himself in the rear view mirror, "I could have found someone I could trust. A professional."

The only flaw in this logic was that any hired private investigator would be used to tracking evidence of the typical variety of crime and intrigue. This espionage required a scientist's eye. It had to be him.

Stan made a U-turn a few minutes after passing the parked car and then returned to the highway. He entered the onramp and continued South, hoping that she hadn't changed course. After speeding up, he caught sight of her familiar tail lights in the distance.

Stan made an effort to stay further behind her but was too nervous about losing her to get completely out of sight. He had been following her for a few days now, since she had left her house in Virginia. He couldn't have known that she would take a trip this long, but when she left her house, he thought she might lead him to a secondary location that housed a lab. His needed to collect as much intelligence as possible on what she was up to. He went about this task as thoroughly and systematically as he approached every other problem in life. Before returning to Cincinnati, he would have to figure out how to get into her house, in case her lab was there. He needed to find the stolen samples, his samples. If those samples were leaked to any kind of government or media organization, Green Future's objective would be jeopardized. The importance of this task cast an equally large shadow of dread in his psyche. This was not his line of work.

He had been rehearsing his story in his head, which grew more elaborate with each moral infraction. He wasn't doing anything illegal. Not yet. That last thought hit him like a wall.

"How far are you willing to go?" he heard his voice ask the empty car.

He shook the question away—he wasn't prepared to answer it yet.

The car in front of him suddenly hit the brakes as it approached an upcoming bend in the road. He could see the angle of the rear brake lights shift as the car slid out of control. He was too far away to hear the squealing of tires on pavement. He saw the car silently disappear off of the cliff as if he were watching a muted television screen. His first thought was that this must be a ruse to shake him off her tail as he watched in disbelief. He pulled his rental car to the side of the road when he arrived at the spot where the guard rail had been effortlessly peeled back. He got out of the car and jogged across the road, his heavy footsteps sounding out of place in the middle of an empty highway.

The car had flipped over while tumbling over the rough terrain. It was laying upside down, with the front end an unrecognizable, tangled mass of metal and plastic. The driver's side window was closest to him as he made his way to the car. The window was closed and a smear of blood obscured his view of the driver. It looked like the front windshield had hit a boulder as the car had tumbled end over end. Stan couldn't bring himself to look at the driver. He crossed in front of the car and went over to the passenger side window, which had been smashed during the accident, lending a clear view of the driver. He saw a woman dangling from the upside-down seat, held in by her seatbelt. The lifeless way her limp, bloody neck was hanging made him look away. She was not conscious.

He thought he was going to be sick.

Stan closed his eyes and turned away from the sight of the woman. He picked up his cell phone to dial 911 and then stopped. His mechanical mind reasoned with him through the panic. What he was looking for might be here—he could hold off for just a moment on alerting the authorities. He looked back at the horrible scene of broken glass and blood. He spotted a black laptop case sitting on the ceiling of the car, below the passenger seat that hung in the air. This scene was horribly wrong, but there it was, delivered to him. Whatever this woman was up to, it was likely housed in that black case sitting simply, incredibly, in plain view.

Stan felt his arms move slowly forward toward the bag without his permission. His body was moving as if ordered by some other power, without the complete consent of his conscience. His hands were shaky, but he managed to pass them through the mess of broken glass and grab the laptop case. He dared not take a second look at the woman. He shook the case free of glass while it was still in the car to avoid creating any evidence that anything had been taken from the vehicle after the crash.

Once the case was free of the car he struggled back up the steep slope, at odds with his out of shape, over-sized limbs. Panting at the top, he looked up and down the highway. He saw no one. He jogged across the road, sweat creating a dark shadow across his back. He opened the trunk of the rental car and quickly unzipped the suitcase inside. He slipped the laptop case inside the suitcase, closed the trunk, and got back in the driver's seat.

He opened his cell phone to dial 911 but stopped abruptly. He had never dialed 911 before. He wasn't sure whether he would be required to state his name and whether or not they would expect him to hang around and answer questions. They would trace his call. He couldn't do that. The sudden realization of who he was, what he was doing there, and what he had taken came crashing down on him. The laptop of an employee of the Central Intelligence Agency. He slowly closed his cell phone and set it on the seat beside him. He gripped the steering wheel with his sweaty palms and then slowly pulled away from the shoulder.

"Dear God, please help that woman," he said through clenched teeth, noticing the sweat pouring down the sides of his face in the rearview mirror. "I can't risk it. I'm sorry."

Stan turned his thoughts back to his purpose as his eyes fell back to the road. This was an accident—an accident that Stan strongly suspected was an act of God. Stan would leave this woman in His hands as well.

"His will manifests itself in mysterious ways that we do not always understand." Stan assured himself as he set the cruise control.

It was an accident. It was an accident. It was an accident.

This was the mantra that accompanied Stan all the way back to Sarah's empty house in Virginia.

Part I

Chapter 1

Wars and revolutions and battles are due simply and solely to the body and its desires. All wars are undertaken for the acquisition of wealth; and the reason why we have to acquire wealth is the body, because we are slaves in its service.

Socrates

Three months before the accident, Sarah's world was measured in quantity and quality.

The hydrological cycle was personal, not diagrams in a textbook, nor the notion of our physical dependence on freshwater for survival—abstract. She could feel pure groundwater in her belly like a satisfying meal, and polluted streams like a cancerous ache running through her veins. Health—and the future—were measured in quantity and quality of potable water.

Sarah was employed by a branch of the CIA tasked with quantifying national resources. Her job was to track potable water within the United States. Her early ambition for the power to make a difference had led her to Washington D.C., where she sniffed out importance and followed ruthlessly. Individuals seek power only to control and sway outcomes; they are on one of two sides: of personal gain, or of the greater good.

A powerless individual can't do much to help anyone. Although Sarah's position in the Agency was as a data collector, it put her into the position of informing those with direct power, and getting to know them personally. She never really felt like CIA, but like an infiltrator accomplishing a larger task.

She was an acutely vigilant detector for individuals in the CIA who were part of the former category, of self-serving power seekers. As a silent infiltrator, she never made her true self known. Instead, she parroted opinions and flew under the radar while keeping to herself.

Her branch evaluated natural resources to predict any shortages. In national security, the two big ones are water and energy, tied together like a fateful couple. Energy is required to clean and convey water—water is necessary to create energy. Fresh water will become scarce long before fossil fuels, due to direct consumption as well as needs tied to the production of electricity. Fossil fuels increase the quality of life, but water supports life itself.

In Sarah's career, she expected to help her country manage the dwindling resource of fresh water. The Great Lakes alone comprise 20% of the earth's fresh water—other countries are not so fortunate. This was why her job had everything to do with national security.

Some things scared Sarah too much to think about, things she feared about herself. She thought about them with the phrase "water wars". When resources dwindled, people fought. When there wasn't enough to go around, every man had to look out for himself. The will to survive was just too strong to resist. When it came down to it, her country would be prepared to defend the resource that kept its citizens alive. It didn't matter whether it was fair that resources were inequitably distributed—they were the way they were, and the haves would fight tooth and nail to keep what they had while the have-nots would fight to take it.

War was fundamentally driven by resources, or their inequitable distribution. Large-scale war had emerged just after the development of large-scale agriculture. Arable land and stores of grain became coveted. With large-scale agriculture, man had the time and resources to create weapons of war. With weapons, one could conquer neighboring areas and appropriate their resources. It didn't matter whether one just wanted enough or more—the result was the same.

Sarah pictured herself defending her land with her pitchfork and wondered whether she would defend her body in the end by taking a life to keep hers a little longer. This was the part of herself that she did not know, and that she feared.

"Aw come on; it's four thirty Friday and you're still working?" A voice trying to be playful cut through her thoughts. It was Charlie, a coworker she thought might be trying to flirt with her but who wasn't even worth officially rejecting. He was an overly-groomed, scented D.C. type who thought the definition of manliness resided in a three-piece suit. She had news for him. From where she'd originated in western Virginia, the young ladies might swoon over a highfalutin fellow like Charlie from the city, but he wouldn't last more than a couple of minutes at the same bar with the men of the back woods. They would send him back to D.C. with his manly pride tucked carefully away in his briefcase.

Typically, guys hit on her because of her startling bright

blue eyes, wide and honest, and her curly blond hair, kept at shoulder length, tucked behind her ears. But she wasn't the stereotype they hoped for. She was nice-looking, but not because she tried to be. She had fine, strong features that were feminine in a very natural way. Her frame was slender and petite but sturdy. If she had wanted to be an athlete she could have been, but had been more interested in intellectual pursuits when choosing her career path.

"I'm preparing for a field visit next week. It's important." Sarah spoke dryly to help him get the clue that she didn't want the conversation to go on any longer.

"Well, a few of us are going out for beers tonight after work if you want to join," he persisted.

She had to keep herself from rolling her eyes. New guys at work were the worst. It took a while to train them that she was not interested. "I don't drink and besides, I have plans."

He got the same look on his face that most people did when she revealed she was a teetotaler. Shock, followed by genuine concern. Was she a recovering alcoholic? An unstable woman who'd end up dancing on the bar? Or a hard-core, to the bone, better-give-up-now-because-there's-no-hope, prude. She wondered if he had enough substance to ask the usual question, "Why don't you drink?"

But he didn't. That would have taken ballsy curiosity, which he didn't have. He just kind of shrank into himself and averted his eyes.

"Oh, okay, that's cool," he said lamely. "Well, have a good

weekend."

She knew she was too hard on people, but she was relieved when he finally gave up and walked away. It was almost five o-clock on a Friday and she'd been at the office since six that morning, so enough was enough. She was prepared for her field investigation next week. She shut down her laptop and packed it into her travel case along with her field notepad and lab gear.

After passing through the layers of security surrounding Agency headquarters she made her way to her car and threw her case down in the passenger seat. Yes, she was grateful she could afford an above-average lifestyle, including a house larger than she needed, with a yard large enough for all the gardening she had time for. Her house was her refuge—she always looked forward to going home. The garden was a constantly evolving mystery. At the beginning of the season she never could guess what would take off, what would rot or get eaten by bugs, and what would overrun the garden and make its way into the freezer to feed her all year long.

Every year was also an experiment in her secret garden.

She chuckled to herself when she realized that she really did, in fact, have a secret garden, one that would get her fired in an instant if her employer was privy to it. Besides organic vegetable gardening, Sarah had a second obsession, which kept her solitary, childless, and completely self-absorbed. Sarah was going to single-handedly produce the scientific evidence that would finally, decisively, bring down the giant company producing genetically engineered crops, the ironically-named Green Future. Her secret garden was the longest-running field trial of Green Future's products in the world. She kept neurotically detailed accounts of weather, fertilizer, bacteria and fungi populations, herbicide and pesticide applications, seed lot numbers, planting dates, insect populations and anything else that might remotely affect what was going on in a small, secluded area of her land.

The test plot was in a perfect position at the top of her remote parcel, located on a small knoll with southern exposure, and far enough away from the fence line that no neighbors could see what she might be doing up there. The test plot was distant enough from her own organic garden, with plenty of physical barriers such as her house, to keep any applied chemicals away from her vegetables.

She began the test plot as a ten-year experiment, planting seeds on one-tenth of the area the first year and filling up an additional one-tenth of the area each year for a decade before the plot was filled. Now, she just kept on planting and spraying the herbicide "Weed Off", Green Future's patented formula, at the recommended application rates. The big news that Weed Off-resistant weeds were appearing in the vast acreages of Green Future monocultures around the world was not news to her. She'd had a hard time keeping tight-lipped about that one. Weeds weren't a deal-breaker. She was holding out until she could prove beyond a shadow of a doubt that the Green Future-based agricultural methods would eventually bring down the food system after wreaking havoc on the environment. Anything short of that wasn't worth the risk of exposing herself and her test plot.

When she had initially joined the CIA as a young scientist, Sarah naively imagined being surrounded by kindred spirits, as she had been at Greenpeace. She left Greenpeace because she realized that the only way to permanently change the world on a large scale was through legislation, not narrow-sighted attacks of individual wrongdoers. Her biggest ally and friend at Greenpeace, Nancy Milcroft, had gone on to cofound the "Organic Consumers Organization". Nancy's mission was to expose the truth behind Green Future's environmental and legal practices, but she didn't have the scientific background that Sarah had to really do damage to the agricultural behemoth. Her journalistic skills could only organize the information produced by others. Sarah and Nancy had kept in touch throughout the years, but Sarah had not told even Nancy what she was up to. It wasn't time yet.

Sarah thought of her job at the CIA as a dance at a masquerade ball. Those she clasped hands with, she knew not what lay behind a colorfully painted visage. Even her boss, Greg Walen, she was not sure about. She recalled the first conversation she had with him when she was talking about modeling the water usage of modern agricultural practices.

"Green Future is already developing drought-resistant crops. By this year in your model, even the increase in land use will be offset by 40% less irrigation of that crop type," Mr. Walen had advised her.

"That's what their marketing literature claims, but we can't actually use that in our model until it is field-proven."

"That won't happen for another decade."

"So why can't we get samples of their drought resistant crops and hire some testing ourselves if we are going to use that assumption? Besides, what if their agricultural products aren't sustainable? If the country goes organic, there is going to be even more land use by that year."

She had unwittingly hit a nerve. Greg Walen's face grew rigid and his voice adopted a tone that Sarah had never heard him use before. "First of all, Ms. Addison, if I find out that you have ordered testing of any of Green Future's products you will find yourself out of not only this job but any other job you wish to pursue in the future. I would also strongly advise you not to pursue the notion that Green Future's agricultural practices are unsound. You have no idea how much bigger this issue is than just water use. My advice to you is to use the water use values that Green Future publishes as well as the reduction targets that they have set for future product development."

Sarah searched his face for a flicker of concern, trying to decipher whether he was saying this as a paternal gesture to protect her, or whether the menacing tone he adopted came from some self-serving goal. She saw nothing; the man was obviously the right man for his job—she couldn't read anything behind his stony visage.

"Are we clear on this, Ms. Addison?"

"Yes sir."

"We are not going to have this conversation again, are we?"

"No sir."

"Good."

After that conversation, Sarah tightened up security around her secret garden. She couldn't let Mr. Walen or anyone know what she was up to until she had found the proof that she needed. After that, even her job didn't matter, but until then, if she lost her job at the CIA she would lose touch with some key information channels as well as a position for enacting change. If her plot were discovered, along with the lack of a written agreement with Green Future to use and test their products, her comfortable life would quickly turn into a downward spiral of attorney fees after losing the position at the CIA that she had worked so hard to attain.

Sarah continued to discretely obtain her annual handful of Green Future seeds from an old family friend in western Virginia who had bought in to the Green Future system. She overpaid for the small amount she requested from him, which kept him from asking too many questions. He probably just figured that she owned so little land that she didn't need much. He was satisfied with her promise to not save seeds from year to year, and her annual purchases reinforced his trust.

Chapter 2

The further the spiritual evolution of mankind advances, the more certain it seems to me that the path to genuine religiosity does not lie through fear of life, and the fear of death, and blind faith, but through striving after rational knowledge.

Albert Einstein

Three months before the accident, Trevor's world took a wide sidetrack into a life of diversion. A brilliant student of chemistry with a minor in mathematics, the tedium of school work at the university and his lack of work ethic left him on the brink of flunking out of the Chemical Engineering department of MIT through sheer lack of challenge and motivation. His focus turned to an online crowd-sourcing protein folding game called "Foldit". Not long after its release to the online community, players collectively helped to decode the crystal structure of the Mason-Pfizer monkey virus retroviral protease, an AIDS-causing monkey virus. They were able to produce a three-dimensional model of the virus in 10 days, a solution which had eluded scientists for fifteen years.

One key to the success of the game was the competitive challenge it posed to the users. Each was ranked according to his or her ability to solve complex three-dimensional puzzles and received points based on the quality of his or her solution. The players worked off of each other's models, thus creating a solution with the dynamics of a group. The myopic solution of each individual was transformed by multiple players, creating a super human computer with problem-solving prowess far beyond typical computing power. With the number of possible solutions to the natural state of a protein, it would require enormous amounts of computational power to do what humans can do naturally, with the innate ability to recognize patterns and perform spatial reasoning.

The small molecule design version of the software was released in 2013 and since that time Trevor rarely left his dorm room. He disheartedly pumped meaning into his life by telling himself that the solutions he was working on could be used to cure cancer and other diseases. He didn't really care about that—it was just something to tell himself to justify his obsession. He prided himself as being the highest ranked player on Foldit, and he had held that position for over six months. That was more important to him than any scientific contribution he may or may not be making, though he couldn't consciously admit this to himself.

Trevor wasn't sure how exactly he had arrived at his present state. Slowly, he supposed, but he didn't really like to reflect on it. The gradual dropping off of each of his friends and his lack of interest in making new ones had helped to create the isolation that a part of him craved and another part of him dreaded. His friends now consisted of an online community of Foldit players, whom he had never met, whom he didn't have any desire to ever meet. The only person he really had to interact with on a daily basis was his eccentric roommate, Scott.

Trevor hoarded his time. While others squandered their time away on each other, he would use his to hone his mind into a tool sharp enough to rival any mind before his. He knew that he was destined to solve something big—he just didn't know what it was yet.

His various intellectual obsessions lasted for different spans of time, depending on how long they would keep Trevor engaged. He was like a detective of concepts and would follow a trail of knowledge until it ended, or until he could build upon it. The mysteries of the world were problems to be solved, some more complex than others, some taking more time than others, some potentially taking a lifetime, or several. The Foldit obsession was currently the longest lasting, but another lingering one that he hadn't yet put down was the obsession with phi.

Trevor never forgot the first time that phi was explained by one of his High School math teachers, Mr. Nerk. It wasn't part of the curriculum, but it was evident by the sparkle in Mr. Nerk's eyes that it was of special interest to him.

"Today we are going to explore something called the 'Golden Ratio', otherwise known as phi. Has anyone heard of this number?"

The class was silent as Mr. Nerk was met with a sea of blank stares.

He continued, "The meaning of this ratio has not yet been completely discovered or understood. What is known is that two quantities are in the golden ratio if the sum of the two quantities to the larger quantity is equal to the ratio of the larger quantity to the smaller one.

"The golden ratio has fascinated intellectuals of diverse interests for at least 2,400 years. It is said that the golden ratio creates aesthetically pleasing proportions and has been used both unconsciously and consciously by artists for thousands of years, even predating the discovery of the ratio itself."

The students looked around at each other, sensing that something was off in their High School algebra class.

Mr. Nerk continued, "The golden ratio can be obtained by starting with nothing and then adding one unit, then adding that unit to the previous value and repeating the sequence, like this:"

Mr. Nerk turned around and wrote the sequence on the chalk board:

0, 1, 1, 2, 3, 5, 8, 13, 21, 34, 55, 89, 144, 233, 377....

"The ratio of one number to the preceding one will converge at the value of phi," he said, "which is:"

Mr. Nerk wrote a string of numbers on the board:

1.6180339887498948482045868634....

"Phi is an irrational number, meaning that the number contains an infinite number of integers. Back in Ancient Greece, the Pythagorean view of the world consisted of discrete, measurable units. The discovery of irrational numbers went directly counter to this view. The discovery of irrational numbers was like a bomb going off in a world in love with peace and order. The square root of two, which was uncovered by the Pythagorean

Theorem, was originally referred to by Plato in Greek as 'arrhetos', or the secret, unmentionable mystery.

"This sequence of numbers," he said, pointing to the series of numbers separated by commas on the blackboard, "represents the so-called 'Fibonacci' sequence seen in nature. The physical manifestation of phi in the natural world is expressed in the arrangement of branches along the stems of plants, the skeletons of animals, the branching of veins and nerves and the shape of galaxies. It underlies the clock cycle of brain waves and is present in human DNA."

Mr. Nerk went on to draw some shapes on the chalkboard and derive the number phi geometrically.

"Who here can tell me why all this is important?"

The students stared at the carefully crafted geometry. Trevor found himself increasingly interested as he soaked in each of the shapes. Trevor looked around the room. The excitement that grew in him threatened to bubble over. Am I the only person who sees where this is heading? He wondered to himself.

Trevor raised his hand. Mr. Nerk's eyes took a few tours of the room before spotting Trevor's raised hand in the back corner.

"Trevor?" Mr. Nerk said with surprise.

Every head in the room turned to look at the weird red-headed kid who had never spoken in class.

"The natural world contains mathematical order," Trevor blurted out awkwardly.

The Newtonian world came alive for Trevor that day. Mathematics was no longer just a set of number puzzles that were fun to solve—the puzzles could provide insight into the workings of life itself.

Trevor explored his fascination with phi throughout High School. To Trevor, the meaning of phi had to do with the existence of life itself. Since he didn't have a belief in any traditional god, his beliefs consisted of mathematical solutions as they exist in the natural world. What kept him coming back to phi was that it had no tangible solution—it propagated itself infinitely. It was found to be the only mathematical configuration that could duplicate itself ad infinitum without variance. To Trevor, it represented growth itself, continued evolution.

Trevor hypothesized that if everything was examined by an appropriate microscope, that the golden ratio would be fundamental to every shape in the universe. It seemed to provide an infinite ratio that, when set in motion in nature, self-perpetuated. He just didn't have any idea why. Most intellectuals throughout history held a very anticlimactic interest in phi, whose significance never revealed itself, and whose usefulness had been limited to architecture and the modeling of financial markets, nothing close to the meaning of life. Like many others before him, Trevor held phi in his back pocket like the photo of an old flame whose allure had never really gone away, but had never really gotten him anywhere, either.

When Trevor got to college, phi took a back seat to the Foldit challenge. Although protein-folding was not likely going to reveal the meaning of life to Trevor, it inspired him. He was learning about how nature organized itself. The point-score system was addictive for his ego, and besides, it was fun. The truth is, Trevor never was good at following rules. The normal course of life for a guy like him was university, then more university, then a position in some laboratory or think-tank where he could put his uncanny problem-solving talent to good use for mankind. The problem was that he didn't like mankind. He also didn't dislike mankind; he just wasn't thrilled about the idea of the human race as it is. So, he preferred to remain in a state of Foldit limbo, where he was not really doing anything wrong, but not really doing what he was supposed to be doing, either.

Trevor didn't come from a family of wealth. His SAT scores were what had earned him a full ride at MIT. He worked as a math tutor to pay his living expenses. His family was still back in a defunct little farming town in Iowa. Fortunately they were too far away to keep tabs on him. His mom would have a heart attack if she knew that he was slowly blowing his ride. He was his family's last hope for a better future, and that kind of pressure didn't sit well with him. The family had slowly sold off their land that had been in the family for generations after his dad got laid off from the factory.

This was after his grandfather had unsuccessfully tried to pass the farming lifestyle on to his son. The ups and downs of the farm, the unending financial struggles, and the droughts that had hit for three seasons in a row had soured his dad to the farm life. A job in a factory had seemed like the only way to raise a family with any kind of security. The lack of capitol and no vision for a farming future kept him from starting the farm back up after he was unemployed, so the land disappeared from the family acre by acre. The vast expanse of what had been corn and wheat was slowly replaced by cookie-cutter tract homes.

Trevor's gray eyes were fixed on the computer screen through his thin-framed glasses. His wavy red hair, long overdue for a trim, lent him a shaggy look in combination with a two-day shadow. A smattering of freckles framed his thin face. His face was one that looked like it belonged on the farm dressed in overalls over a plaid shirt, but the intelligence that shone through his eyes set him apart from the generations of farmers who had come before him. His kind of mind would never have been satisfied sitting on a tractor. He sometimes thought, but not without some guilt, that he had scored a lucky break by the farm going under a generation before him. It saved him being the cause of his parent's heartache.

It was time. He couldn't procrastinate any longer. If he didn't pull himself away from his computer now, he would be late for his tutoring appointment. A meat head Civil Engineering student at Northeastern was struggling with Statics. He didn't have the heart to tell this guy that he was destined to flunk out once he reached Calculus so he shouldn't even bother, but Trevor was perfectly happy to collect a paycheck before that happened so he kept his mouth shut.

Trevor reluctantly got up from his desk and threw on his backpack. His tall, lanky frame made every movement seem slightly awkward. He quickly left his dorm room and took the steps two at a time down to the bike rack. He unlocked his bike and stood on one pedal as he pushed off with the other foot, throwing his leg over the bike at the last minute. He dodged students as he made his way off campus toward the Harvard Bridge that would take him across the Charles River toward Boston.

Chapter 3

All the variety, all the charm, all the beauty of life is made up of light and shadow.

Leo Tolstoy, from "Anna Karenina"

Three months before the accident, Loren stood in a near empty hall with a guard posted stiffly in the corner. Tears welled up in her dark brown eyes and she was careful not to let them slip away from her, revealing herself to the ambivalent stranger in a uniform. She was standing in front of a painting by Rousseau, in front of a world that had existed over 100 years before she was born. She was standing in front of the soul of a man now dead, looking at a part of the world that was likely now paved over.

In the gilded-framed painting, the sunlight was filtered through slightly ominous clouds, gracing the meadow below with silver-flecked puddles. A collection of cows stood silent as monks. They were composed of no more than sienna brown brush strokes, but she could feel the warmth of their fur through a coating of recent rain. Her heart glowed in response to beauty expressed so perfectly. The delicate tree leaves backlit by the few glints of blinding sunlight proved to be tentative brush strokes on close inspection, quivering as if on the verge of being taken by a slight breeze. She blinked hard, becoming aware that she was actually standing in a hallway, looking at nothing but a fading collection of oil and pigment. How this object had the power to transport her, imparting a feeling like the Buddha must have felt under the Bodhi tree, she had no idea.

Paintings like these were part of the reason she gave up on painting years ago. She spent her 23rd birthday in a sequence of three rooms at the Louvre full of Corot paintings. Everything that her soul had been yearning to say was already sitting here in the basement of this enormous concrete and marble complex. One or two stragglers hurried through the rooms on their way to more popular aesthetic marvels. The crowds were four or five rows deep at the Mona Lisa, but here was Corot down here on his lonesome, the lesser-known father of the impressionist movement who can't be found in a single compilation of impressionist painters. He was the first plein-air painter, before the phrase was coined. His was a love so profound of the natural environment that his paintings spoke more to her on environmental preservation than any green movement or environmental policy. This was what she wanted to do—to make love to the trees, the sky, the soil, the wind, to stay so long in a place that you still smell the pollen and the musty leaves after you have brought your canvas home, to feel the placement of shadows behind your eyelids so tangibly that you can continue painting from memory for days, to disappear into something pure. The painting was merely a remnant of the experience.

Painting was what she wanted to do with her life, but the inadequacy of her statement when so much greater a voice had said the same thing, and failed, left her deflated. Landscape paintings weren't popular anymore. Loren had learned in art school that one had to say something outlandish and clever with art, or even better, political, but as far as she was concerned, real art addressed the eternal struggle of the human soul, not modern politics, whatever they happen to be at the moment.

Then there was the whole commercial aspect of modern art. People bought paintings to match the color of their sofa. It was all too heart-breaking. If she was going to sell her time, it wasn't going to be painting—it just didn't feel right. Instead, she joined the bulk of art school graduates in a career of minimum wage jobs, mostly in the food industry. She eventually found herself living in a suburb of Boston, working in a food processing facility. She would sometimes visit the Museum of Fine Arts or the Gardner Museum when she wasn't working. Although there were only a few paintings of these collections that truly moved her, she never tired of them. The modern artists of Boston didn't interest her, even the more traditional ones. She found them either too technical and not passionate enough, or too passionate and not technical enough. They were out of balance; how could they not be? The world was out of balance.

The slick look of oil paint squeezed out of tubes, bulked up with filler, gave all modern oil paintings a look of cheapness. Something had disappeared from the world of painting— something that the cell phone and the television destroyed. It was impossible to get back the monastic life of the nineteenth century landscape painter. Life had a different pace back then. Life was palpable, discernible to the true seeker. In modern times, life had a sleek coating on it enforced by modern distractions.

Loren felt that she was somehow born at the wrong place and time. She knew that with practice and application, along with isolation, she could be a modern day Corot, but to what end? She couldn't find it in herself to drive at that goal relentlessly like Van Gogh did with his singular vision. She couldn't go so forcefully against the grain of the judgment that modern life shackled her with. She didn't want to waste her life, and yet, by not having the courage to let her vision carry her she was, in essence, wasting her life along with her singular talent.

There was a soothing monotony to the food processing plant. There was the hum of the machines, the textures and smells of the food product, the automated system geared for massive amounts of perfectly packaged fake-food product. She culled the line for defects, found a rhythm with the pace of the conveyor belts, and spent the whole day with nothing other than the quest for a perfectly packaged, unblemished product.

Those were the good days. On the bad days, the rhythmic, metallic thumping of machine parts was cacophony that was too relentless for her to get in sync with. She grew apathetic to perfection and even fantasized about smashing every one of the perfectly packaged products as they were wheeled away to fat kids. But she didn't because those stupid little packages paid the bills. She had a simple life and not many material demands. A modest, steady paycheck kept her body alive. But every year she let the sterile monotony of the days lull her artistic passions to sleep.

Whenever she felt down, she went to the museum to remind herself how much was possible from an evolved human soul. She wanted to remind herself that there were people who could deeply appreciate the beauty and goodness that this earth provided. She wanted to revel in the depth of skill attained through years of quiet movement and pure love of nature and craft.

There weren't that many places in the world that she could visit that were as perfect as the Rousseau at the Museum of Fine Arts. That was the world she wanted to be in, even if only on her days off. The Boston Commons didn't cut it. There was a pond she sometimes walked to near the room that she rented in a house in the suburbs, but she couldn't go anywhere without feeling the heavy hand of man on it. State parks had posted signs demanding fees, public parks were overrun with kids and dogs, and everywhere in between had a fence around it.

After the Rousseau, Loren didn't feel like visiting the rest of the museum. She decided to walk around in the Fens before catching the T back to the suburbs. She descended the steps of the Museum of Fine Arts and turned left, but then rather than turning left again toward the Fens, she kept walking. She changed her mind about going to the Fens suddenly. She was on Huntington Avenue, a main artery leading toward downtown. Cars sped brazenly by the crowds getting on and off the T. She headed toward downtown, then took a left toward the river after passing Northeastern University. She decided that what she needed was a view—a view consisting of mostly water and sky. It was at least apparently clean— a place where she could erase the people in her mind and be momentarily in the infinite expanse of a landscape.

Chapter 4

He who is not contented with what he has, would not be contented with what he would like to have.

Socrates

Three months before the accident, Dr. Stan Cobald was a proud man. The things about himself that he might not be so proud of he never allowed himself to think about. He had a reason to be proud. He was the Director of Bioengineering of a company that needed no introduction.

"Good Morning, Dr. Cobald." Stan's secretary Nancy called out as he entered the pristine lobby.

"Good Morning, Nancy." He replied as he had nearly every working day for the past twenty five years.

Nancy stood up and handed Stan a neat pile of papers as he approached her desk. "That report you've been expecting came over from the development team."

Stan's eyes lighted up as he took the stack of papers from Nancy. "Great! Thank you."

The top sheet of the report contained the words: "CONFIDENTIAL: THIS DOCUMENT AND THE INFORMATION IN IT ARE PROVIDED FOR THE SOLE USE OF GREEN FUTURE, INC.". Stan briskly tucked the stack of papers under one arm as he navigated deeper into the impressive structure that was the Green Future biotechnology building and his home away from home.

The towering corridor led him through a series of offices, laboratories, and climate-controlled greenhouses. He chose to place his office at the back of the building so that he could survey the goings-on of every team in the building at the beginning and the end of each day. The building was alive with busy white coats measuring, titrating, recording and poring over data at computer consoles.

Green Future had revolutionized agricultural methods. Just as technology had improved the lives of humans in nearly every other aspect of the modern day, Green Future had applied these same principals of engineering and efficiency to agriculture. In terms of market share of world-wide seed supply, Green Future was the undisputed leader. This hadn't happened by accident. The undeniable efficacy of herbicide-resistant crops coupled with the use of Green Future's crop-compatible herbicide "Weed Off" had increased food production for every farmer that had bought into the system, increasing overall farming income despite the higher cost of seed and herbicide.

Being Stan was a whole lot like being God. By manipulating the protein structure of a plant's DNA, he could actually give birth to a whole new set of plant traits, which might have taken thousands of years to evolve on their own if they had evolved at all. The evolution Green Future crafted was focused on serving the agricultural needs of man. Stan was leading teams of engineers to design crops expressly for the purpose of making farming easier and more productive. Green Future's goal was to answer the problem of dwindling resources and a growing population with more efficient farming methods. This Herculean task thrilled him.

Stan felt that he had the best of both worlds—a challenging and interesting career coupled with an absurd amount of compensation for doing it. Green Future's leaders had an unrivaled business sense. Every day, the company spent over $3 million on research and development. Through a shrewd process of patents and patent enforcement, Green Future had managed to protect the intellectual property it had spent a quarter of a century building.

The company's success was bittersweet. There was a large resistance to the idea of genetically modified crops. The popular imagination for the potential harm in consuming genetically modified crops knew no bounds.

New technology has always been met with fear and suspicion. Early inventions were seen as sorcery, and their inventors burned as witches. The technologies invented by the research and development team at Green Future did not have an impeccable track record. The chemicals they had invented had performed their intended purposes, from pesticides to herbicides to industrial chemicals and preservatives. The subsequent surface and groundwater contamination, cases of cancer, and decimated aquatic ecosystems couldn't have been foreseen. At the time of the development of those chemicals, the testing mandates simply were not in place. There was a demand for the technologies, and Green Future provided.

The complete consequences and side effects of a new

technology can never be known at the beginning. Green Future was boldly forging ahead with the conviction that improved farming methods were not only going to improve human life on the planet, but also make every principal of Green Future very rich in the process. In Stan's mind, there was no more brilliant business model than applying technology to agricultural methods, which directly benefitted all of mankind and at the same time made all of mankind dependent on the technology.

The original agricultural technologies were born in the Fertile Crescent, the cradle of civilization. Without the food surplus, the human race would never have been able to develop the arts and the sciences. The provision of an abundance of food, which was easier and faster than hunting and gathering, gave humans the time needed to develop culture, societies and civilization including canals, roads, sanitary sewer systems, large buildings and government. Without agricultural technologies, humans would still be hunting and gathering, scraping up a meager existence within the confines of the daylight hours.

A business model that supported more agricultural production with less work not only enriched food-poor areas of the world, but also promoted further technological developments in other areas of the world. Western society could spend more time on advancements in other areas as the labor and resources required for creating basic sustenance were reduced—the cure for cancer, outer space travel, a perpetual energy machine. Green Future was fueling the minds of every next great inventor and thinker.

Opponents of Green Future had vilified the term

"genetically engineered", but plants could be engineered to be identical to a plant that has been modified by selective breeding. Selective breeding was in fact considered genetic engineering by some scientific communities. Direct manipulation of the genetic code was a more efficient means than selective breeding to obtain beneficial traits, but to say that it was unnatural was not correct. Nature could be considered the greatest engineer, refining plants and animals through evolution. *What was the difference between the products of natural selection and artificial selection if both processes resulted in the same end product?* Stan smiled to himself at the irony.

Considering himself a man of both God and science, Stan had no problem with accepting both the theory of evolution and the existence of a creator. The belief in God and His forgiveness and the church system of right and wrong with a clearly-defined way of life kept his conscience clear. He didn't have to think about the meaning of life or how he should be living because the path was already spelled out. Ever since he was young, the word of the Lord and the word of his father were set in stone and there was no getting around either of them. Stan kept his nose to the grindstone, making his grades in school, going to the best university, never missing a Sunday at church, and ultimately landing a dream job. His life really couldn't have gone better, and he attributed his success with never straying from the word of God.

Stan had met his wife at church. They didn't wait long to tie the knot and three perfect children arrived soon after, one after the other. His family never had the misfortune of needing a second income, so they were blessed with the same lifestyle that he had grown up with—matriarch at home and patriarch working hard to provide.

The public opposition to Green Future personally incensed him, as a man of God and as a man of science and human progress. The environmentalists naively protested what they did not fully understand, but they had been completely unsuccessful in the United States in stopping Green Future's undeniably effective products. Green Future's farming innovations had been so successful that their genetically engineered staple crops made up more than 90 percent of what lay on U.S. soil. If Green Future's customers were unsatisfied, it would not be the multibillion dollar, global leader that it was. Green Future controlled the genetics of nearly 80% of five major commodity crops. Making farmers more efficient put more money in their pockets so that they could send their kids to college instead of living the hand to mouth existence so typical of family farms.

The world's population was estimated to grow to over 9 billion by 2050. Farmers would need 300 million acres of additional farmland brought into crop production by 2030, an area equal to the current cropland area of the United States and China combined. The goal of Green Future was to double yields in the core crops by 2030, while achieving this with one-third fewer resources such as land, water and energy. Allowing the population to expand without making agriculture more efficient was certain to result in food shortages, more forest land burned and converted to agricultural land, and most importantly water shortages. One key target that Stan's group was focusing on was a drought-resistant gene in the core crops. These crops would have significantly less watering requirements, and in many regions would not require irrigation at all. With agricultural water consuming approximately 70% of all freshwater resources, typical irrigation requirements would create water scarcity in many areas of the world with the increase in food demand by the growing population.

Stan believed he was doing God's work, and he enjoyed the engineering challenges and scientific breakthroughs that he lived with day in and day out.

"Dr. Cobald." A voice from the doorway of a laboratory broke Stan's train of thought. One of the newer staff engineers, a recent graduate in her mid twenties, looked up at Stan with obvious professional admiration.

Stan's thick frame hovering at 6'6" dwarfed the slight frame of the young engineer. He was in his early 50's and already mostly bald, with gray hair that used to be a glossy chestnut brown, matching his eyes. He had never considered himself an attractive man, but decent enough with plain features that would never attract notice in a crowd. He was overweight, like most men his age, but he was gratefully able to ignore that fact by comparing himself to the grossly obese. The contrast between Stan's aging bulk and the young, wiry engineer disappeared as soon as they started to talk shop.

"I'm working on the genetic sequencing for GF-6840. The trials keep failing on me overnight. I need to monitor them after hours until I figure out what's going on. I know I'm fairly new here, but I need to get 24-hour access to do this. Dr. Gerard said that all requests need to go directly through you before I submit the paperwork, so..." The young engineer's voice trailed off as she looked at Stan expectantly.

Stan scrutinized the young, earnest-looking young woman. The security measures getting in and out of Green Future had to be on par with the CIA headquarters. This was necessary to protect intellectual property and also to avoid saboteurs. In addition to video monitoring triggered by motion detectors and a state-of-the art alarm system, there was a guard on the premises around the clock. Key personnel had 24-hour access codes, since most files could not be taken off of the Green Future premises and lab trials often required monitoring at odd hours. Employees signed confidentiality agreements in exchange for persuasive salaries.

It was unusual for new employees to gain permission for 24-hour access, but the drudgery of monitoring new genetic sequencing specimens was not typically in the job description of higher level personnel.

"Go ahead and submit the paperwork, but I need a referral from Dr. Gerard. Have him call me."

"Okay—thank you for your time Dr. Cobald."

"Not a problem."

Stan gave the young engineer a weak but polite smile before continuing down the hall. The mandatory background check would have to be run, but even so he doubted he would grant the permission. He would likely ask Dr. Gerard to assign this work to one of his higher level staff. Young folks were not to be trusted. They were full of ideals and not yet dependent on the monetary security of a healthy salary.

Chapter 5

In wildness is the preservation of the world.

Henry David Thoreau

When Sarah arrived home from work she headed to the back corner of her property with her laptop. She opened the gate in the chain link fencing that separated a large meadow behind her house from the back corner of the lot. The chain link fence was overgrown with thick wisteria, entwined throughout the steel chain links. The wisteria created an impenetrable visual barrier from any part of the front of her property that was accessible from the road. She figured a concrete wall might attract too much curiosity but folks don't tend to notice a wall of green within the landscape of her small piece of land, which she kept intentionally overgrown.

She jotted down data from the wireless weather station, made some notes on how the plot was looking, and grabbed a soil sample to bring back to the house with her. The border of barren soil around the test plot was oddly vacant of weeds due to the applications of herbicide that she regularly applied per Green Future's recommendation. She tucked the soil sample into her pocket as she made her way back through the chain link fence.

The light brownish gray stems of the wisteria growing up from the fence had just barely started their new spring growth. A few weeks ago they could have passed for a completely dead tangle of branches. The thin arms of the delicate wisteria shoots shook in the wind and she looked up at the clouds. A storm might be brewing. It was early spring and the summer thunderstorms that trampled through the region could come as early as this time of year. She realized with a pang that she missed them, and yearned for how they could suddenly seize the sky with a low rumble and command every soul underneath to run for cover.

She crossed the yard feeling the accelerating wind across her face and silently urging it on. She accessed the basement from an outdoor hatch and reluctantly closed it behind her to seal herself off from the fresh air. She had a rudimentary lab in her basement where she could measure biotic and abiotic indicators in the soil samples. She could estimate the ratio of bacterial to fungal populations, which could determine an unhealthy imbalance in the soil.

She set the soil sample down on her workbench. A faded newspaper article pinned to a corkboard read "Indian River Lagoon mystery ailment killing dolphins, manatees, pelicans". She kept articles like this one in eyesight at all times, to reminder herself why she chose to spend all of those long hours in her basement. The "mystery" ailment wasn't a mystery to her at all. The deaths were at the end of a long chain reaction that started with fertilizer runoff and led to algal blooms, resulting in massive oxygen depletion, ending in fish kills. They couldn't pin down the exact cause because it is systemic. The whole system is sick—out of balance—the same kind of imbalance that Sarah measured in her soil samples year after year.

She booted up her laptop and clicked on a folder called

"M10". She opened up an excel spreadsheet and put in the new entries, populating a single row after thousands of rows of data entered previously. The spreadsheet was an input file for modeling software that she had "borrowed" from her workplace. Technically it wasn't piracy—she just used the software during extended business hours for a task that wasn't specifically outlined by her job description. She used the software for her job in the CIA to model the hydrological cycle, point and non-point pollution migration, and the effect of climate change on water resources. It was a powerful program, which could be modified by the user to account for reactions occurring simultaneously along with the default time-based reactions.

She had created a model within the software program that she had been building upon for over ten years, since the inception of her test plot. Actual data collected from the test plot was used to calibrate the model. When she could get the model to mirror what she was actually seeing in her backyard test plot, she would have the means of extrapolating the effect of Green Future's agricultural practices into the future. It would still just be a guess based on a computer model, but it would be the most accurate guess anyone had made so far. It was an enormous amount of data collection over the years, but she had done it bit by bit, day by day. An experiment like this couldn't be rushed—it might take twenty years to gather enough data to make sure that the model was accurate, but this twenty-year task could save humanity from a mistake that might take fifty years to discover, after it was already too late.

She was compelled to collect this research by a force that she felt was bigger than her. She knew what the outcome would be—she just didn't know what the specific mechanism would be that would bring it about, and she needed more than her gut feeling to go public with. She was already able to measure an imbalance in her test plot soil at year two. Year after year, the imbalance in the soil was allowing new species to flourish, which had never had a niche before. She noted that when she allowed the test plot areas to lay fallow for a couple of years that they were able to come back into balance. The longer Green Future's system had been used on the land, the longer it took to come back into balance, but at some point she guessed there would be a tipping point. Once the imbalance reached a tipping point, it would be too far gone to come back. The Indian River Lagoon had reached its tipping point. The diversity of the ecosystem had become so impaired that the system could not regain its balance.

Balance was a kind of obsession for Sarah. When she had graduated from high school, back when she still had a family, her mom treated her to a vacation anywhere of her choosing. She chose to go on a safari in South Africa.

The bush of South Africa was in complete, dynamic balance where it escaped the touch of man. Removing just one component or adding one component had immediate, observable effects. She recalled a story that the park ranger had told of one of the many private game reserves outside of the national park system. These were relatively small tracts of land where large game were kept by private owners, usually as a tourist attraction or for controlled hunting. One private game reserve owner had purchased a leopard and added it to his "collection". He immediately noticed that his antelope population was dwindling too rapidly and he at first wondered if poachers had gained access to his land. He started patrolling the fence line every day at all waking hours. He knew that he had more than enough land and prey to support a leopard and that the population decrease he was observing was disproportionate for one leopard.

One day he happened to be at the corner of his property. It was after dark—killing time for the leopard. He heard the scatter of antelope through the brush and the cry of a baby antelope. He directed his jeep toward the sounds and quickly spotted the leopard. The leopard was using the corner of the fence line to trap a whole family of antelope. In this way, he could make multiple kills at once, since the poor souls had fewer escape routes. The game reserve owner realized then that either the fence or the leopard would have to go. This man-made boundary had shifted the favor to the leopard just enough to make him too effective at hunting, thus upsetting the balance that the land had spent ages evolving.

After entering the day's data, Sarah updated the data set for the model and hit "RUN". It would take about five minutes to complete the computations for a ten-year cycle, which she always used to check the model's output with the data that she had collected two years ago when the oldest part of the test plot was ten years old. She glanced at the corkboard behind her work bench and her eyes wandered across the dozens of articles collected throughout the years—layers upon layers of bad news.

A glassy-eyed frog stared at her from the corner of the board with the headline: "Study: Amphibians in U.S. disappearing at alarming rate". It was no longer a question of disappearance, but how fast they were going. The bat article was old news and had been covered up by some other layer of distress, but she couldn't get the image of a pile of dead bat carcasses out of her mind. The food source of amphibians and bats was bugs. It couldn't be a coincidence that the more widespread the use of pesticide became, the more frequent colony collapse disorder among the bees and mysterious ailments in animals that fed on bugs.

When the focus of the media had turned to the application of pesticides as the cause for declining bee populations, Green Future acquired an organization called "Society for the Investigation of CCD", which had been dedicated to restoring the health of the bee population. It disheartened her to think that most people, even good ones doing good work, had a price tag. Not her.

It wasn't just pesticide application, but some of the crops that Green Future engineered contained some kind of protein that killed bugs when it was ingested by them. Green Future supposedly went through rigorous studies, including feeding the pollen of their crop-generated pesticides to bees and supposedly the bees remained unharmed, but Sarah was a skeptic when it came to scientific studies. *How long were they fed for? What it their sole source of nutrition? How long were the bees monitored for? Who funded the study?* These were the thoughts that fed her skepticism.

She recalled a moment in grad school where she had realized that there were so many factors that could mold scientific conclusions that you could come to any conclusion that you wanted to by manipulating those factors. As a student, she thought she wanted to be a researcher, but changed her mind once she realized how impotent that role would be. She wanted to be closer to the people that made the decisions. Besides, she had a fight in her that didn't belong in a passive researcher. At the time she didn't know what it was, but she felt in her gut that it lay in Washington D.C.

Between her work for the CIA and her vigilante occupation at home, Sarah had this abstract equation she was trying to solve. She was trying solve the set of equations that would yield the solution to a question that burned inside her in the form of a number. She called it the balance number—the number of humans who could sustainably live on the planet. There were many dynamic factors in this equation such as lifestyle, but population values could be generated for each type of lifestyle in various places on the planet with their unique available resources to arrive at the balance number. It would be a tool that could be used to inform controlled population growth. Just the concept of controlled population growth hearkened on Nazis and Communist China—this was the conversation that no one was willing to have. In Sarah's mind, it was the one that mattered most.

She was already doing the major work for this equation for her job with the CIA, but the work for the CIA was centered on water resources. She wanted to know—she felt she had to know—what the limiting resource would be for human life on earth. This would ultimately determine the balance number, so she considered other parameters when she wasn't on the clock. Her test plot project centered on the most widespread agricultural practices—those of Green Future. She didn't know whether or not she could finish it before her lifetime was over, but she felt that this was the major factor in sustainability. Politicians were always sweating over fossil fuels, but she knew from only cursory research that fresh water would become scarce far sooner than fossil fuels. If the human population managed to burn through all the fossil fuel resources on earth, the environment would be so degraded by that time that the viability of human life would have already ceased.

"Click Here to view Output File" appeared on the screen suddenly, snapping her out of her thoughts. She clicked on the box and a spreadsheet opened. She scanned through the cells of data.

"Damn," she spat aloud.

She didn't know what was wrong with the model. It wasn't the input—she knew she had researched every documented parameter that could affect the model output and she believed she had chosen reasonable reaction coefficients. She had even done a sensitivity analysis by varying the coefficients. The problem could be the equations in the model itself, but modifying those equations was mathematically a bit over her head. She felt like she was hitting a wall, one that she had been hitting over and over for the past few years as the model refused to yield the output she was seeing in the test plot. She felt like she had looked at everything and the faint panic of helplessness flitted in her chest. She needed a new angle, and she would keep at it until that angle revealed itself to her, but it wasn't going to happen tonight. The day had been long enough. She turned off her computer and closed the laptop with the disgust of one giving up for the day.

Sarah took the stairs leading from the basement to the first floor of the house. The sun had set completely while she was in the basement and the house was dark and silent. She knew she may seem odd to others for living so alone—it wasn't natural. She had thought about getting a dog for companionship, but there was no one to care for the dog when Sarah had to do field work. She preferred to be as self-reliant as possible and couldn't picture herself allowing a caretaker into her world for a dog. Between her job, her test plot, and her organic garden she really didn't have time to get lonely. When she did get lonely, she read. The company of dead old white guys like Tolstoy and Thoreau was much better than the people she met in this day and age. Those guys spoke directly to her soul. That was what she needed to not feel alone— not the chatter of small talk.

She noticed that it was long past dinner time as she turned the lights on in the kitchen and her stomach grumbled. This was probably why she never had a problem with weight gain—she simply forgot to eat a lot of the time. It was early spring so most of her current food stores had been frozen since the harvest last fall. Her spring crop of spinach, which had spent the winter in a covered row, was currently picked over so she needed to give it a few more days before thinning gain. The broccoli in her greenhouse was just starting to get to picking size and she noticed a few days ago that it was almost ready to start harvesting.

She grabbed a flashlight and headed out to the garden with a buck knife and a basket. She set down her implements to unlock the fencing she had up to protect against the deer and other garden raiders. Once inside, she headed to the greenhouse. The rows of broccoli were planted in the ground perpendicular to a center walkway. The broccoli heads were no larger than about two inches across. She hadn't discovered the secret to organic broccoli growth yet. She held her flashlight in her teeth as she sliced off the heads, one by one, and made her way down the rows.

She knew she could temporarily increase yields by using petroleum-based fertilizers, but she refused. She obstinately hauled compost and concocted mixtures of blood meal and greensand year after year, working the soil by hand and watching for its needs. Her goal was the long-term health of the soil, not gigantic broccoli heads. Her system meant more rows of broccoli and thus more sweat labor. Sweat labor seemed the appropriate price to pay for the dark green abundance laid out before her.

Work in the garden wasn't work at all to her—every moment was pure enjoyment. The garden changed every day—it was an ecosystem in itself. She shared her spoils with the insects reluctantly, and silently rejoiced when those same visitors disappeared with the arrival of the ladybugs. She weeded everything by hand, transferring the weed mass to her giant compost pile. It gave her satisfaction to observe, year after year, the soil becoming darker and fluffier as its health and fertility slowly improved from the sandy silt it started out as when she had initially bought the property, a 3-acre lot surrounded by typical D.C. suburbia. She had turned her piece of suburbia into a wild oasis, much to the dismay of her lawn-flanked neighbors. She placated them by planting deep rows of trees and thick shrubs as a visual barrier around her entire lot.

Sarah believed in the system of organic gardening as if it

were her religion, not just because of the science or the philosophy, but because of a feeling that she could never quite articulate. The closest she could come to that feeling in words was "internal compass". It was something inside her that guided her, and when she followed that feeling life just worked. When she let her machinations get the better of her actions and tried to direct her life out of worry, selfishness, short-sightedness or second guessing, everything became difficult. Organic gardening felt right to her just as sitting in the sun or drinking a tall glass of cool water felt right—just as kindness to a stranger felt right. She couldn't live any other way once she started on this path.

When she had completed walking along her rows of broccoli and her basket was half-full of modest green heads she headed back to the house, closing up the greenhouse frame and securing the garden gate behind her. For dinner she added the fresh broccoli to her usual staple of bean stew, originating from the beans and onions she had stored from last fall's harvest. She cooked a large pot of beans on the weekends so that cooking during the week consisted only of heating up a scoop from the large pot she kept in the fridge to accommodate her long days of work. It had taken a few years, but she had finally perfected growing for all of her nutritional needs on about an acre of land, including the garden, greenhouse, berry bushes and fruit and nut trees.

She recalled the new guy at work trying to get her to go out and have beers in the city as she sat in her modest kitchen at a small oak table with the bowl of stew in front of her. He was clearly trying to hit on her and it tickled her how far off he had been about her, thrown off by her wavy blond hair and professional attire. She imagined what he would look like at the table across from her, eating bean stew every night. She laughed out loud and the cackle filled the otherwise silent kitchen as she stirred fresh broccoli into the week-old bean mush.

Chapter 6

The most beautiful thing we can experience is the mysterious. It is the source of all true art and all science. He to whom this emotion is a stranger, who can no longer pause to wonder and stand rapt in awe, is as good as dead; his eyes are closed.

Albert Einstein

Trevor's tutoring session had been predictable. The Northeastern student had a problem visualizing how a force acted on a structure and the equal and opposite reaction force was given back by the structure. If the student didn't completely give up, Trevor was sure he could get him into the passing grade range by spring break. Trevor needed to keep him from giving up for as long as possible so that he could prolong this tutoring gig.

When he had wrapped up the session, he left the Northeastern campus and then turned left onto Massachusetts Avenue to cross the Charles River back to MIT. He was in no rush to get back to campus. He slowed his bike and coasted onto the sidewalk before crossing the bridge.

He was walking his bike across the Harvard Bridge when he noticed something awry. She was a tiny thing—her limbs were so delicate she looked almost insect-like. She leaned on the hand railing and looked out toward the Atlantic, which lay just beyond the Boston skyline. There was something otherworldly about her, like she didn't belong there. Maybe it was her old-fashioned way of dress or her serious expression, as if her thoughts were trained on the world beneath this world. He slowed to a stop without even realizing it, as if in a trance, one hand lightly holding up his bicycle and the other hanging limply at his side.

The young woman looked over her shoulder directly at him so quickly that it made him jump.

Trevor suddenly realized that he was staring at her and immediately became self-conscious. She must have felt his eyes on the back of her head and here he was gaping at her like some kind of creep. He quickly looked away from that intense stare and commanded his feet to regain their forward motion. He averted his gaze from her as he continued walking past her. He avoided looking back, but then couldn't resist the temptation once he was a few hundred feet past where he had seen her. A group of students was walking toward him and he could see the back of the girl walking away from him through the figures clad in backpacks and sneakers. He bobbed his head around to keep his eye on her, but the closer the group got, the less he could see of her. She had walked away briskly, toward the side of the bridge he had just come from. He had probably scared her. His heart suddenly felt seized by a strange ache. The girl had seemed sad—lost. He felt like he had recognized something familiar in her.

He turned back around and hopped on his bike, cranking down on the pedals. He was deeply disturbed, but not sure why. He sped back to his dorm room, narrowly avoiding pedestrians along the way. He couldn't get her eyes out of his head. They were such a dark brown that they looked almost black. Her light brown hair was long but pulled back into a bun that seemed too large for her tiny face. In retrospect, she was extremely plain-looking so he didn't know why she had made such an impression on him. She wore solid, dark hues and a long skirt. It was her face—no—the look in her eyes. There was no falsity, no flinch, in fact, no reaction to him at all. It was as if she were looking right through him.

He shuddered as he recalled it, locking up his bike outside the dorm. He quickly scaled the steps back to his dorm room. His odd roommate wasn't there and he felt relieved by that. He headed straight to his computer out of habit, setting his backpack down with a thud on the floor. When he nudged his computer mouse, the screen lit up on the protein structure he had left off on and he sat down. He stared through the computer screen without seeing it.

"Did I just see a ghost?" he asked himself, his voice sounding strange to himself.

After all, she looked like she was dressed kind of old-fashioned and Boston is an old city. He didn't see anyone else taking notice of her and she definitely looked out of place. He racked his memory for every detail about her before his reason started to talk down on him. *So what if she was a ghost? Big deal. Move on. She was probably just some weird girl that you noticed looking different from a typical college student. It's a waste of time to think about any more.*

He pushed thoughts of the girl out of his head and went back to the protein he was working on. He could see why most people couldn't grasp the concept of protein folding. Getting to the natural protein states definitely followed its own set of logic. Until you figured out that logic, the manipulations required to solve the protein folding puzzles seemed completely random. When he first started, he would tug at various parts of the protein to see how they moved and when the program would reward him for tugging the correct way, he slowly learned the logic. The beautiful thing about the way proteins are folded is that they can technically be folded in an infinite number of ways, which makes the novice's head spin, but they always take the path of least resistance to a more energetically favorable state. Once you can identify the path of least resistance, protein-folding is completely logical. Trevor rotated the protein in three dimensions, peering into the structure. He made a couple of manual tweeks and then shook the protein. Done.

Trevor looked at his cell phone and noticed that one of his lectures was starting in about fifteen minutes. He still had time to get there before it started, but he had no intention of going. He wasn't sure what it would take for him to get interested in school work again. He was less than a semester away from graduation and he couldn't care less. Maybe it was the reluctance of leaving the shelter of college that kept him dragging his feet. The reality was that he couldn't afford graduate school but couldn't stomach the idea of working just yet. He was biding time as if he were just waiting for something to happen to him. When it did happen, he would feel almost like he had been expecting it.

Chapter 7

Only through independence can you know yourself. And only through knowing yourself will you be able to ask the key questions of your life: what is it that I am destined to accomplish, and how can I make it happen?

Eustace Conway

The sky was heavy that day, laying like a protective blanket over Boston. Loren was grateful—this kind of weather left the active types uninspired, holding out for a sunnier hour to linger on the shores of the Charles or go for a jog. She walked slowly toward the Harvard Bridge like a sleepwalker, without a clear goal in mind. She felt like a ghost, unacknowledged in this city, drifting between crowds. The Harvard Bridge was much emptier than it typically was on a Saturday at this time. The restlessness that stirred her to head this way seemed to ease up once she got further and further away from the Boston side of the bridge. As half of her view became water, the sound of cars passing to her left faded into the background and she turned her head to get them out of the picture completely. She watched the water float past at its own pace a half a dozen yards beneath her, ignoring her own legs and their awkward rhythm.

Loren kept walking until she got to the middle of the bridge and turned to face the water. Somewhere behind that mess of a city was the ocean. The blanket of grey above her picked up speed like it had a mind to rain. The river disappeared into the sky in the far distance and she matched the color of the water in her mind with an imaginary set of watercolors. The pigments in her imaginary set of watercolors were made from ground up bits of nature. She thought of them as being elements captured from life and concentrated into little tubs that came alive when water was added; blood, flower petals, glaciers, smoldering coals, sunlight. She started at the shore on each side, cleaning off her brush to remove the pigment before picking up the wet stroke and going from shore to sky in one wet puddle, solid earth dissolving to air. She added ochre to the sky to add warmth to the grey clouds and shared some with the reflections of sky in the foreground.

Painting in her mind kept the sentiment eternally fresh. When really painting, the painted object often died on the page once the pigment had dried. But the mind paintings were as ephemeral as the moments—utterly personal, and then completely gone. She wondered if poets sometimes didn't pause to write down inspired prose.

A sensation of being watched snapped her out of her thoughts and her head involuntarily jolted over her shoulder. A young man, probably a college student, stared at her blankly without moving. He stood with a bike at his side—utterly forgotten as he faced her. He looked lost. Not lost like a tourist with the panic-stricken groping for the nearest passerby to show him the way—lost like he never had a place in mind to head to. She recognized that look. It made her uncomfortable to see it reflected back at her and she suddenly remembered herself.

The young man seem embarrassed as soon as he realized

the absurdity of standing there staring at her. He quickly looked down and grabbed at his bicycle convulsively. He spun around to continue across the bridge, making an obvious attempt to avert his gaze from her. She followed his movements a moment longer and turned back to the river that had gone pale, dissolving the painting in her mind. She turned back toward Boston, shaking off the awkward moment, and gratefully passed a group of students, placing a barrier between her and the startled young man. There was something disquieting about the whole chain of events. She wondered if she looked crazy to him. *Can he see the thoughts that I don't share?* She wondered.

She had no place in the modern world. She was a voluntary outcast—unwilling to accept the modern world as it was.

She recalled her time in art school, where she was sure she would revolutionize the art world. No one worked harder than she did. She felt like every minute of her life was leading her somewhere, to some pinnacle at some point in time, where she would think to herself "I have arrived". It would be some unique masterpiece that would change people just by looking at it— making them kinder, more caring—spiritually enlightened in a glance. She painted without cease. Her teachers had never seen anything like it. The smell of turpentine was soaked into her faded sweatshirts. Every article of clothing she owned had splotches of paint on it.

Everything else in her life fell away in the constant drive for that masterpiece and one day she realized that she had something close. It was a simple thing—a haiku if you will—but it was perfect. It was a tiny water color of a pond reflecting sky and the mere suggestion of an aged wooden fence line. A footpath led to distant mountains, which disappeared into the sky. An oak tree cast a shadow on the pond, turning half of it dark, the counterweight to the other half reflecting sky—a yin and yang in light and shadow. She didn't particularly remember doing it—it was one of dozens and dozens of tiny water colors she used to carry in her back pocket for plein air painting. Her watercolor brush was one of those giant ones that magically came to a point when wet. She still didn't know how her hand remained steady enough to position each of those tiny fence posts with a gigantic brush like that, lightly dashed across the middle ground.

She recognized the specialness of that little painting from its conception. It never died for her, but it also remained a mystery. It captured the perfection of nature, unmolested by petty grasping at making a good painting, which she had managed to capture for only an instant. She never could replicate what she had done. Anything she attempted on a larger scale failed—its charm was in its simplicity and humility. She kept it like a postcard from a dear friend, a reminder of something beloved that visited once but didn't stay.

Loren was told by her painting teachers that the painting wasn't important. It couldn't be—it measured two inches by three inches. All serious work had to at least be the size of a sheet of paper, if not much larger. She tried to replicate it larger, even trying to use larger brushes, but the larger size made the entire composition break down. She finally gave up and let it be—a haiku whose symmetry only she could hear.

From that point on, her attitude changed. She still worked

hard, but she lacked some of the drive that she previously had. She no longer counted on being able to succeed as a commercial artist. She knew what commercial artwork was like—gaudy, ego-driven crap. She didn't count on people understanding what her message was. It was too quiet—it got lost in the myriad of other voices demanding to be heard. It had no motive, no audience to convince, no cause to support, no injustice to avenge. Its cause was beauty and simplicity—admiration of the natural world—as loud as the sound of the sun illuminating the leaves of a tree.

Loren didn't mind honest work, so she accepted that painting would be no more than a hobby for her. It was actually a relief. She kept her work to herself and never had to turn it over to critical eyes carrying an agenda. The work no longer needed to be great. It was only what it was. And that was more than okay with her. She painted less and less, and lately not at all. When the painting stopped there was nothing to fill the space it left. She had her mindless day job at the food processing plant, which she didn't hate—it kept her busy. She visited the paintings at the M.F.A. with the devotion of a widow who could never move on. She wondered half-heartedly what was next, but didn't see what it could be. It seemed an insurmountable challenge to muster up caring what it could be.

Chapter 8

There are two tragedies in life. One is to lose your heart's desire.
The other is to gain it.

George Bernard Shaw

The results of Green Future's trials of the drought-resistant crops were more than promising—they were astounding. Stan grinned widely as he read the concluding remarks of the development team's report. These crops could be grown in areas of Africa that probably hadn't seen crop production for a thousand years. This could be the rebirth of areas like the Fertile Crescent, where unsustainable agricultural practices had left a desert wasteland. Stan thought about the swollen bellies of African children on those infomercials that tried to get you to sponsor a child for a few dollars a month and he felt a wave of pride. This was something that he could help with, not just one child, but a whole country of children. He was pleased with himself and the success of the engineering under his direction that could make this possible.

The Green Future corporate strategy was to provide a multi-faceted approach to the future of food, dubbed the 2030 solution. The target was to set up food infrastructure for the population of the earth in the year 2030 with current trends in population growth. This could be achieved through three avenues. The first was to increase the efficiency of current agricultural land, which Green Future had already done and continued to do through new innovations in genetic crop traits. The second was to take areas of the earth, which are currently considered arid or semi-arid, where agriculture is currently not possible, and engineer drought-resistant crops for these areas. The report sitting on Stan's desk showed him the glowing success of this second target. The third target would be far more controversial than anything Green Future had produced to date, and would also provide Stan with the biggest engineering challenge of his career.

He had to admit to himself that he had been dragging his feet about starting it, since it was so different than anything he had worked on before. He would need a protein specialist who had a background in chemical engineering, for starters. There could be an astronomical number of effects that chemicals can have on a protein—pure computational power wouldn't help him. No one currently on staff had the kind of talent it would take to pull off this kind of engineering. If he were to try to come up with a solution experimentally, it would likely take a few decades of experimental research. He would need someone who understood protein structure intimately so that he could guide the experimentation and potentially land on an effective chemical after a few lab trials rather than a few thousand.

He leaned back in his overstuffed executive armchair and clasped his hands behind his head, staring at the ceiling in thought. He looked out the large picture window that came with a prestigious corner office. The neatly manicured lawns and perfectly shaped geometries of the mechanically pruned shrubs made his view more like a modernist, geometrical painting than a landscape. The early sun was working on erasing the morning dew making the perfectly sculpted shrubs glitter in the slanting light.

He closed his eyes and imagined what mechanism might unfold the structure of a highly specific protein while leaving all other similar proteins untouched. Something clicked into place in his memory bank as he visualized the unfolding of the protein. There had been an article in a popular magazine not too long ago. He sat up quickly and moved his oversized body as quickly as it would take him to his towering bookcase of magazines and scientific journals.

A neatly organized row of the magazine "Scientific American" was crammed between "Science Now" and "The Scientific Journal of Plants". He grabbed a handful of issues with his large hands and spread them face up across the floor. He scanned the covers and observed the shape they were in. He remembered reading that article during a business trip where he was folding the magazine nervously while waiting to board. The article had been short but he had found it extremely fascinating, and had thought about it long after the plane landed. He had stuffed the magazine into the seatback pocket once he had finished it midflight and had made an effort to not forget it there after the plane had landed. This made that issue unique among the pristine covers of the other issues, only some of which he had carved out enough time to read.

The first handful yielded nothing, and he shoved that pile out of the way before grabbing another handful from the shelf and spreading that on the floor next to the first pile. The folded issue made an awkward lump toward the edge of the second pile. He grabbed it and it folded back in half in his familiar grip. He flipped through the magazine and landed on the page that he recognized. This was the tool that he needed. He brought the magazine article back to his desk after returning the other magazines to the shelf and turned to his laptop. He typed a couple of search terms that got him to the Foldit website. He saw that he could download a version of the Foldit software, but that wasn't what he needed exactly. He needed one of the top performers at this program—someone who had already mastered the nuances of unlocking the keys to proteins.

Stan clicked on the "Players" tab from the Foldit home page. The top fifty Foldit players were displayed in descending rank. Clicking on each screen name led to the personal profile of each player, including their Foldit achievements such as "Master Evolver—achieved rank of 10 or better in at least 15 puzzles" and "Master Soloist—achieved soloist rank of 10 or better in at least 15 puzzles". Stan clicked on the number one ranked Foldit player and scanned his profile. He was leagues ahead in points of any of the other players.

"Phi_guy who the hell are you?" he mumbled to himself as he scrolled down an impressive list of Foldit achievements. He copied his screen name and pasted it into a search engine. Pages from the Foldit website came up and he meticulously combed through each one. The pages were all bits of chat and folding tips on the Foldit forum posted by Phi_guy. He had left no online clues to his real identity through his screen name. It took Stan about thirty minutes of reading through forum posts until he found the lead he was looking for. One of the search engine hits took him to a page with a large logo reading "Boston Science Festival".

The post read:

> *Calling all Foldit players in the greater Boston area! Come see us at the Boston Convention & Exhibition Center on Friday April 25 from 10:00am-6:00pm for Science Expo Day! Talk shop with our scientists and come see our currently #1 ranked Foldit player Phi_guy in action. We'll be located just inside Zone 2. We'll see you there!*

"Well I'll be," Stan grinned and then chuckled to himself generously after checking the date of the posting.

Stan slapped the intercom on his desk to life and shouted into the speaker, "Nancy, book me a trip to Boston this Thursday." His voice held the excitement of a man fifteen years younger than himself and Nancy was taken aback—she had never heard him sound quite like this before.

"Why, yes Dr. Cobald," she stuttered a bit after a short pause, "When would you like to get there and when would you like to return?"

"I'd like to be there Thursday evening. Book me somewhere near the Boston Convention Center. Return flight...hmm. Let's make it Friday evening. It won't take long."

"It is as good as done. I will email you flight, hotel and rental car information in a few minutes."

"Thank you, Nancy."`

"Yes sir."

Stan leaned back in his chair, satisfied with himself. This was the inspirational break he needed to kick off this round of research. He clasped his hands behind his head and looked out the window. He felt the direct hand of God working through him. He was engineering a path to tame the wildness, to turn chaos into something useful and productive for man. He would give new shape to vast areas of wilderness. He looked at the neutered bush outside the window. It would be a ragged, overgrown specimen if it weren't for the hand of the gardeners. As God had given shape to man, man's role was thus to give shape to the earth.

He snapped out of his triumphant reverie and turned back to his computer to start writing up an offer for this guy, whoever he might be. He hoped this guy was still a college kid who would jump at the opportunity, but whoever he was, he was about to receive an offer that he wouldn't be able to refuse.

Chapter 9

Our inventions are wont to be pretty toys, which distract our attention from serious things. They are but improved means to an unimproved end.

Henry David Thoreau

It was early Spring—time to prepare beds for the Spring plantings. Sarah dug new rows with a spade-tipped shovel before mixing in compost, greensand and bone meal. Rows left over from last year were freshened up with a layer of compost, mixed in with a tined hoe. Sarah took careful notes of what was planted in each row each year to ensure that she followed the succession: legume—brassica—root. Cover crops were planted in rows that would lay fallow for a spell to rest and replenish the soil. Sarah felt like the director of a symphony, each character in the garden contributing to the various tones while the weather dictated the tempo.

Over the weekend Sarah managed to finish one more new row, which was no small feat. Her wiry arms had task-specific strength gained through years of gardening. Her garden rows were thirty feet long and two and a half feet wide, dug to a depth of eighteen inches. She had trenched seventy five square feet of soil and mixed in the equivalent of about four inches of compost over that area. The digging and mixing had taken most of Saturday and had trickled into Sunday.

Sunday mid day, she dragged her dirt-covered, weary body

gratefully into the oversized outdoor chair that was perched at the edge of the garden. She propped up her throbbing legs onto a tree stump she had fashioned as a foot rest and tea cup holder. There was nothing quite like being filthy and exhausted from working the soil. Her whole body worked at moving dirt—leaning in to drive the shovel into the ground—lifting and pivoting to move the soil away from the active trench. Her biceps were the weak link in the whole process, and she accepted that they would be sore tomorrow.

She took a moment after the hard work was done. Although the birds didn't disappear completely during the winter, the majority of them came trickling back from winter vacation this time of year. She noticed the bird calls that had been absent since last November coming from the trees. The emergence of leaves after winter filled a deep longing in her. She loved the seasons, each one for its unique qualities, but she supposed that what made them so dear was that they never lasted. In winter, one longed for greenery. During the riot of summer, one longed for the silence of snow. It was an endless cycle of yearning and momentary fulfillment.

Sarah experienced moments of complete happiness that seemed to be unique to being outside in the garden—maybe not happiness, but a kind of complete peace. It was a feeling that everything was as it should be. The closer she lived to her ideals, the more frequently she felt the tiny peaks of this feeling. The feeling mostly came at times like this, when her body was exhausted by physical labor. Some would say she was a workaholic, a goody two-shoes, and that she didn't play enough—

that her lifestyle must be a burden.

"On the contrary," she said aloud, "it is exactly what frees me".

A cardinal responded with a melodic affirmation from a nearby tree branch.

"I'm glad you agree." She said to the brightly colored male who eyed her cautiously. "But I would rather be you, my friend— you are truly free. No house, no clothes, no sense of time other than the passing of the seasons."

The cardinal cocked his head at her before flying away distrustfully.

Sarah took that as a cue to get up from the garden chair. There were still house chores to complete before packing for her field work the next day. She would be driving North to Vermont. The field work there should be finished within the week so that she could make her way back home for the weekend to continue her Spring work in the garden.

Field data from Vermont was required for her computer model at work. The model accounted for the way water quality was affected by the major flooding events that were getting more and more frequent with the increase of global warming. The area of Southern Vermont hit by tropical storm Irene was a perfect location to monitor. The flooding had been considered to be a thousand-year storm event for the area. She had begun inspecting the areas hit by the swollen river around Wilmington, Vermont as soon as non-emergency personnel were allowed in.

Initially she had taken water quality samples from the floodwaters downstream. With the upheaval of fuel tanks, septic tanks, and the massive movement of debris and structures, the water could nearly be classified as hazardous. The sludge left behind the floodwaters was also significantly contaminated. Ideally, the contaminated soil would be properly hauled and landfilled, but with the financial constraints of these little towns and the dire emergency of getting the towns back on their feet, that just didn't happen. She had been visiting Wilmington ever since, taking soil and water samples from the downstream side of town where the river had swelled to its deepest point and documenting the populations of aquatic organisms. With the tremendous flooding, the course of the river changed, scouring the flanks of the already steep mountainsides. Downed trees across the river made the river change course completely in areas. The fish spawning areas in the shallows of the river had been destroyed when the town reinforced the eroded riverbanks with rip-rap after the floods. The river bed had been completely barren of life for the better part of a year after the flood. It was just beginning to show signs of recovery, starting with the tenacious growth of algae over the surface of the rip rap.

It was ironic that after the careful environmental regulations set in place to mitigate the impact to the environment through engineered septic systems and double-contained fuel storage, that Mother Nature herself came along and made a mess of all of it practically overnight. If there were a Mother Nature, she must have an overwhelming urge to shake us off of her back.

When people asked Sarah why she didn't want kids, her

answer was toned down to suit the ears of the person asking the question. To avoid sounding like a radical, anti-American, she didn't usually say she couldn't bear the thought of introducing another parasite to the world with the appetite of an American. A simple "I've never wanted them" usually sufficed. A follow up was often prompted, so she continued with a politically correct version of the truth. "Everyone is just meant to do different things in life. I was meant to do something else. It doesn't leave time for kids. Besides, it kind of requires a partner, which I don't have, so I have never had to make the choice." People were usually satisfied with the last part of her response. Of course she would want kids if she had the right partner. Of course it was understandable that she wouldn't want to have a child alone like some liberal feminist lesbian. Sarah thought that that line of questioning would stop after she reached the age of forty a couple of years ago, but apparently she had a baby face and was usually mistaken for ten years younger. She had fresh eyes and a ready smile, and had never adopted the weary look of most other women her age. Then there was the memory of what had happened to her family, but this memory was tucked away so deeply that it rarely surfaced consciously anymore.

Looking at mothers with their children, she wondered what had happened to her—to leave a void where the desire to mother was supposed to be. Perhaps it was her ambitious nature, which left room for nothing else. Perhaps her disgust for a consumer society had spread to the view of family itself. It wasn't that she didn't like kids. It wasn't their fault they were brought into the world. It was the entire system that she refused to feed by injecting more humans into it—she couldn't, in good conscience, bring someone into a world with more problems than people willing to incorporate solutions. Especially when the problem that made all other problems unmanageable was overpopulation.

In Sarah's mind, the technical solutions to all of society's problems were available—the regulatory policy was just lacking due to the will of individuals to do the right thing. With companies like Green Future funding the campaigns of political candidates, a company that cared more for the company's stock price than the greater good, she no longer had faith in the power of the people in the U.S. The more money a company had, the more political persuasion they enjoyed. The will of the good did not shine through policy anymore—it was rather the will of the wealthy. Until enough evidence could be compiled against Green Future's agricultural practices, they could not be stopped. No politician could keep face in public by backing them if the evidence were irrefutable. This Sarah did believe. If she didn't hold a hope for this possibility, she wouldn't be able to maintain the will to keep working for it.

Sarah daydreamed about her upcoming trip as she packed up her field gear. It was always a relief to be in an area without the urban sprawl she had grown grudgingly accustomed to. With every trip up North, the Vermont landscape sank its tendrils into her skin a little deeper.

The rugged terrain of Vermont never lent itself well to development. This was both its salvation and its curse. Agricultural land pushed up against the Green Mountains in rolling hills and valleys, recalling another day when Vermonters didn't import fruits and vegetables from Chile or Argentina. The old town centers with skeletons of mills and hydro-powered tool making factories straddled rushing rivers and streams coming off of the surrounding mountains. The old tool factories would run their lathes and saws off of belt drives, driven by the massive rivers squeezed between vast mountain ranges of wilderness.

Driving through Vermont was like having a conversation with an old woman about the olden days. She would smile through her wrinkles with a faraway look as she talked about how family values used to be, when doors remained unlocked and free time was spent with neighbors. The community was sewn together by the local country store where everyone knew everyone and everyone's business. Local farmers tended small herds of cows, free range on land that looked like it was straight out of some nineteenth century European landscape painting. There was still such a thing as homemade and hand-crafted. When something broke, it was fixed. The people were strong and self reliant. A weak pulse of this old life could still be felt along Vermont's country roads winding through its mountain towns.

Perhaps Sarah would retire up there one day, like so many New Englanders did who grew weary of city life. But retirement wasn't yet on the radar for her—she had too much work to do. She did think about it, especially in terms of water security. Vermont was a water-rich area of the U.S., and predicted to become even more so with the increasing effect of global warming, while much of the other parts of the country were expected to undergo more and more severe droughts. With contamination dwindling fresh water supplies along with increasing population, fresh water would become more scarce and expensive. The water poor areas would spend enormous amounts of fossil fuels to convey water from the water rich areas, leading to more pollution, more environmental disruption and more greenhouse gases. Something drastic was imminent within her lifetime if water conservation was not implemented very soon and probably even if it was implemented immediately.

For the water resources prediction model that she was creating, all she could do was to provide best-case and worst-case scenarios reflecting whether or not action was taken. The future would be decided by environmental policy. If Sarah didn't give a crap about anyone but herself, she would quit her job and move to Vermont to go off the grid. Perhaps someday she would hit a wall and realize that she had done all that was in her power to do, but that day hadn't come yet. She still felt a narrow window of opportunity for her to make a difference and she felt that if she didn't act immediately, the window would close and it would be too late—the earth would be too far gone. Despite the overwhelming evidence that continued to show that the majority of governments around the world cared more about economy than sustainability, she preferred to stay naively optimistic. If she could provide the hard evidence, she believed that she could convince enough people in power to develop sound environmental policies.

Chapter 10

The path up and down are one and the same.

Heraclitus

Trevor enjoyed the smug satisfaction of being at the top of the pyramid of Foldit players. It was the pursuit of this position that was likely a large factor in him failing nearly all of his classes.

Going to the expositions that Foldit participated in across the country to attract more players was one of those cheap thrills for him. They treated him like he was some rare form of animal threatened by extinction—tiptoeing around him in admiration and deference. He graciously handed out tips that he had invented over the years, never fearing that his skill would be surpassed because he knew he would invent others.

The Science expo would last all day and he was obligated to hang out at the Foldit booth. He was only missing one class and a lab to stay there all day, not that it really mattered anymore. He arrived at the Convention Center in the morning and the hall lined with booths was still fairly empty. The hall had opened fifteen minutes prior to his arrival. He tried to get there on time, but missed the mark slightly as usual. He navigated his way to Area 2 and spotted the bright green Foldit logo from a distance.

Two lanky guys with Foldit t-shirts were standing inside the booth. Laptops were set up for members of the crowd to come by and try their skill at protein folding. A man was standing at the booth, chatting with one of the Foldit booth crew members. He was a large-framed man with over-sized features. He appeared to be in his fifties, though Trevor wasn't good at guessing that sort of thing. Trevor walked up to introduce himself to the Foldit guy who wasn't engaged with the man.

"Hi I'm Trevor," Trevor held out his hand but there was no recognition on the Fold it representative's face.

"Hi I'm Chris." The representative said as he shook Trevor's hand.

"Oh," Trevor realized that not everyone knew him by name. "My screen name is Phi_guy. I promised you guys I'd hang out all day."

The conversation between the other Foldit guy and the man went silent. "Oh, okay, right. Thanks for coming. This guy actually came early and was looking for you," Chris said, motioning to the man.

Trevor looked over at the man with a question on his face as the man's face broke into an oversized grin.

"Well, Phi_guy, um.... Trevor," his large hand came forward for a handshake, swallowing Trevor's bony fingers, "it is a real pleasure to meet you. I'm Dr. Cobald, but please call me Stan. Tell me about how you became the number one ranked player of Foldit."

Trevor shrugged his shoulders. "Well, I'm a student and it's more fun than schoolwork, you know?"

"Ah, I can see that. Where are you a student?"

"MIT. I'm sure you've heard of it," Trevor jested.

Stan chuckled too loudly and seemed too eager for the conversation to progress. "What's your major?" Stan continued.

"Chemical Engineering."

Stan's eyes came alive. "Excellent. I majored in Chemical Engineering as well. You are no doubt an excellent student?" Stan prompted, assuming that Trevor would be proud to talk about his school accomplishments as well.

"Well I guess I could be. I dunno. I'm doing okay I guess." Trevor all of a sudden became self-conscious—the over worn jeans he couldn't afford to replace, the traces of bed head from being too lazy to shower that morning, the five-day shadow that was well beyond fashionable, and his wild hair that was about three months overdue for a haircut.

Stan felt the promise of the offer he held in the briefcase next to him. The quick jolt of the same kind of knowingness he had when he had read about this expo online ran through his body. The kid had no interest in school work but was brilliant, young, obsessive with puzzles, and at this moment looking like he didn't have a single direction in life. He was perfect.

"Say, I would really like to sit down and talk to you," Stan said. "Would you mind terribly if I bought you lunch this afternoon? I don't want to get in the way of what's going on here. I can come back at noon for you if you would find that agreeable."

Stan noticed a shadow cross over Trevor's face in distrust. "I'm sorry, I haven't completely introduced myself. I work for a global leader in biotechnology, where I head the biochemical research and development department. I would like to get to know you better. We need young men like you who have the kind of skill it takes to solve these kinds of puzzles."

Trevor relaxed and his brow raised. "Oh really?" He cleared his throat a bit before continuing. "Well in that case, sure, I don't see why we couldn't have lunch together." An embarrassed smile spread across his previously rigid face.

"Excellent. I'll be back here at noon to pick you up so we can go somewhere decent to eat." Stan continued, "Meet me out front on Summer Street."

"Sure, you bet. See you then," Trevor stammered. Now it was his turn to sound too eager.

"Damn good way to start the day," Trevor smiled to the Fold it representatives after Stan had left. Stan's easy manner and impeccable dress suggested that this was the real deal. Trevor had known several fellow students who had been recruited by major companies, but he had never heard of anyone actually being stalked and met in person. Trevor supposed this was a unique case. His grades at school were never going to get him noticed and there was no other way that this guy would have been able to find out the identify of Phi_guy except to track him down in person at an event like this. Trevor recognized that this had been a pretty clever way of finding him, and let go of his initial distrust. The prospect of a potential job opportunity started to lift an enormous burden off of him. He felt like someone had thrown him a rope down the hole he had been digging for himself since he had started skipping classes and missing assignments.

The next hour and a half dragged past. Trevor was not interested in the Foldit crowd—his mind was at lunch already. That man could be the perfect solution to his situation. If he could get a job solving puzzles like protein-folding, he would gladly take a leave of absence from school. It wasn't too late to take a leave of absence this semester if he filed his paperwork right away. His parents would certainly be happier with the news that he got a job rather than that he flunked out of his last semester at MIT. He would reassure them that he would finish later—that this opportunity was time sensitive.

Trevor walked to the front of the Convention Center on Summer Street to meet Stan a few minutes before noon. Stan pulled up in a large sedan and waived to Trevor from the driver's seat. The thought flashed through Trevor's mind that this guy could be some psychopath, but he forcefully pushed that thought away—he needed this opportunity. When Trevor got into the passenger side he was put at ease by the gentle manner of Stan. He certainly didn't seem like a psychopath—he seemed like someone's nice old uncle.

"I made reservations for us at a place not too far from here that looks pretty good," Stan said. "I'm not from Boston, but the online reviews were good."

"Sure—anything is fine with me." Trevor fidgeted.

The restaurant was about a mile from the Convention Center. It was upscale—somewhere that Trevor never thought he would be eating, especially today. He was dressed all wrong and he felt all wrong.

A tall waiter with slick, dark hair greeted them without expression. The lighting inside the restaurant was made to resemble the low candlelight of an underground wine cave. The white tablecloths were complimented by dark red roses in crystal vases on each table. As Trevor and Stan sat down, the waiters assisted them with their chairs. Trevor had never felt so out of place in his life. Stan didn't bat an eyelash at the treatment they got and the waiters tactfully paid no heed to the way Trevor was dressed. Trevor couldn't decipher anything on the menu.

"Apparently you are supposed to understand French to order here." Trevor jested uncomfortably. "I'll just have whatever you're having."

Stan ordered for them and then handed the menus back to the waiter.

"Thank you for joining me," Stan started. "As I mentioned, my company is always looking for bright young men like you. Have you thought yet about what you would like to do with your professional life?"

Trevor was silent for a while, forming his thoughts. "I haven't been planning too much for the future. I was actually considering taking some time off of school. It hasn't been very challenging for me lately. I spend most of my time on Foldit puzzles, to be perfectly honest." Trevor felt like he was confessing to this guy, to this guy who he should be impressing to get a job offer. Dishonesty and bravado just wasn't in his repertoire.

"Well it is just fine to take some time off. I am looking to hire someone right away for an immediate need we have for someone with your skills. You could always go back to school when things slow down a bit."

"Yeah, that makes sense." Trevor was trying not to sound too eager. This seemed too good to be true. "Say, what company did you say you were from?"

Now it was Stan's turn to pause for a moment before answering. "It's a company called Green Future. Have you heard of it?"

Trevor's heart dropped. This would explain the creepy stalking, the fancy restaurant, and the overly nice man. Even though Trevor wasn't an activist, no one in his generation could have avoided hearing about the evils of Green Future. His eyes fell to the table cloth in front of him, and he grew silent. Part of him wanted to stand up, take the starched white napkin off of his lap and throw it in the guy's face before storming out of the restaurant. But the truth was, he was starving, and he wasn't the confrontational type. It also wouldn't hurt to just hear this guy out. He didn't have to go through with taking the job if he didn't want to.

Stan noticed the change in Trevor's expression as if he had expected it, and just patiently waited for him to compose himself.

"Yeah I've heard of it," Trevor said cautiously. "There are a lot of folks who don't like you guys too much."

Stan laughed a hearty laugh and the table shook a little. "Very true, but there are a lot of folks who are great supporters—they're just not as vocal as those other folks that you're talking about."

Trevor was curious. He was looking at a human face behind the supposedly evil mega corporation. The man seemed genuinely nice. Trevor wasn't a pushover—he didn't think this guy could fool him. He could fact check the guy's claims when he returned to his dorm room. He could also eat a free lunch on Green Future. He suddenly perked up and grew interested in the whole situation.

Stan noticed him relax and took that as a good sign. Rather than butter Trevor up with the typical candy-coated elevator speeches, he got straight to the point for someone as intelligent as Trevor obviously was.

"I love my job," Stan stated simply. "There are a lot of people out there who really want to believe that villains exist and that Green Future is one of them, and that's just not true. We are a bunch of hard working Americans with a real desire to improve the technology behind food production, and there is simply no proof that our agricultural methods harm the environment. Now, I'm not saying our methods are perfect, but they provide food for a whole lot of people who would go hungry otherwise. The numbers tell the real story. You cannot feed the entire population of the earth with organic gardening practices. Would you rather let the rest of the people on the planet starve to death?"

Trevor listened to him, not interrupting. It was clear that Stan was sincere in what he was saying. If he didn't believe it himself he was a damned good actor, and Trevor didn't think he was that type. He was a scientist—not a greasy salesman type.

Stan continued, "I work in a challenging field, making engineering discoveries that no one on the planet has made yet. My work is fun and interesting. I go to bed knowing that I am making a positive difference in peoples' lives. There isn't one study out there that shows conclusively that our herbicides or pesticides cause cancer, or that GM crops kill bees. If there was, we would not be allowed to do what we do.

"We have had incredible success at patenting the IP that we have spent millions of dollars creating. Yes, I get paid handsomely for what I do. Yes, Green Future is a huge economical boost for the American economy. Does being good at making money also make us the bad guys? We are living the American Dream."

Stan paused to let his words soak in and then looked at Trevor for a reaction. Trevor didn't quite know what to say—he needed time to do some research for himself. Just then, the grim waiter brought their meals, easing the silent pause that had formed.

"Bon Appetit," Stan said to Trevor.

The delicious meal lightened the intensity of the conversation. Trevor welcomed the distraction of the food and turned to occasional chit chat as they ate. When they had finished eating and the table had been cleared of plates, Stan leaned forward and addressed Trevor in a serious tone.

"We are doing ground-breaking research at Green Future— research which may sustain the future of mankind," Stan said. "You have a gift, Trevor, an uncanny gift. I want to give you the opportunity of tapping that gift in order to reach your full potential. You have already proved your mastery inside the world of Foldit—just imagine the entire globe as your arena. I would like you to come work for me at Green Future as part of the research team for a new product."

Stan paused, searching Trevor's face for a reaction. "What do you think Trevor?"

"Dr.... I mean Stan," Trevor stammered, "I am going to have to think about this. It's all just a bit overwhelming."

"You don't have to answer me right now," Stan said quickly, reading Trevor's hesitation. "I'm going to leave my business card with you along with an employment offer. You can take as long as you'd like to get back to me, but of course I would prefer an answer sooner rather than later. If you have any questions for me, please call me or email me. I'm an open book, Trevor, and I would be thrilled to welcome you into the Green Future family."

Trevor's face didn't indicate one way or the other how he was feeling. He said finally, "Thank you. I will look at this when I get back to my dorm room and I'll let you know if I have any questions."

Stan was satisfied that he had done all he could do to entice this young man into the fold.

Despite the oddity of the situation and Trevor's predisposition against a company like Green Future, Trevor realized with a kind of amazement that he liked this man.

Chapter 11

After Stan dropped him off at the Convention Center, Trevor was in an exceptionally good mood. No matter what would happen with the offer, he was flattered. But he wanted to wait until he could do some research on Green Future before making any kind of a decision. Again, the hours could not go quickly enough at the Science Expo—he couldn't wait to get back to his dorm room to scour the internet for anything he could dig up on Green Future.

When he finally did arrive back at his dorm room, his roommate Scott was there. Trevor was slightly on guard whenever his roommate was around. The guy was weird. He majored in Theoretical Physics with a minor in Philosophy. But he was someone worth talking to if you don't mind getting sucked into hour-long conversations about the meaning of life. This was one of those times when Trevor desperately needed someone to talk to, even if that someone was Scott.

"Hey," Trevor said as he put down his backpack.

Scott was propped up on an elbow and hunched over a textbook with a tangle of black hair over thick-framed glasses. Scott raised his normally tightly bunched eyebrows at Trevor, who rarely ever addressed him. Obviously Trevor wanted to talk.

"Something strange just happened to me," Trevor said. He knew this would get Scott's attention. Scott put a piece of scratch paper in the text book to mark his place and sat up.

"What was it?" Scott prompted.

"I just got offered a job by someone from Green Future—the head of Biochemical Research and Development or something."

"Bullshit!" Scott smiled like he thought this was enormously funny.

"No, it's not," Trevor countered with sincerity. "Look; he gave me his business card." Trevor handed him the impeccably designed business card with the familiar green logo.

"What the hell..." Scott said. "Well, was the guy a creep or what?"

"No he was actually pretty nice. I mean, I'm probably not going to take the job or anything."

"You're not? What the hell else are you gonna do? Play video games in here all day? You're a frigging burnout, man."

Trevor was taken aback. Scott usually poised himself as anti-establishment, which included corporations like Green Future. Now Trevor was really confused.

"Isn't Green Future supposed to be some evil corporation that sues poor farmers and creates Franken food?" Trevor asked Scott.

"Maybe, but everything is relative. Is Green Future going to be the cause of the end of the world? I highly doubt it. For all we know, a solar flare could send our whole society back to the Stone Age tomorrow. Are they an evil corporation that only cares about profit even at the expense of the future of the human race?

Probably, but what is evil anyway? I tend to think that evil has a gray scale and to label someone as evil is like a shade of gray calling out a darker shade. It's part of what it is to be human. Think of the ascetics who isolate and starve themselves at the top of a mountain. Those extreme measures are what it takes to cleanse the human soul, and even that doesn't always work." Scott stopped himself suddenly in the midst of his tirade. "How much did they offer you anyway?"

"I don't know."

"What do you mean you don't know? You didn't tear up the offer, did you?"

"No, it's in my backpack. Wait a minute I'll look." Trevor opened his backpack and took out a large, crisp envelope. He took out several pieces of paper and quickly scanned the text of the first page. Trevor's already pale face grew paler.

"Holy crap," Trevor said.

Scott took the pieces of papers from Trevor's hands, which had gone limp. He looked at the numbers and broke into a wide grin.

"You got it made, man." Scott laughed and threw the papers back at him. The papers fluttered around Trevor and then fell to the floor.

Trevor picked up the pieces of paper one by one. The last page was some kind of nondisclosure form that he was supposed to sign if he was going to accept the employment offer.

"Money isn't everything," Trevor said half-heartedly,

staring incredulously at the offer.

"Of course not," Scott responded. "But it *is* just a job. If you hate it or feel weird about it, you can quit. Besides, you know what they say. Keep your friends close and your enemies closer. That nondisclosure form, well, you could always pull a Snowden. Look at the big picture. Getting paid by someone doesn't mean that you agree with what they're doing. This is an opportunity for you to find out what they're doing. Don't you want to know? I would. Maybe they are an evil empire that needs to be stopped, or maybe the hippies have it all wrong. They don't let reporters anywhere near their headquarters. You could be the Snowden of the corporate empire Green Future."

Having a conversation with Scott was like having a conversation with two different people sometimes. Scott would take two different sides of an issue, one after the other. He seemed to not have his own opinion—he expressed all possible opinions on the matter. One of Scott's one-liners was "the root of ignorance is being chained to ideology". Any stance he appeared to have on a matter seemed momentarily summoned from the cosmos and as quickly discarded without attachment.

Scott's advice seemed practical enough, though. What could be the harm in just trying it out? His other options in life right now consisted of flunking out of school or acing all of his finals and then he might get good enough grades to graduate. He didn't really see the latter option panning out for him.

Trevor spent the remainder of his Friday doing online research on Green Future with Scott hovering over his shoulder.

There really was very little substance that could be verified from what they read. Because of "inconclusive" studies, you could make almost any conclusion you were predisposed to. The fact was that Green Future had won every court case ever filed by farmers against them. It was either because the justice system was working, or because Green Future simply had better lawyers.

Trevor grew exhausted from scrolling through articles. He was too far removed and the available information was too biased to make any kind of judgment. There were experts out there who could evaluate whether or not Green Future was threatening the environment or human health, and as far as he could tell they were working on it. For the first time in his life, Trevor considered the possibility of having money. He could take care of his parents. He could have a place of his own and maybe even start a family. A new and improved Trevor starting forming in his mind—the successful man he could be rather than the awkward young man on the brink of failure that he currently was.

When Trevor's head hit the pillow that night, it was filled with a drive that had been absent for quite a while. The feeling was suspiciously akin to happiness—it was a momentum to do something with his life. The decision was made.

Chapter 12

Man cannot stand a meaningless life.

Carl Jung

Loren wasn't able to sleep. Recycled thoughts replayed themselves all night as she lay awake. Her body felt exhausted and her mind burned but sleep would not come to relieve her. The act of painting had dried out to a trickle and then stopped altogether. She thought that this might be why she couldn't sleep, but she had no desire to go back to it. She felt like all those years she had spent painting had been wasted. The numerous daily tasks like eating and brushing her teeth seemed like enormous burdens. She couldn't imagine repeating these chores hundreds of thousands of times until she was an old woman.

Loren was not a seeker of company—she preferred to be alone. But lately, the aloneness weighed on her. The silence became unbearably loud. She preferred to be at work, among the pounding of the food processing machines. Each day, she was relieved to put on the mandatory white smock, hair net and plastic gloves. She was no longer herself but a blank canvas, a robot systematically removing imperfections from the line of shiny plastic packages. When her shift was over she felt like a prisoner must feel when finally set free. She didn't know where she wanted to go—she felt impotent in the face of making a decision. No one path seemed better than any other. She could do almost anything and nothing would make any difference.

Whether or not Loren even existed, the world would continue on the same path toward irreverent self-destruction. She was only one person—nothing she could ever do would change its course. Skipping meals and not sleeping were taking their toll. Sometimes she thought she saw someone out of the corner of her eye and on a double-take realized that no one had been there. Sometimes she swore she could hear someone talking to her, but no one was there. She wondered if she might be going crazy, but figured that crazy people didn't wonder such things.

She was in the break room one day at work. She hadn't brought a lunch, as was her custom as of late, and was just waiting for her lunch break to be over to start her next shift. The second hand on the lunch room clock slowed down until it stopped completely. The barely audible ticking sound started ringing, like a crystal glass when a finger is circled around the rim. The glass broke and it cut her face. She was face down in a puddle of mud, rubbing her face into the mud and broken glass. She knew she had lost her face, and would never be herself again. She belonged in this hole in the ground.

"Loren, Loren," She could hear someone saying her name from far away, then closer and closer. "Loren, wake up." A hand was shaking her shoulder and she jolted into reality.

"What..." Loren mumbled.

"You were asleep, and I think you were having a bad dream." It was Margie, an overweight motherly type who had always been kind to her.

"Oh, sorry." Loren lifted her head from her arms and blinked the sleep out of her eyes.

"You were saying something. Sounded a little bit like crying," Margie said. "Are you doing okay? Are you sleeping? You sure have been looking really tired at work lately."

"No," Loren said simply. "I haven't been sleeping. I don't feel well."

"Are you sick? Why don't you take a few days off and rest up?" asked Margie.

"I just haven't been able to sleep."

"Have you tried taking anything for that?"

"I'm not going to take some drug to make me sleep," snapped Loren.

"Oh honey, I'm sorry. I know you like to keep things natural, but maybe there's some kind of homeopathic remedy or something for sleeplessness."

"Yeah I guess you're right. I'll look into it Margie. Thanks." Loren spoke mechanically, trying to sound believable. "Well I gotta get back to the line."

Loren's eyes were red and underlined by dark circles. She squinted into the fluorescent lights as she walked back onto the processing floor. White smocks floated between the steel conveyor belts—angels in an operating room. She rubbed her eyes and blinked.

"Stay awake," She whispered to herself, biting her lower

lip.

She clenched the cold steel of the railing. Colorful packages raced by on the conveyor belt in front of her. She commanded her arms to move but they remained attached to the railing.

A large, firm hand suddenly encircled her elbow.

"Loren, I'm clocking out and I'm going to drive you home," Margie said. "Really, you can hardly hold yourself up."

Loren had no will. Whatever this woman wanted to do with her was okay. Margie gently wrapped her enormous arm around Loren's shoulders and nearly picked her up off of her feet as she guided her back to the break room.

Loren curled up like a cat in the passenger seat of Margie's Lincoln. Margie marveled at how tiny and delicate Loren seemed, like you could knock her over if you breathed too hard. It looked like Loren had lost weight in the past couple of weeks. She had gone from thin to emaciated. Margie knew that Loren wasn't the type to get into drugs, so maybe it was boy or family troubles. She stopped at the grocery store while Loren stayed in the car. She came back with a Styrofoam bowl of hot soup and some crackers. Loren jumped when Margie shut the door after getting back into the car.

"Now, we're going to sit in this parking lot until you finish that soup and crackers. I know a hungry girl when I see one," said Margie.

Loren sat up, disheveled. She looked around her at the people rushing in and out of their cars in the parking lot. "Margie, do you ever feel like there's just no point, that the world is such an ugly place that it's not worth any effort at all?"

"Loren, it sounds like you've been at the plant for too long. You need a break. The world is what you make of it. There are beautiful places and ugly places. Sometimes we all go to dark places, but when we come out of them, we're better for it."

Loren blew on the soup. "What kind of beautiful places?" she asked.

"Well, I haven't traveled much. I mean, I was born and raised here in Massachusetts. I never went to school or nothing. I've seen plenty of places on T.V. Europe is supposed to be real pretty—all those old castles and stuff."

"I've been there," Loren said dryly. "There isn't a place on earth that doesn't have a McDonald's. If they find a beautiful place, they put a fence around it and charge you admission."

Loren knew that Margie wasn't the person to have this conversation with. She set her mind to finishing her soup and crackers so that she could go home. Margie was sweet, but everything she said made her feel worse somehow.

"Boston is beautiful, Loren. The architecture, the Commons, the bay—people come from all over to see our city."

"Yeah, you're right," Loren said weakly. Margie wasn't going to understand.

No inch was unmolested—no inch sacred. Nothing remained wild. Loren's spirit felt as shackled as the land under her feet.

Loren struggled to finish the soup and crackers and then instructed Margie where to drop her off.

"I already told Roger that you have some kind of a bug and would need to take the next few days off," Margie said as she pulled up in front of the house where Loren rented a room. "He said to just give him a call once you know when you'll be back."

"Thank you, Margie."

"No sweat, kid. Get some rest and make sure to eat something."

"I will. See you later."

Loren got out of the car and made her way through the front door and up the steps to her room. She walked over to her drawing table and opened her sketchbook. She sat down and flipped through the notebook. It was filled with idyllic landscapes that had been done in various parks around Boston. The streets had been roughed in to make them look like dirt roads rather than concrete, with the cars deliberately omitted. She had ignored the litter scattered around the water's edge at the creek in the Fens. She had drawn the water's surface like it reflected the sky perfectly, rather than being the murky, sulfide-laden stream that it was. The things that she loved weren't really there. She had been reaching for them through her imagination, but the only proof of their existence was the tentative strokes of graphite lining the pages of her notebook. There was nowhere for her to go but inside, and inside her internal landscape was withering.

She was ashamed of what people had turned this place into. She sometimes wondered what it must have looked like when the pilgrims first came—when the Native Americans lived seamlessly with the land. She would give anything just to see it once—to smell the air, to taste the water. It was a land that still had its dignity. She was sorry—deeply sorry for what the generations before her had done. She did not want to be part of it. She was part of the perpetual machine of exploitation.

Loren flipped through the sketchbook until she got to an unused sheet. She grabbed a pencil and then rested her chin on the blank page. It was a piece of beauty—untouched, undreampt, endless possibilities. She closed her eyes and put her head on her hands. Just before falling asleep, a tear rolled down her cheek and landed on the otherwise spotless sheet.

Chapter 13

The covetous man is always in want.

Horace

Trevor called Stan the Monday following his trip to Boston. Stan wasn't surprised. A kid straight out of college couldn't earn the kind of salary that Stan had offered him without any work experience. They established that Trevor would work for Green Future remotely from Boston. This would give him the chance to attend classes if he wanted to return to school at some point. For the work he would be doing, he didn't need to be in Cincinnati. Trevor would tie up loose ends at school right away and start work for Green Future by the following week.

With Trevor an imminent part of the Green Future team, Stan was confident that they could have a product to test by the end of the year. The next step was to work on Washington so there would be no issues once the full-scale trial was launched. Stan phoned Senator Roger Bly. Senator Bly said that he would be happy to meet with Stan for lunch on Thursday. Stan always met with Senator Bly in person to discuss legislation. Nothing could be in writing.

Stan didn't face a moral dilemma for reimbursing Senator Bly for helping out Green Future. Political persuasion such as lobbying was after all a part of the American legal system. Everyone had the right to lobby governmental officials. In the case of Senator Bly, extra work would be required to draft legislation. In case payments made to him came under scrutiny, the funds were paid as campaign contributions. Individuals, companies, and all kinds of private interest groups contributed to the political campaigns of candidates that they felt best represented their interests. Green Future had been scrutinized for spending more on lobbying than any other agribusiness, but without the support of American farmers, they obviously wouldn't have been able to spend millions of dollars on lobbying every year. In a way, Green Future represented the interests of all of the farmers who supported them with their business.

Stan enjoyed visiting Washington D.C., which he did at least several times a year. Green Future had to stay on top of pending legislation and political favor, especially since their major victories had been won with only a narrow margin. Being in D.C. reminded him what privileged soil he was born on. The United States was still the land of opportunity, where a man without a penny to his name could take a revolutionary idea and build an empire out of it.

The U.S. patent system was the backbone of Green Future's success. All of their court victories had come down to protecting patent rights, which was far more straightforward to defend than whether or not private ownership of genetic traits of food crops was morally correct or not. If the United States stopped protecting patents, it simply would not be the great nation of innovative thinking that it was.

The ingenious ideas of people creating revolutionary products and methods would probably never come to light without the U.S. patent system. Innovators oftentimes made extreme personal sacrifices in order to bear their ideas into the world. In a communist-type regime, there aren't those kinds of breakthroughs in technology. There was no benefit to working harder than the next guy in a communistic society and without an incentive, there was no reason to cultivate unique ideas. The great nation of the United States was shaped by the brave innovators.

The afternoon that Stan met with Senator Bly was a beautiful crisp Spring day in the Capitol. They met at an upscale restaurant and wine bar near the Capitol building. Senator Bly was late, as usual. He didn't overtly acknowledge Green Future's contributions to him. Rather, he acted like it was he who was conferring the favor on Green Future. In truth, it was. By writing legislation for Green Future, he was putting himself up for public scrutiny and even risking the office he had worked so hard to occupy. This predicament also dictated the magnitude of Green Future's payments to him.

"Good Afternoon," Senator Bly said as he took the seat opposite Stan in a booth at the back of the restaurant.

"Good Afternoon," Stan responded, eager to get right to business but careful not to push too hard too soon. "Thank you for meeting me on such short notice. This is quite time sensitive."

"My pleasure," Bly responded, but his face suggested otherwise.

"We need to get some wording into the Forestry Bill that is coming up." Stan got right to the point.

"Forestry Bill?"

"Yes. This is a bit different from what we have done before and because of the public outcry to the additions we made to the Agriculture bill, I think it would be a better fit in the Forestry bill."

"You think it won't be as scrutinized."

"Well yes, but it is also a better fit there. The chemical applications will be to forested land, so it would make sense to put it in there."

"Chemical applications to forestland?" Bly's eyebrows raised.

"Benign chemicals—it will be an improvement on current land clearing practices. You know how the environmentalists can misconstrue anything."

"The less I know about the specifics the better. Chemical application for land clearing purposes—that should do it. I can add the same kind of wording we did last time to allow for large-scale applications without a mandatory monitoring period of field trials. The art of slipping this through the House of Representatives will be to address the multitude of avenues that might thwart the applications in as succinct wording as possible. It should also appear to address another, more acceptable product, rather than a completely new product. I have used some similar wording in other legislation before."

"Perfect," Stan responded, his eyes scanning the restaurant for anyone within earshot.

The low din of the lunch crowd and the distance between their booth and the next occupied tables reassured him. Stan looked around at the upper echelon of Washington D.C. He wondered how many of these people would be outraged at the conversation he was having with Senator Bly and whether they would feel that their rights were being violated.

Stan held the resolve that if it were anyone else running this research, the public might have something to fear. He had no intention of harming anyone. He trusted the rigorousness of his laboratory methods and testing program because he oversaw them himself. If his laboratory determined Green Future's products to be safe, Stan was satisfied. And he stood by his word. He didn't select organic food for himself or his family. He was his own living proof, which enforced his faith in the conclusions he reported.

Stan recognized that his methods would be dissected and construed as wrong by some, but he was doing this for the greater good. If it had to happen this way to avoid mass starvation in the future, in a hushed conversation toward the back of an expensive restaurant, then it was still the right thing to do.

The lunch conversation ended with a handshake. The wheels were slowly turning and everything was falling into place.

Chapter 14

Whenever quantum system A meets quantum system B, their phases get mixed up.

Nick Herbert, from "Quantum Reality"

Sarah arrived in Wilmington, Vermont and was astonished to see the town's progress in recovering from Tropical Storm Irene since she had last visited. It was impossible to tell that the town had been nearly destroyed not long ago. The historic buildings had all been lovingly pieced back together, reinsulated, rewired, and repainted.

Sarah checked in to the same little Inn as usual, located just outside the center of town. The Inn had been operating for over 150 years. The floorboards creaked, as old structures do, and the matronly woman who owned and operated the Inn proudly detailed how much damage had been done by Irene and how hard they had worked to get this old lady back into shape.

The worst flooding had occurred in the middle of downtown, where the river had overwhelmed the bridge along Main Street. She only needed to take a short walk to gain access to the river to do her field surveys. The town had only two choices of restaurants to eat for dinner, both of them right in town. Not having a commute made her days seem longer. She could walk back up to town from the streambed for lunch and walk straight back to her hotel after eight hours of daily field work. The free time she usually spent in the garden or her laboratory basement could be spent on walks along the river or in the expanses of nearby farmland. Just outside the quaint downtown, hundred-year-old landscapes had been frozen in time. Aging barns and silos were worn like beloved crowns by the expanses of now fallow fields.

Spring was considerably colder in Vermont than in Washington D.C. Vermont could still get snow this time of year, especially on the mountain. Sarah realized with dismay that she hadn't kept this fact in mind when she packed for this trip. The morning after her arrival in town she felt the nip of frost as she exited the old hotel on her way down to the streambed. As she passed through the center of town, she noticed that the stone pavilion creating the focal point for the main intersection was being rebuilt. The stone mason working on the project didn't seem to notice the cold that chilled her bones. She didn't know that masonry could be done at freezing temperatures. She was feeling lighthearted this morning—happy to be in such lovely surroundings for the week.

"Do you have any problems mixing the mortar with this cold weather?" Sarah surprised herself by addressing the mason on a whim.

The mason stood up and looked at her and laughed heartily. "You aren't from around here, are you?" he said, with that distinctive Vermont accent.

She was a bit embarrassed, but she was curious. "No I'm not. Is it that obvious?" she smiled and blushed. After the stone mason had stood up, she noticed how striking he was. His strong jaw set off a deeply tanned, muscular build. His laugh had cracked open a contagious smile on his face, like opening the curtains on a sunny day. His smile was framed by deep dimples to compliment the ruggedness of a two-day shadow. He wore a flannel, but she could see the shape of chiseled biceps through the light material. She was filled with unexpected warmth.

She hadn't escaped his notice, either. He took a minute to drink her in with his eyes before he continued. "The Portland cement reacts with the water and gives off heat," he explained, like someone who is pleased to share his love of his craft. "It's a perfect day for masonry. The heat of summer is what'll kill ya."

"Well it looks nice," she said, noticing how stones of various sizes seemed to fit magically together like they had all been one stone at one time, then shattered into pieces, only to be put back together again piece by piece. He was creating a low wall, which would surround the whole pavilion.

"Dry-laid is much better. If you do it right, dry-laid will last forever, but you need better stone than this. This is what the town wanted. People think that mortar is going to make the wall stronger, but the secret to strength is that if the stones are placed just right, you don't need the mortar. Then, water can travel right through the wall instead of getting stuck in the cracks, turning to ice and eventually heaving the wall apart."

"Oh really? I never knew that," she said. She was genuinely interested, her analytical mind dissecting the thought of the water turning to ice in all of the cracks between the mortar and the rock and slowly creating chaos of the perfectly cemented stones. It was interesting that even in man-made structures it was better to work with nature rather than fight against it. She hadn't thought of it quite like that before.

"Say, what are you doin' here anyway? With all that gear you don't look like a tourist." He motioned to her water sampling get-up, which made her look a bit like a traveling snake oil salesman.

"I'm here for work. I'm doing a field survey of the riverbed. It's because of Irene—I'm monitoring how the ecology was affected by the flood. Specifically, I'm gathering data on how it is recovering. It's important for the potable water resources downstream."

"You some kind of biologist?"

"No. I'm a water resources analyst. I work for the CIA."

The mason broke into a wide grin. "The CIA is in Wilmington, VT. Now the world really has gone crazy. I always wanted to be in the CIA or the FBI. If you're in the CIA why the hell are you counting fish instead of catching bad guys?"

"Well, there are many different branches of the CIA," she explained. "My job is keeping track of water resources. Floods like the one that happened here affect our fresh water supplies so they're important to understand. You know how much wastewater got dumped into Harriman reservoir because of the flood? At lot of it is still probably there and will continue leaching downstream for a while."

"Humph," he said as he looked at her with amusement. They stood there for a moment in silence, him with his trowel in one hand and her with an armful of instrumentation. He didn't seem to have any intention of going back to the mud he had just mixed.

"Well I better let you get back to your wall—I've got some algae to quantify," she said abruptly. She turned away and continued down to the riverbed as he stood there and watched her walk away, looking spellbound and yet slightly confused.

That morning while she worked Sarah couldn't get the mason out of her head. She kept hearing his contagious laugh, open and wild. He had a boyishness about him, like the world around him was still something fresh and new, that there was a new adventure to be found in each day. Sarah's days tended to be a ceaseless stream of work and gloomy thoughts about what the future might hold. She considered actions for the sake of pure fun to be foolish, and he seemed like the type to revel in them. Strangely, she didn't dislike him for it and even wondered if that was part of the attraction.

When lunchtime came, she purposely walked back through the pavilion to eat at the restaurant on the east side of town, rather than the one that was closest to where she was working at in the stream bed. The mason was sitting on a red cooler, drinking a cup of coffee.

"Hey CIA!" he hollered as she approached. He got up from his cooler and walked toward her.

She smiled and said, "You don't have to call me CIA. My

name is Sarah."

He smiled and stuck out his hand to shake hers. "Hello." He took the Vermonter out of his diction and pushed his jovial face into a serious expression. "My name is Darin. It is a pleasure to make your acquaintance." He then he reverted back to his Vermont-ese. "See—I can talk like a civilized person if I feel like it. I just don't feel like it. As far as I'm concerned, the best things in life are uncivilized."

Sarah smiled as he gripped her hand. His palm was coated in thick calluses and his grip felt strong enough to break every bone in her hand, but he held it gently, holding it for a bit longer than is typical.

"I was just going to have lunch. Would you care to join me?" Sarah realized the words that came out of her mouth only after she had said them. This guy already felt like a friend and the offer had just flown out without her thinking about it.

"Lunch with a CIA agent? Wouldn't miss it for the world," he said, smiling.

She felt a thrill through her body at his acceptance. *It's just nice to have company sometimes*, she told herself to placate the logical part of her mind.

Darin made Sarah laugh through a single lunch more than she could remember laughing for the past few years. For that lunch hour, she seemed to forget who she was and what she was doing there—she was just enjoying herself and the lightheartedness of this stranger. She couldn't remember when the last time was she had enjoyed someone's company this much. As a young woman, she had been introverted, awkward and absorbed in the pursuit of her studies. Her internal world was rich enough that she didn't need to reach to the outside for fulfillment by others. She had tried dating as she got older and blossomed into a beautiful young woman, but she found herself spending her few free evenings with dull-witted guys and ultimately dismissed the whole pursuit as a waste of time. It wasn't that she intended to become an old maid—she just no longer expected that the universe would conjure up someone interesting enough for her to make time for. That was okay with her—she had more important things to do in life. It baffled her how she could have attracted the attention of this young, attractive man. She couldn't be that much older than him, but she felt much older than her years, with the problems of the human race continually weighing on her.

"You're really somethin', you know," Darin said to her as they left the restaurant and headed back to the pavilion.

"Me?" Sarah asked incredulously. She was a stick in the mud compared to this guy. He seemed like the kind of guy that any woman would be crazy over with his easy manner, sense of humor and good looks—he was the polar opposite of how she viewed herself.

"You know many Vermonters?" he asked, addressing the perplexity in her face.

"No, not really."

"Well we have a saying here in Vermont. What do you call 32 women from Vermont? " he asked her.

"What?" she asked.

"A full set of teeth."

Sarah laughed after a short pause and then he looked at her with a sincere expression for the first time. "But really what I mean is... not very many people around here have motivation like you do. You're actually doing something with your life. You're smart and you're passionate." Darin smiled at her, then averted his eyes and put his baseball cap back on. "You're mighty easy on the eyes as well."

Sarah blushed. She felt so awkward from the compliment that she couldn't think of anything to say back to him. She had butterflies in her stomach like a schoolgirl and felt almost foolish.

They walked back to the pavilion after lunch. "Have a nice rest of your day, Miss Sarah," Darin called to her as she continued her walk down to the river bed and he picked up his shovel to mix up a new batch of mud.

Sarah was still smiling when she arrived at her survey site. She chuckled to herself again at some of his antics during lunch, deliberately embarrassing himself in front of the waiter to get her to laugh. There was a small part of her that wanted to pull back, as if romantic happiness could threaten her goals, but she was drawn to him in a way that she had no control over. She finally resolved that all she could do was enjoy the way she was feeling and resist the temptation to form expectations. Whatever was going to happen would happen. She was just going to enjoy her time here and she would be back in D.C. in no time at all.

He can't be too dangerous. She silently tried to persuade herself. *After all, he's young. He will soon grow disinterested in me once he realizes how much work my life is.*

Chapter 15

There is neither happiness nor misery in the world; there is only the comparison of one state with another, nothing more. He who has felt the deepest grief is best able to experience supreme happiness.

Alexandre Dumas

It was one of those days that exhausted Loren. The sun was out in full force. Glaring white clouds hovered like static explosions in the distance. She was walking toward the Harvard Bridge. She remembered her moment of forgetfulness here— forgetting where she was as she focused on the water flowing continually out to sea below her and the sky effacing the outline of the city. Today was different. With the sun out, it seemed to be magnifying the city like it was under a gigantic microscope. Cars whizzed by beside her, uncomfortably close. She felt like there was nowhere in the world left to go. She hadn't called in to work—she didn't know what to say to them. She hadn't been back since that embarrassing evening last week when Margie had taken her home. She never wanted to go back.

She got to the center of the bridge and her eyes squinted against the glare coming off of the water. The drop to the water didn't seem too bad at about fifty feet. But it didn't seem like the jump alone would do the trick—unless the water was freezing. She had read a newspaper article about a guy who had jumped from the Harvard Bridge on January 1. His body must have gone into shock when it hit the water. There was no turning back then. It took them until March to find his body. No one could say why he did it. They were trying to call it an accident. Though the water wasn't freezing, it had to be very cold this time of year.

Her mind was spinning and she gripped the railing. If she could think of one way to make her life useful she would reconsider, but she had gone to the depths and resurfaced with nothing. She knew she had lied to Margie when she said that there were no more beautiful places in the world. The truth was that there might still be beautiful and remote places, but humans were slowly destroying them, even from afar.

"The world isn't ugly; the human soul is ugly." Loren whispered to herself, squinting at the blazing sky. "This is the only noble action that I can do."

Her heart sped up at hearing her own words—whispers that had been immediately consumed by the sound of cars speeding by. She looked down at the water, and then up at the outline of the city. She turned around one last time at what she was leaving behind and her mind suddenly froze. The thoughts that were spinning through her head fell at her feet like sick bees. When she turned around, she was being stared at by that guy, that same guy who she had seen at this very spot before.

She knew she was seeing things now. The sleep deprivation had taken its toll. She had crossed the line of sanity but she was strangely not bothered by it. As far as she was concerned, she was already dead.

Chapter 16

Trevor would be starting with Green Future on Monday. He had filed his paperwork with MIT to take the semester off, and he had located an apartment in the Fenway area of Boston that was available immediately.

He had been biking back and forth between his dorm room and his new apartment all day, his backpack and bike panniers filled with his belongings. Some of his items would be too bulky for the bike, and he wasn't exactly sure how he was going to get them to his new apartment. He supposed he could wait for Scott to get out of class to help him.

It was on one of his trips back from his new apartment when he noticed something that made him stop immediately. That same girl that he had seen a while back that had troubled him so much was there again, standing in the same spot on the Harvard Bridge. He felt like that was eons ago. Back then, he had been a struggling student with no real plan in life. He had his first real job now, and now he was somebody with something to offer.

The girl was completely lost in her thoughts, unaware of him this time. Trevor felt a swell of courage and stood there, waiting for her to turn around and notice him. When she did finally turn around, he took a step backward. Her way of looking right through him unnerved him. She seemed equally as surprised to see him standing there.

"Hi," said Trevor lamely.

"Hi," Loren said. She looked confused.

"I'm Trevor. I, uh... saw you here before. It's kind of strange you know... I ride by here all the time and don't usually see the same people twice."

She looked at him as if he were speaking Greek. "You're not trying to pick me up, are you?" she said flatly.

"Oh um... I just, I don't know... I thought you looked... I don't know."

"Lost?" she said. Then she snapped, "It takes one to know one, doesn't it?"

The look in her eyes frightened Trevor. Tears suddenly sprang from her eyes and she didn't seem to notice them. She looked at him as if she were drowning and were pleading to him for help.

"Hey, I didn't mean to upset you," Trevor said, coming a little closer to her. "What's wrong? Are you okay?"

There were no more pretenses for Loren. She wasn't sure whether or not this guy was a figment of her imagination. Her soul was ripped open—this was her last attempt to connect with the world before she would ultimately reject her place in it.

"I'm sorry," She said quietly.

Trevor could barely hear her voice over the roar of the cars passing behind him. She didn't seem to care whether or not he could hear her—she seemed to be talking to herself rather than to him.

Trevor instinctively moved toward her and grabbed her hands. As soon as his hands closed around hers she clutched at him fiercely and opened her eyes at him, widely.

"What are you sorry for?" he urged her. She seemed to snap to the reality that he was not an apparition once his hands closed around hers.

"What are you doing here?" she questioned back at him. "Who are you?"

"My name is Trevor. I'm just moving out of my dorm room. Hey, look, whatever you're going through right now, it won't last. Just last week, I had no aim in life. I was basically flunking out of school. My parents would have been crushed. Now, I've got a job, a real job, and I'm going to take some time off school to get my head straight. Your life can turn around too. Whatever it is that's bothering you, it won't last." Trevor surprised himself. He was the last person on earth to approach a strange girl and ask her to open up about her life. This girl was different, though. There was something so painfully honest about her, the way she looked at him, that he trusted her implicitly. She was open to him, and that made him open to her. However it happened, he didn't know, but it happened. His soul had chosen her, and her soul had chosen him.

"I... thank you," she said quietly. She let her head fall, as if in defeat. She realized that she was no longer completely in control of the course of her life. Something else was happening to her, something that her intuition had led her into.

Trevor squeezed her hands and told her "I'm not going to leave you alone right now. Come with me. I'm just on my way back to my dorm to pick up some of the last of my things. Then I'll cook you dinner at my new place. Don't worry—I'm not a creep or anything. You look like you need some company. I'd like for you to think of me as someone to talk to. I don't have many friends. My guess is that you don't either. I don't mean that there's something wrong with you, just that, you know... most people suck. What do you say? Will you come with me?"

Loren smiled through her tears. Her answer was a nod.

Chapter 17

Loren didn't tell Trevor that he had saved her life, but he knew that he had. It wasn't something that needed to be said. That afternoon Loren helped Trevor move the remainder of his belongings to his new apartment. She was very quiet at first, slowly getting used to his presence until it started to feel natural to her. Her first impulse was to be completely open to him, which was different from her reaction to most people. This was a new feeling for her. She wasn't used to being around someone like this, but the longer she spent with him the more she realized that she belonged with him.

She couldn't help but be open to him. His boyish, freckled face with his mop of red hair looked almost out of place with his serious grey eyes, which frequently clouded over in thought. He was so completely gentle to the point of being physically inept. She had never felt less threatened by a guy in her life.

They finished moving his belongings to his new apartment and Trevor took out a corkboard that he kept over his desk. "Hey can you give me a hand with this?" Trevor asked her. "I just need you to hold it up so that I can get these screws in."

"Sure," Loren said, and held the corkboard up while he fastened the screws into the wall. She looked over all the various geometric structures and drawings of chemical and protein structures.

"Phi," Loren said simply.

Trevor stopped for a second and looked at her. "Amazing," he said.

"What?" she asked him.

"Not many people know about phi," he said. "What do you know about it?"

"I just know about it from art school. You know, it started with the ancient Greeks. You can take just about any masterpiece and find phi geometry in it. It's kind of like this magic proportion that we are just attracted to for some reason." She paused for a minute in thought and then asked. "Why do you think that is?"

"Well, if you ask me, you're going to get an answer that's going to make you think I'm crazy."

"Sounds interesting. Go on."

"All kinds of natural structures are built upon the Fibonacci sequence, which converges on the number phi. That means that if you divide one number of the Fibonacci sequence by the one that precedes it, you will get something close to the number Phi. The ratio of the two numbers gets closer and closer to phi the further down the Fibonacci sequence. Even human DNA measures 34 angstroms long by 21 angstroms wide for each full cycle of its double helix spiral. Those are Fibonacci numbers; their ratio is 1.619. What I think is that phi is the ratio for perpetuating life itself—perhaps all aspects of life."

"Wow—I just thought it was something that painters used because it looks good."

"But it gets even crazier than that. If you really want to learn about this, you should talk to my old roommate. His major is theoretical physics so he really gets this stuff. I only sort of get it but it goes something like this. You know about Planck's constant? You might have learned about it in a physics class."

"Uh... no. I was an art major, remember?"

"Right. Okay, so some really smart physicist named Max Planck was trying to figure out why metal glows with different colors at different temperatures—you know how you heat up steel and it gets cherry red? Then you heat it up some more and it gets yellow, then some more and it gets blue?"

"Yeah."

"Well, that's called black body radiation. All the classical physicists of the time did the math and the math kept saying that the steel should glow blue at any temperature, but we know for a fact that it changes color with temperature. Well, it turns out that the math works out if you put this seemingly arbitrary number into the equation for black body radiation, which we now call Planck's constant. Planck proposed that energy is emitted in clumps; he called each clump a quantum of energy. The energy of a quantum depends on Planck's constant multiplied by the frequency of vibration. No one took him seriously because it seemed too weird to have this arbitrary constant in there. Having some constant thrown in seemed too messy to their purist thinking, just like the discovery of irrational numbers was heresy to the ancient mathematicians.

"Anyway, it turns out that energy emitted from an atom

has to do with how electrons jump from orbit to orbit around the atom, called a quantum jump. The energy is emitted in clumps because the energy is the result of these quantum jumps, which occur in discrete amounts because of the sizes and energy levels of the orbits.

"Really small objects like electrons and photons act really strange. Photons can act like both a particle and a wave, which to our Newtonian understanding is mutually exclusive. You can also get something called non-locality, where if you do something to an electron in one location, it will instantaneously affect an electron in another location.

"Planck's constant is about 6 times 10 to the negative thirty fourth power Joule seconds. That's a really, really small number. That number sets the scale for quantum phenomena. So the weird way that reality behaves on a really microscopic scale doesn't happen to the phenomena that we experience on our scale because of that one, seemingly random, tiny number. That's why it took us so long to realize the strange quantum phenomena—we will never see it in our daily lives. Our classical brains can't understand the logic that governs the scale of atoms.

"My question is this: Why is Planck's constant the number that it is? It looks like an irrational number, just like phi. Is it an irrational number? I think so; we just don't know exactly what it is because it was derived experimentally. We have only figured it out to about ten decimal places.

"The point of all this is that how the universe behaves is related to these constants, and these constants are all very specific irrational numbers. Some guys even think that phi is somehow related to Planck's constant but my roommate Scott says that their derivations are convoluted—that basically they only find phi in there because they are looking for it.

"I don't know if phi is somehow tied into Planck's constant, but that so-called golden ratio seems to dictate how stuff grows in nature, including us, on our scale of phenomena. You would think that it would somehow be more useful than just to make stuff look good."

Trevor paused for a moment after his monologue to check to see if Loren was following him.

"Just to make stuff look good?" she asked him. "There are some people who spend their entire lives trying to just make stuff look good."

"That's true. I guess I never thought about it like that," Trevor said, suddenly feeling embarrassed.

"Trevor, have you ever looked at a painting or another kind of work of art, and had it blow open your world, or touch you in a way that you couldn't explain?" she looked at him and he stopped to consider her words.

"No I don't think so. I don't get art. I don't mean to sound like an ass, but to be honest it does nothing for me."

"Hmm. That's weird. It does something to me; something significant. It changes me, even if only for a moment. It lights me up completely, from the inside. Sometimes the feeling lasts for days. It transforms the way I see things. The world becomes more beautiful, enchanted even. I see perfect compositions everywhere I look. I feel it in my whole body. And the strange thing is, I think that this is what makes my paintings improve, slowly over time. I seem to make major leaps when I study the old master paintings. Maybe I'm seeing phi because I'm looking for it, but there's this tool that the old masters reportedly used. It's like a compass, you know, the thing you use to draw circles, only this thing will retain phi proportions and you can make it bigger or smaller. It was used to create compositions, but can also be used for us to look at old Master paintings to find the features that align with the phi geometry. All of the masterpieces have the phi geometry when you check with this tool. It's uncanny. It's no coincidence that they become masterpieces. I'm not the only one who gets this feeling from them. Some people have thrown away everything else in life to be in continual harmony with phi proportions through painting. I know; I have been there."

Trevor looked at Loren as if to discover her for the first time. Her face seemed so much more alive than any other he had ever seen. It seemed to change before him constantly—one moment as open and innocent as a child's and the next moment deep and wise like a woman beyond her years. She was an entirely new creature to him—he felt like he could just sit and watch her, mesmerized, all night.

"You do that to me," he said.

Loren looked up at him. "You're sweet," she said frankly.

"No, actually I'm not," he told her. "I'm really quite cold to people, introverted, uninterested. I don't really have any friends anymore and I really don't care. I don't really like people, to be honest. It seems to me everyone is out for himself, and basically I am too when I take a hard look at myself."

"Well it's true that people can be selfish," she responded to him. "But you're sweet to me."

"You're different. You're not just anyone. Don't take this the wrong way since I just met you today, but I feel like we're the same, somehow. I mean, not the same, but it's like we're... I don't mean to be too forward, but..." Trevor paused, stumbling over the words.

"I like you." Loren interrupted him.

"I like you too. You're like me somehow, but I don't know exactly how. I think we can understand each other. I think we don't really fit with a lot of other people, but now we have each other. We don't have to be alone anymore."

Trevor's lips quivered and he went to speak, but his voice failed him. He took her hands gently in his two hands. He looked down at her, towering over her tiny frame by over a foot. He composed himself and continued. "Will you stay with me? I mean, it doesn't have to be tonight, and it doesn't have to be like that. I don't want you to ever be alone again."

Loren smiled and looked up at him. This was the first time he had seen her normally tense face smile and it lighted him up.

"I'm not going anywhere," she said to him, and squeezed his hands. For the first time in months, she no longer felt like a ghost. She felt like she had a place in the world among the living.

Chapter 18

We are part of this universe; we are in this universe, but perhaps more important than both of those facts, is that the universe is in us.

Neil deGrasse Tyson

It was Friday and Sarah was wrapping up her week in Wilmington. She had lunch with Darin every day since making his acquaintance on her first day in town. When she had lunch with Darin earlier that day, she had told him that this was her last day in town. She had to get back to her house to make some more progress on her garden for the Spring plantings. It was going to be a full day of driving so she wanted to get an early start Saturday morning. She had lightheartedly promised to let him know the next time she would do field work in Wilmington.

On her way back to the inn from the river bed, Sarah noticed that the weather was shifting and she shivered inside of her inadequate sweater. She was approaching the stone pavilion with an inkling of hope, though she didn't really expect to see Darin again. He usually started his work day before her and also ended before her. At the end of each day, she would see the stone wall getting longer every day after he had gone and admired it thoroughly. The way he cleaned every joint and fit the stones together so perfectly made it look like they were born next to each other. Dark clouds were moving in overhead and the wind was picking up. When Sarah got to the pavilion and noticed Darin waiting for her, her heart sped up, pounding noisily in her chest and flooding her face with heat.

"I thought you might like some company for dinner, seeing as how it doesn't seem like you know anyone but me in these parts," Darin addressed her once she came within earshot.

Sarah was glad to see him—too glad. It wasn't like her to prefer company to solitude. Solitude kept life simple and dependable, but she couldn't deny the enjoyment that this week had given her by providing a short respite from it.

"I would like that," she said. "Just give me a moment to put my field gear away. Can I meet you somewhere in about a half an hour?"

"How 'bout I pick you up at the inn? There's nowhere decent to eat in this town."

Sarah paused for a moment and wondered what she was getting herself into and decided that for once she would let go of some of her cautiousness. She enjoyed his company, and that was a rarity.

"Sure. I'll wait for you outside the inn," she told him.

Sarah walked away from the pavilion with an eagerness she hadn't felt in years. She quickly changed out of her field clothes in her room at the inn and wondered what she was supposed to do to make herself presentable. She looked at herself in the mirror, at the wind-blown shoulder length blond hair that was probably long out of fashion.

"Forget it," she said to herself in the mirror, "all I'm gonna do is be myself and have fun. I don't give a crap what this guy thinks of me. This isn't a date. I don't know what it is, but after tonight I'll probably never see this guy again anyway."

By the time Sarah went back outside to wait for Darin, tiny flakes of snow had started to fall. She cursed herself for not checking the weather. Hopefully this was a little squall that would blow over by morning. Darin pulled up in a large dump truck with his masonry company's logo on the side. He got out of the truck and approached her. "That the only coat you got? Didn't check the weather, did you?"

"No, I'm afraid I didn't," Sarah replied, feeling foolish.

"I have something in the truck that won't fit you, but you can float in it. In this weather, there's nothing safer than this thing on the road. It's supposed to keep coming down tonight," Darin said, looking up at the clouds moving in overhead.

"Really?" she asked him with a worried look.

"It's just snow." He answered her worried look with a smile. "It happens all the time in these parts. Don't you worry. Come on—hop in." Darin opened the passenger side door for her.

Sarah felt out of control—she would have preferred to take her own car but she didn't have snow tires. She was starting to feel like this might be a bad idea, but Darin's light-hearted demeanor reassured her. He was so at ease that it was impossible to second guess him. Sarah climbed into the truck and Darin got into the driver's seat.

"Yeehaw!" he hollered as he took off the parking brake and put the truck into drive. "This thing will drive through anything."

The truck roared as they pulled forward. Sarah could feel the engine rumbling through the seat underneath her. Darin drove east, deeper into the Green Mountains. Sarah had never been this far into Vermont before. The houses grew sparser. Historic homesteads looked out onto the road, as lights turned on one by one in response to the fading daylight. If there hadn't been cars parked out front of the homesteads, it would have seemed like they had travelled back to another era. Smoke curled out of a chimney of a sugar shack that started to collect snow on its old tin roof, its wooden walls bleached gray by years of sun. Cordwood was stacked floor to ceiling under awnings around the sugar shack.

The snow was slowly erasing remnants of driveways and sticking to the tree branches. The snowflakes were becoming larger and starting to stick to the road. They travelled about twenty minutes outside of town when Darin pulled off the main road and onto a dirt road that ran along the ridgeline of a hill. After a few hundred feet, Darin parked amidst at least a dozen other cars in what was a small parking lot.

"We're here," Darin said and hopped out of the truck.

When Sarah got out of the truck she noticed an enormous barn with an impressive stone foundation. Old fashioned lanterns lighted a path to the main entrance with the daylight now just about gone. The words "The Barn" were painted on a sign next to the entrance and surrounded by white Christmas lights.

"This place has the best steak in the state," Darin said as he held the barn door open for her.

"Wow—look at this place." Sarah looked around at the inside of the old barn, which had been converted to a restaurant. A giant fireplace had been built on one side of the barn, open to the dining room, and a huge fire crackled as it radiated warmth.

"We better get a seat by the fire before this place fills up," Darin suggested. "On a Friday night there will be a waiting list by seven o'clock. Good thing we got here early."

Darin saw to it that they were seated next to the fireplace and the waiter left them to look at the menus.

Sarah couldn't stop looking around her at the gigantic old beams and the worn barn board. It was her idea of beautiful architecture—simple, natural, functional. She imagined hundreds of years ago when this place would have been filled with sheep and cows, smelling of manure, earth and straw. The fireplace was enormous, yet every stone had been perfectly shaped and set.

"You like it?" Darin asked Sarah, snapping her out of her concentration as she studied the stonework.

"Absolutely. I mean, I don't know much about masonry but it looks amazing." she said.

"Well thank you," he offered.

"Wow—that is your work? How did you learn how to do that?"

"I learned from Mennonites in Pennsylvania. I guess you could say I was an apprentice. Except for the religious stuff, those guys really know how to live."

"You lived with Mennonites?"

"I didn't live with them. My ex wife and I rented an old barn that had been converted to an apartment behind of one of their houses. I spent a few years with them and once I learned everything I thought I needed to know, we moved back to Vermont."

"Where is your ex-wife now?"

"Who knows. She's a big drinker, like most people around here. I'm over 10 years sober myself. I was a horrible drunk. Or a good one—depending on who you ask."

"Really? I don't drink either, but I was never a drunk. I just don't drink."

"You don't say! Well that's pretty rare. Good for you. Geez, you're pretty damn boring aren't you?"

"I'm afraid so. I work. A lot. In my free time, I garden and I read. I'm pretty much a wet blanket. No kids, never been married. A regular old spinster, and happy to be one."

"Well here's to a beautiful spinster," Darin said as he raised his water glass.

Sarah raised her glass as well and responded, "and here's to teetotalers."

"Damned straight," Darin said as they clinked glasses.

"So no kids, but what about family?" Darin asked Sarah, and he could tell immediately that he had hit a nerve. It should have been an easy question to answer, but Sarah lowered her eyes to the table and started fidgeting with the edge of the tablecloth.

"There was an accident when I went off to college," Sarah said, deliberately choosing her words. She knew that it wasn't her fault, but she carried around guilt and embarrassment. After all, he shared her blood. "I don't have a family anymore. I mean, I have aunts and uncles, but no immediate family. After the accident, the extended family drifted apart."

"I'm sorry to hear that," he said, not wanting to pry further, and sorry that he had unintentionally dampened the mood.

"It's been a while and I don't dwell on it anymore. In a way it's nice. I don't have to go anywhere in particular for holidays—I get to selfishly do whatever I want with my time. I like it that way. There's too much to do and too little time to do it. Life is short. Every moment counts."

"Well then I'm very honored that you are spending tonight with me."

Sarah smiled at the compliment. This guy had the uncanny power over her to make her actually feel giddy. She didn't know she could feel giddy after all that had happened to her in her life.

When the waiter arrived, Darin ordered a steak, while Sarah ordered a vegetarian pasta dish. Darin looked at her after the waiter left. "I knew there had to be something less than perfect about you," he jested.

"I know, I know, a complete cliché—a vegetarian on top of all the other things that make me completely boring."

"Hey, I don't care if you're vegetarian—just don't make me

eat that kale stuff. I don't care how healthy it is—I'd rather have a short, happy life than a long one eating kale."

"Fair enough," Sarah smiled. "You're not allowed to touch the kale in my garden. I get it all to myself."

"Does that mean I'll get to see your garden someday?"

Sarah paused for just a second, but Darin noticed. She realized that she completely clicked with this guy, regardless of their differences, and maybe even because of them.

"Maybe." She smiled at him, but then realized as she said that word that it hung on her lips like a lie. There was an uncomfortable pause in the conversation, and Sarah went back to admiring the fireplace and the gentle way the light from the flames described the faces of the stones.

She was glad that he hadn't asked her why she didn't drink, because she realized that she would tell him the truth, and then she would feel like an even bigger cornball than she already felt like. When Sarah had been a teenager, she became interested in Buddhism, to the point where her young self even considered becoming a Buddhist nun. She had spent one summer in a Buddhist monastic community, where she had taken lay precepts. The concept of the precepts was different from a promise, where you would be punished or have to repent if the promise was broken. A precept was an ideal that you strove for, usually imperfectly.

The Buddha believed that the ultimate goal in life was to attain enlightenment. Performing self-destructive actions was contrary to that goal, so the Buddha prescribed five precepts that one should strive to follow. They were: no killing, no stealing, no lying, no sexual misconduct and no intoxicants. The ultimate goal was living a life without harming, and the five precepts made the concept more specific in order to be easier to follow the path of no harm.

Buddhists believed that every action had consequences. In addition to manifesting as negative consequences, negative actions would manifest as guilt clouding the mind and preventing the attainment of higher states of consciousness.

After Sarah had put the five precepts through her rational wringer, she decided to take the precepts that summer. After over two decades of keeping the precepts, she could say firsthand that it constantly improved her experience of life and had transformed a rather cold, analytical young person into a compassionate woman. She didn't think of herself as being morally strict because the precepts had become so much a part of her being. The hardest one to keep was the no killing. There were a lot of bugs in the world. When she accidently killed one by a clumsy move, she said a quick Buddhist prayer, a reminder of the preciousness of all life. Although she didn't anticipate achieving anything akin to enlightenment, she did believe that the path of no harm would lead to achieving her highest potential as a human being.

The easiest precept to keep was the no intoxicants. Being a naturally introverted person, she often used this as an excuse to indulge in anti-social behavior. She had heard all the arguments— antioxidants, relaxation, a social lubricant. She felt that all of those benefits could be achieved by other means, without the negative side effect of acting like an ass. Just watching people after they had a few cleansed her of any illusion she might have had about the "positive" effects of alcohol.

Sarah enjoyed Darin's company and they were even able to share silence without feeling awkward. Sarah kept having the feeling that she had known Darin for a lot longer than the five days that she had been working in Wilmington. No one in the restaurant would have picked this couple out as complete strangers as of four days ago.

Just as the waiter arrived at their table with their meals, the lighting cut out in the restaurant. The light from the fireplace and the candles on the tables were now the only source of light in the restaurant and the cathedral ceiling of the huge barn suddenly felt claustrophobic as a dark shroud dropped down to hover just above the table tops.

"Well it looks like you will be eating in the dark," the waiter shrugged. "Hopefully you brought cash—in this storm the electricity probably won't be back until morning so our credit card machines won't work."

"Yup—no problem," Darin said as the waiter placed their meals in front of them. He looked up at Sarah and her eyes were wide in the candlelight as she looked around her.

"Is this normal?" she asked, "I mean, the electricity going out?"

"Yeah, pretty normal if a snow storm hits this time of year. It'll be fixed by morning, most likely."

"What about the hotel? Will it have power?"

"Probably not. Wilmington is pretty small. When one line goes down, it usually means the whole town."

"Am I going to be able to drive out in the morning?"

"Yeah—the plows will be through by morning. Don't worry. I'll follow you out of town with my truck to make sure that city slicker car of yours makes it down the hill. Once they plow and salt it won't be bad."

"No one seems to be bothered by this."

"A lot of us who live outside of town are off-grid anyway. Those of us in town, well you saw what Irene did. You can't intimidate a Vermonter with the weather. We always make it through somehow. I swear, if the whole outside world ended, Vermont would be better off for it. It would go back to the way it used to be. All these old farms would get started back up. People lived without electricity for a whole lot longer than we have lived with it. City folk seem to think that life would end without electricity. Life might end without the sun, but life as I know it would just keep on going without electricity. It would slow down a bit, that's all. It's about time it did."

"I guess I never thought about it like that. A lot of my life revolves around electricity. Electricity enables me to get information for my work, and to be able to do computations that would otherwise take lifetimes to do."

"So what kind of computations do you need to do that are so important?"

"Well, my main job is trying to figure out when we're going

to run out of resources to sustain the population. The idea is that if we know more about it, that we can manage the resources more wisely."

"You smart people are so stupid sometimes. Why not just manage the resources wisely? Does it really matter when they will run out? If they're gone, they're gone. What's the point in worrying about it? Sounds to me like the government higher ups want to know all this stuff so that they can make sure they get their fill before the whole world goes to hell in a hand basket."

"Yeah, that could be. I wonder about that sometimes. I mean, when people like me put these reports together, the government then knows where the resources are and how much there are. If a report landed on the President's desk one day and it said that we have ten years left or else we need to whittle the population down to 50% of what it is right now, what do you think he would do?"

"Well, If I were President, which maybe I will be someday," Darin winked at her, "I would say, 'Boys, get the guns and the pizzas and I'll meet you downstairs in the vault while we wait out this war that's about to take place upstairs.'"

Sarah smiled, but she felt a sadness come over her in realizing that there was some truth to his words. She looked around her at the dark restaurant. The candles on the tables just barely lit up the faces of the guests filling the dining room. There seemed to be nothing amiss in this scene. In fact, the guests seemed to be more animated by the change in lighting.

"Okay folks listen up." The waiter hollered into the dining

room from the entrance to the kitchen. "The cooks are all cooking with candlelight now, so no complaints are allowed about whatever might end up on your plate."

"Oh great," groaned a voice from the dining room amidst chuckling.

The analytical little girl in her who cringed with change, was mortally afraid of the dark, and wanted control of all variables, seemed to be utterly absent in Sarah that night. Her twenty-line TO DO lists sitting on every surface of her house as she led her life in a mad rush to achieve the most in this lifetime were completely forgotten, along with the rows and rows of data recorded and yet to be collected. She oddly felt safe and at peace here, in a dark room with strangers gathered in an old barn on the side of a mountain being slowly covered by snow, while time seemed to be standing still. This felt like a real place, not one tenuously dependent on outside resources, the international stock market, and political climate. This place had been here long before her time, and would be here for long after she was gone. This old barn begged the question of her as she sat there in the candlelight:

Just what kind of life are you so obsessed about preserving?

Chapter 19

Darin drove Sarah back to the hotel through a very dark and quiet downtown Wilmington. Due to the electricity outage she had agreed with him, to her astonishment, that it would make more sense to spend the night at his place.

"Where I will make you breakfast and coffee in the morning and send you back to your dismal life in the city," Darin had convinced her.

"I don't live in the city. I mean, I'm near the city, but it's pretty rural," she contested.

"If you see more concrete than dirt on a daily basis, you live in the city," he continued to tease her.

"Okay—it's pretty suburban," she finally conceded.

The inn proprietor provided Sarah with a flashlight so that she could navigate through the dark hallways to her room to gather her belongings. Sarah was grateful that she would not be staying in the hotel, whose walls creaked ominously in the weak glow of the flashlight.

When Sarah exited the hotel with her overnight bag, the snow was coming down unlike anything she had ever seen. The huge flakes were relentless, completely overwhelming the landscape, the houses, and finally the road as they made their way out of town. When they got to Darin's driveway he put the plow down on the front of his dump truck and carved the way for them up a moderately sloped hill. She could see the house in the light of the truck headlights. It was a cape-style house built of stone—modest but charming.

"You'd never guess, but this is new construction. I finished it a few years ago—it was something I always wanted to do," Darin told her as he helped her out of the truck. Darin hurried ahead with her overnight bag to turn on a porch light so that she could see where she was walking. She could feel the freshly fallen snow creeping up on her ankles—she hadn't brought appropriate shoes with her.

"Solar." Darin answered the question in Sarah's eyes when she looked at the illuminated porch light.

When they entered the doorway that looked like it had been crafted at least a century ago, a Burnese Mountain Dog greeted them at the door. She was a strong, handsome canine and she greeted Darin with an excited whine and then set to investigating Sarah with her nose.

"Don't worry about her. She knows you're with me. She's just checking you out," Darin said to Sarah. "Her name is Adah. She has an amazing sense for people. She knows you're one of the good ones so she's fine with you. You should see her when some people come to the house, though. Adah turns into Cujo. She would die before she let anyone hurt me."

"She's beautiful," Sarah said, and then took her eyes off of the dog to scan the inside of Darin's home.

The small stone house, a simple rectangular shape, had an

open floor plan. Fashioned to look like a cape on the outside, rough-hewn wooden beams framed the open space on the inside. A massive stone chimney with a wood stove served as the focal point of the room.

"Make yourself comfortable while I get the stove going," he said as he opened the wood stove and set to work with some kindling. "I don't have guests too often, so forgive the mess."

"Are you kidding? It's absolutely perfect," Sarah exclaimed. "I feel like I have been whisked out of my banal existence and thrown into a fantasy world. It looks like my idea of heaven in here."

"I'm glad you think so. I feel the same way."

"Actually, it seems like I'm just waking up from a recurring dream. This feels more real to me than my own life."

"It is. Your life in the city would end if the power went out and the food stopped being trucked in."

"Actually, I do grow my own food, but you're right about the power. The whole city would become dysfunctional."

"I've always wanted to farm up here, but I don't have the time. After laying stone for eight hours a day I don't have much gas left in me."

"It is work to grow food for sure, but I enjoy it. I don't have to lay stone for a living—I sit in front of a computer all day most of the time and I think if I didn't garden my body and spirit would waste away."

The scene seemed too perfect to Sarah to be reality—the

snow, the perfectly crafted house, the warmth of the woodstove. She wanted to prolong the moment as much as possible before she had to return to the life that she had known for so long. The snow kept falling outside, and she secretly wished that it would keep falling, sealing them both up in this cozy paradise indefinitely.

They drank hot tea and watched the fire through the glass of the woodstove, talking in low voices and laughing occasionally. Darin reached out and took her hand in his and she didn't resist. After years with her nose to the grindstone, she wanted to allow herself this time, this man. She didn't know how it had happened and she didn't care. This brief time they were granted together was a gift that may never happen again and she was going to gratefully enjoy every last moment of it.

Chapter 20

When morality comes up against profit, it is seldom that profit loses.

Shirley Chisholm

Stan called a meeting with Jack Sims, Green Future's CEO, as soon as he arrived back from Washington. He walked briskly down the corridor lined tastefully with potted plants at regular intervals. The corporate building of Green Future had a much different look than the bioengineering wing where Stan worked. His building was much starker—more function than form in the clean, bare spaces. No doubt one of the best interior decorating firms in Cincinnati had been hired to turn the Green Future corporate offices into a place where one felt awkward without a suit and tie.

Stan was greeted by a very attractive young woman wearing no expression as she greeted him. She was the CEO's secretary, no doubt chosen with the same thoughts in mind as the interior decorator—to instill a sort of awed respect. It was apparent that she felt that overt friendliness would be a violation of professionalism.

"Please, have a seat in the conference room. Mr. Sims will meet you there shortly," the secretary said briskly.

Stan led himself to the conference room where he had been on surprisingly few occasions considering how long he had been working for Green Future. As soon as he sat down in one of the enormous, plush seats, a woman entered the room with a silver tray filled with an assortment of items. She looked to be around retirement age, with tired skin, and an expression matching that of the secretary.

"Will you have coffee, sir?" the older woman, dressed impeccably, asked him. Her uniform was almost an exact match to the dark gray paint chosen for the walls of the conference room, accented austerely by white molding.

"Yes, please, with sugar and cream. Thank you," Stan replied, and made himself busy with pulling the documents he brought out of his briefcase.

The woman silently prepared his coffee for him, the teaspoon clinking awkwardly in the silent room, before disappearing as quickly as she had appeared.

Once Stan had arranged his documents into neat piles on the conference room's oversized dark mahogany table, the CEO entered.

Stan stood up abruptly and unconsciously bowed slightly as he greeted the CEO and shook his hand vigorously. Although Stan had worked under the CEO for decades, he still felt a stranger to him. Stan was naturally inclined to want to please his superior. He always felt smaller in this man's presence, even though his hulking frame was a good deal larger than the CEO's in every dimension.

"I hope this meeting means that things are progressing well in the lab." Jack Sims started right off without concern for warming up with small talk.

Stan smiled eagerly, "Yes. I am happy to report that major progress has been made. In fact, we are just wrapping up our work on the second target of the 2030 solution. I have brought you the final lab report in person. Our drought-resistant crops are ready for retail. But that's not all. I'm excited to report that we have also made a major move forward on the third target of the 2030 solution."

Jack raised his eyebrows, but showed no emotion that Stan could discern.

"I believe we have the major pieces in place that are going to help us solve this chemical puzzle," Stan started. "In fact, I'm so confident that we are going to knock this one out of the park that I already have Senator Bly working on some legislation that will ensure that the immediate application of the new product isn't derailed by activists."

"That is good news." Jack offered the words with joyless eyes. Then his eyes narrowed and he leaned toward Stan and spoke in a lower voice. "I do hope that Senator Bly realizes how carefully he needs to word this legislation."

"Yes, yes," Stan quickly replied. "He understands the sensitivity of the situation. The legislation will look like it is describing a chemical already in use. The intent of the new chemical will be well hidden—I will make sure of it. I will proofread thoroughly whatever Senator Bly authors."

"Good," Jack replied, and then added quickly, "what is your timeframe for lab testing?"

"That's hard to say just yet. This legislation is imminent. In fact, our timing is perfect—Senator Bly will slip it into a Forestry bill that should get signed within two months. The legislation shouldn't hold anything up. I'm guessing we'll have something to start internal testing within the month." The look on Stan's face hinted that he doubted his own words. This was a tall order, but he had faith in the boy. He only said that they would have something to try out. It may take many trials before they had something that might work in the field. Lab testing could start as soon as Trevor came up with a single possible solution with the Foldit software.

"When are you starting your patent paperwork?"

"We'll start this week. We'll be patenting the intent of the process, not the chemical exactly. This will keep others from coming up with different versions of what we're doing."

"Perfect."

"About the lab testing..." Stan groped awkwardly for words at this point. "Something like this needs to have some component of long-term testing, at least for our own internal review. It..."

Jack cut Stan's words short, "That's the point of the legislation. Why should our products require more testing than other products out there on the market? Long-term? How long-term? One year, five years, ten years? We don't have the time, Stan. Every day about 370,000 people are born in the world. Are you going to tell them to wait a few years before they can eat?"

"Well no, sir, but..."

"Just do the testing you are hired to do. This one is no

different than the others. The next time you walk in here, I want to see the final lab report that shows that this thing works."

Stan stood in stunned silence. He realized how different the daily challenges were for Mr. Sims than his own. Mr. Sims would never really understand the intricacies and implications of what this chemical might do. It was his responsibility to keep the company profitable.

Stan was silent for a moment before responding. "Of course, Mr. Sims. You're absolutely right. I will keep you updated electronically on our progress."

"Good. Thank you Mr. Cobald." The CEO got up from the conference table, letting Stan know that their meeting was over.

Stan quickly shook his hand, and then looked down at the conference table while the CEO turned away and headed for the door.

"Don't forget these." Stan picked up the piles of papers and practically chased Mr. Sims as he was heading out of the door of the conference room.

"Ah yes, thank you," Jack said as he took the papers without looking at them. "Good Day, Mr. Cobald."

With that, Mr. Sims left the room.

Stan suddenly felt a chill despite the full suit he had donned especially for this occasion.

Chapter 21

Jack Sims was annoyed at Stan Cobald, though he couldn't put his finger on any one thing that Stan had done to cause the irritation. Stan reminded him of a fat little boy he used to enjoy tormenting in grade school. He remembered stepping on the fat kid's lunch one day and then as the kid started to cry he had laughed. "You don't need it, fat ass," he had said to him. The group of kids who obediently followed Jack around all snickered.

Jack smiled to himself at the memory, at his entourage even at that young age, thinking about what a natural leader he was. He was born to direct a company of this magnitude. Ironically, he directed a company where he had to depend on the innovations of sniveling geeks like Stan Cobald. Stan Cobald was excellent at his job, Jack had to admit. Jack chose to put up with him for no other reason, but he did attempt for as few in-person meetings as possible. He preferred to stay out of what went on the lab—all that mattered were the company's financials and even more precisely, his own financials. As far as the lab was concerned, he just needed enough data for marketing purposes. As for long-term testing, that was not Jack's concern. Most of this product would land on foreign soil and what happened to the world after Jack was done with it was of absolutely no concern to him. He had never been the family man type. He hadn't even been the marrying type. Having to put up with other people, deal with their issues, and support them had never appealed to Jack. Jack was too busy owning the world, acre by acre.

Jack considered his world view realistic. The natural environment was a naturally competitive place, where only the strong were destined to survive. The maladapted and the weak would get weeded out, sooner or later. Jack was at the top of the food chain. He had fought hard to get where he was, and continued to do whatever it would take to stay there.

"Mr. Sims." The voice of his secretary cut into his thoughts through his phone speaker as Jack sat at his desk.

"Yes, Simone."

"A Mr. Jacques Thibaudeau is on the line for you."

"Tell him I am not available."

"He said you would say that. He wanted me to tell you that he is not going to give up until you speak with him. I'm just relaying the message, Sir. If you don't want to take the call that is fine but he may be tying up my phone line until I can get IT to block his call."

Jack's face soured. "Fine. Put him through."

Jack picked up the receiver and answered curtly, "Yes?"

The voice on the other end was thick with a French accent. "Mister Sims, I am sorry to bother you but I must insist that you listen to me."

"Go on," replied Jack flatly.

"My absence in the kitchen is due to my wife's illness. She has cancer. Her condition has deteriorated quite suddenly."

"If you don't show up to work to do your job you are replaced by someone who will. The circumstances do not matter. I can't very well eat if there is no head chef in my kitchen."

"Mister Sims, I have served you faithfully for twelve years. You know that I am dependable. Please, I ask that you allow me some time to be with my wife while she has a treatment of chemotherapy. I will return as soon as is possible."

"You either come to work or you do not. You have exactly 24 hours before I find your replacement. If you are not in the kitchen when I come home from work tomorrow evening then you will no longer have a position with me. There is no discussion about it. If I had already found a replacement then we would not even be having this conversation. Lucky for you, I have not gotten around to it yet. You decide Monsieur Thibaudeau."

"But Sir..."

"Good bye." Jack hung up the receiver and then pressed the button for Simone's line.

"Yes, Mr. Sims."

"Go ahead and block his number."

"Yes sir."

Chapter 22

Where there is love there is life.

Mahatma Gandhi

Loren slipped into Trevor's life as if she had always been a part of it—she was the little cog that had been missing in his clockwork. Once it popped back into place, all systems sprang to life.

He had one nagging concern. He hadn't told Loren who he worked for. She wasn't nosy about his work. Though he worked from home, there was no way for her to tell who his employer was. But he had just passed the two-week mark of his employment, and he knew that a pay stub was due any day now. He was afraid that she would get to the mail before him. He didn't want to keep secrets from her—he had just been postponing a conversation that he wasn't particularly keen on having. It might not even be a big deal—he just wasn't sure. She could be really sensitive about things that never would have occurred to him as touchy subjects.

Soon after moving in with him, Loren had resumed her shifts at the food processing facility. Margie had covered for her and told their boss Roger that Loren had become extremely ill. With how thin and pale she was, their boss didn't doubt her.

Loren had just gotten home from her shift and let herself in to the apartment. She set her bag down in the entryway. It was a one bedroom apartment and had a small kitchenette overlooking a living room. Trevor had set up his home office in the far corner of the living room. He was deep in thought, hunched over his desk. When he heard the apartment door open and close, he forced his eyes away from the computer screen.

"Don't mind me," Loren said. "I'll go ahead and start dinner. You just keep on doing whatever it is you do."

Loren walked over to his desk and gave him a kiss before going to the kitchenette. Trevor smiled gratefully at her, but didn't go back to looking at the model he was working on. Instead, he watched her as she opened every cupboard to scan its contents, going back and forth to the refrigerator to assess what was there. She stood in the middle of the kitchen with her hands on her hips. He could see her mentally processing all the potential ingredients and trying to figure out new combinations. He saw her jump slightly, as if seized with an idea, and then she methodically went for her target ingredients, pulling pans out of the cupboards and taking items out of the refrigerator as she amassed a heap of items on the kitchen counter. Loren had a gift for taking whatever she could find in the kitchen and making something surprisingly delicious. She named each meal as she served it, intent on never cooking exactly the same meal twice.

"What's it going to be tonight?" Trevor asked her with a smile.

Loren's eyes twinkled. "Tonight's dinner is going to be called 'Three Cheeses to the Wind', featuring three-cheese alfredo sauce over pasta, topped by a dusting of herbs tossed at random."

Trevor smiled and got up from his office chair. He took a

seat at the breakfast bar which served as their kitchen table. The breakfast bar was perched over the kitchen counter where Loren was busily preparing dinner. He could have afforded a bigger apartment with his new salary, but didn't want to change his lifestyle too much right off the bat. He also wasn't sure what the future would bring.

Trevor sat quietly watching Loren prepare dinner as he tried to figure out an opening line to what was sure to be an awkward conversation.

"What's on your mind?" she said to him plainly, reading the workings of his thoughts in the spots of tension on his face.

"Oh, it's nothing really," he answered, grateful for her noticing that he needed to talk. "It's just that you have no idea what I do for work. I mean it's just a job. It's fun. My boss is a good guy. But the company itself, well, it's fairly controversial."

Loren stopped what she was doing, her interest instantly piqued. Her hands, which had been engaged in chopping a block of monterey jack into neat squares suddenly stopped. "Well, who do you work for?"

"A company called Green Future."

"Yeah, right," she said in disbelief, but then she paused to look at his face and instantly realized that he was being sincere. After a moment of silence, she blurted out "Why the hell do you work for them?"

"To be honest, mainly it's the money. But the work is fun, too— it's what I'm good at."

"Why in the world would you help them?"

"I couldn't come up with a compelling reason not to. I mean, there's so much misinformation out there. I'm not sure that they're the bad guys that everyone makes them out to be. There are also public safety requirements, such as product testing. If what they're doing really is so bad, I don't believe that our country would let them continue."

"It's called corruption. All governments have it. The people that end up in politics aren't the Mother Theresas of the world. They're power and money-hungry people. They get paid off to allow Green Future to do what they do."

"So what if they do? Isn't one of the greatest things about this country the freedom of choice? No one is forced to buy their products. As long as they can show through testing that their products aren't harmful, why shouldn't they be allowed to sell their products?"

"You really think a test paid for by Green Future would show that their products are harmful? Besides, there are no long-term test results out there—our planet is their long-term testing lab and if the results are harmful, it will be too late. I don't care about America and how great it is to have our so-called freedom. I care about the fact that humans are slowly destroying everything beautiful and wild in the world."

"I don't know, Loren—I don't have all the answers, but I can tell you that if I didn't take this job, I was going to flunk out of MIT, blow my full-ride scholarship, and have to move back to Iowa and live with my folks, who can't even afford to pay their mortgage. There weren't a lot of options for me."

Loren's eyebrows knitted together and she scrutinized Trevor's face. She was trying to understand, but mostly she was trying to keep her anger from welling up inside of her and spilling out all over him.

"You guys are all the same, you know. You only care about yourself. Why am I even here?" Loren's form slumped as her eyes scanned the apartment helplessly.

"I know it's not perfect. I'm not fully convinced myself. I just needed to get out of the slump I was in. It doesn't have to be for forever. I plan on going back to school eventually. I just needed a break, okay?"

"No, it's not okay. Not with me. "

The conversation left the air feeling thick and the apartment was suddenly filled with unbearable silence as Loren looked expectantly at Trevor. He averted his eyes from her, feeling like his heart was being ripped from his chest. He wasn't sure what to expect when he told her, but this was worse than what he had imagined.

"I love you Loren," he said to her, simply. "I'm not a perfect guy and I'm certainly no hero, by any stretch of the imagination. I'm just doing the best I can with what I have been given. For all I know, this is just temporary. I mean, they haven't relocated me or anything."

"I love you too," she said to him. Her anger started to melt into sadness as she realized what was at stake.

After a long pause she said, "I don't subscribe the idea of having strings attached to love—like I love you but only if you resemble the person I want you to be. I know I love you, and I know you're not perfect, and that's okay with me. I want you to know how concerned I am about the future of what remains of our environment, but I also realize that I am not perfect. I'm sure a lot of what I eat is GMO, as careful as I try to be. I wish you didn't work for that company and I hope that it is only temporary."

"I swear, Loren, if I come across anything at Green Future that makes me think that they are not above board, I will become a whistleblower," Trevor offered sincerely.

Loren grew thoughtful for a moment and then her eyes started to sparkle. She smiled at him. "You may not be a big dummy after all. All right, we'll see where this goes."

Chapter 23

The world is a dangerous place to live; not because of the people who are evil, but because of the people who don't do anything about it.

Albert Einstein

Arriving back at her desk in Washington D.C. felt like being slapped back into a cold reality after her time in Vermont. Sarah's mind kept wandering back to Darin's house on the mountain, wrapped in snow and warmed by fire. She had a pile of data to enter into her model from the notes that she had taken in Wilmington, but every time she picked up a sheet of paper from her field notebook, she could see Darin's dimpled cheeks laughing at her.

"What are those numbers going to tell you, little lady?" she could hear him saying with a laugh in his throat. "I'll tell you want they say—there are too many goddamn idiots in the world."

"Looks like someone had a good weekend," Amanda said, snapping Sarah out of her reveries.

"Yeah, I did," Sarah responded quickly, realizing that she had been smiling to herself when Amanda had appeared in the doorway of her office. "What's up Amanda?"

"Hey, you know how you asked me to keep tabs on that Senator? Well, it looks like Bly is working on some new legislation."

"Is he? Is it agricultural?"

"You know, I can't really tell. It is in the Forestry Bill. I guess it could be agricultural. It sounds pretty vague, really. You should take a look at the draft yourself. I just emailed it to you."

Amanda was a legal aid to the CIA, and had taken it upon herself as a personal favor to Sarah to keep her privy to upcoming legislation. Sarah had given her a whole list of items that she wanted to be alerted about, including any legislature that Senator Bly had authored.

"Thanks a ton, Amanda. I owe you one."

Sarah's mood suddenly shifted as her mind came into focus.

"Yeah, no problem." Amanda lingered in the doorway as Sarah started to nervously tap her crossed leg. "What's his name, anyway."

"Oh god, is it that obvious?" Sarah rolled her eyes.

"Sarah, how long have we been working together? Fifteen years? I've never seen you with that goofy look on your face. Well, it's none of my business, but I'm happy for you. Enjoy it while it lasts. I hope he deserves you."

"Thanks," Sarah responded self-consciously.

Amanda smiled and then finally left the doorway.

Sarah took a deep breath and smiled to herself. "Yup," she said under her breathe before turning back to her computer, "I am an idiot."

As soon as Sarah read the carefully crafted wording of Bly's legislation, she knew Green Future was up to something. The fact that they chose the forestry bill was not good news. This would fly under the public's radar. With the timing of this upcoming legislation, she knew that Green Future would probably be doing some initial laboratory testing very soon of whatever god forbidden chemical they had come up with this time. This legislation would essentially allow them to commercialize the product without having to wait for the results of any field trials.

Sarah knew that the field-scale tests would be ineffectual anyway. It was easy to manipulate baseline levels of contamination and average occurrences of sicknesses like cancer by simply sampling selectively. The Green Future scientists were simply too clever to be trapped by that kind of concrete evidence, especially if their chemicals caused a sickness that may take decades to appear, in an area of the world where the members of the population are constantly shifting. It would be impossible to chase down a single culprit for cancer since carcinogens are ubiquitous in the modern environment. Any required field-scale testing would likely not be run for long enough to identify the long-term effects on the environment as well.

This legislature being in the forestry bill posed the possibility that Green Future had its eyes on extremely large tracts of land, especially forested tracts of land. This worried Sarah. The world's largest terrestrial biodiversity was housed in forests. She suddenly lost interest in the pile of data she had collected in Wilmington. As she absent-mindedly flipped through her field notebook, she slowly formed a plan in her mind for gaining access to Green Future's laboratory. She realized that her mind was working like a criminal now, desperately trying to find an in to that corporate fortress.

Chapter 24

Numbers are the essence of things.

Pythagoras

Trevor was told as little as possible about what he was working on. He was provided with a specific assignment, without being informed what his solution would be used for.

Trevor had been at his desk for about fifteen hours straight, obsessing over the visual riddle. Loren had gone to bed a while ago after kissing him and telling him not to stay up too late. Several times throughout the night he thought he had hit a wall, but then he took a short break and found himself running back to the computer model with a new idea. The particular protein that Stan had given him to unfold wasn't a difficult puzzle to solve, but after solving it, he had to take the chemical structure responsible for the unfolding and enter it into a second program to see how that molecule would react to some common elements.

Although Stan did not explicitly reveal to Trevor what the aim of this project was, Trevor thought he might have figured it out. It seemed like Green Future was trying to come up with a chemical that would rapidly degrade cellulose and then quickly biodegrade. This could be used for all kinds of industrial applications where fibrous waste products needed to be swiftly and economically broken down. For Green Future to invent a chemical like this and then patent it would be hugely useful for many industrial processes. Trevor didn't yet understand where it fit into their agriculture-centric plans for the future, but if the chemical could become completely unreactive after a few days, it would not pose any environmental problems.

The idea that this puzzle he was working on could have an application in the real world was nothing short of thrilling for Trevor. Trevor's curiosity of whether the chemical would act in the lab as it did in the model was overpowering. Trevor's vision started to blur as his eyes settled on one point on the screen and became heavy with the desire to close.

"Maybe it's time to stop for the night. For the tenth time. For real this time," he said aloud to the empty room. He quickly turned off his computer before he could change his mind and then rubbed his eyes as he sat hunched over his keyboard while the purr of the computer went silent.

When he opened his eyes again, he looked up at the corkboard that he kept above his workspace like a shrine to phi. "You provide the ability to grow infinitely," he said to the geometric figures as if they could hear him. "What would your opposite look like? Something that spontaneously unravels."

The yin to the yang of the protein puzzle flashed in his mind like a photo.

"Of course that's it!"

Trevor slapped the power key to his computer with a grin— delirious from lack of sleep and drunk from the excitement of discovery.

Chapter 25

"I've got it," the excited young voice in the receiver said. "I've been up all night just waiting 'til morning to call you."

Stan leaned forward in his chair, the phone cradled to his ear and his eyebrows pressed together. "I'm pleased to hear that you have a potential solution," Stan said in a metered tone. "But just so you know, these things don't happen overnight. We might have twenty different chemicals worthy of lab trials before we figure out which one is going to do the trick. And maybe none of them will, but I appreciate your enthusiasm."

Stan smiled at the voice on the other end of the phone. He knew he had found the right match when he had first spotted Trevor. He was immensely pleased that his instincts had panned out, and that they had panned out this quickly with a possibility.

"We can start lab trials right away. As soon as I get the lab data, I'll send it over to you so you can compare it with your model's results. Good work, Trevor. Send me what you have so that I can put together a testing plan right away."

When Stan got off the phone, he leaned back in his chair and tucked his hands neatly behind his head, mentally piecing together the testing schedule and assembling appropriate staff members. He pictured telling Jack Sims that testing was already under way, ahead of schedule. He gazed out the window of his corner office and felt a flutter of excitement. He may shortly receive the information that could revolutionize the conversion of forestland to agricultural land. The dark, impenetrable reaches of the jungle would soon be tamed by the hand of man using unprecedented efficiency.

The third target for the 2030 solution was now underway. The burning of the rainforest to plant palm oil and other crops in tropical areas generated air pollution, killed animals, and more importantly, created bad PR. That method would hopefully be a thing of the past. Green Future would create a chemical that could rapidly degrade the plant and tree material in forested areas in lieu of burning them for crop production. This was no small challenge—there were many factors to consider. The chemical could only affect plant and tree matter, it would have to be extremely potent but short lived and would have to rapidly biodegrade once the plant matter had been degraded. The end product of the chemical reaction would have to be a source of fertilizer for subsequent agricultural crops. This would reuse the nutrients for subsequent crops rather than converting them to particulate pollution in the form of ash, such as with the slash and burn agricultural method.

During the Vietnam War, Agent Orange did its job inelegantly, leaving behind a trail of birth defects and contamination that no doubt still existed. The new chemical could not leave behind a toxic residue because food crops would subsequently be planted there. It would indeed be a huge challenge—a chemical so powerful it could take down a forest, but then it had to biodegrade quickly enough to make it more cost effective than the slash and burn agricultural method. Slash and burn was not incredibly efficient. The deep roots of trees may not burn, and the land still required a lot of energy to get it into shape for modern agricultural practices. Enormous amounts of fossil fuels were required to go from virgin forest to fields worthy of agriculture even after burning the land.

He couldn't imagine what kind of a chemical it would have to be—he just hoped that it could be applied in low concentrations and that it would not be a deadly rerun of the Agent Orange fiasco. Trevor had sounded confident on the phone, with the excitement of discovery in his voice that Stan knew so well. Stan hoped that his excitement was well-founded.

Within a few hours, he would have the lab trial schedule outlined and the staff assembled. Lab testing could begin as soon as tomorrow, as long as the chemical didn't contain any exotic components. Stan eagerly anticipated the next few months, when the most exciting aspects of his job would unfold. He would put his head down and doggedly keep to the testing schedule until a solution could be found, emerging from the other side a sort of technical superman for the progress of mankind on earth.

Chapter 26

Trevor slept until the afternoon after his long night at the computer and his phone call to Stan that morning. Loren had already gone to work and wasn't due back home until dinner time. Trevor was too excited to stay put and had nothing to offer to his job today. He already emailed the chemical composition to Stan and had only to wait for the initial lab results and be available for consulting in case the chemists had questions during the formulation of the chemical solution.

After eating a bowl of cereal, he decided to hop on his bike. It wasn't like him to aimlessly bike around the streets of Boston, so he formulated a plan as he pulled on a pair of jeans and a sweatshirt. Nothing appealed to him until he thought about visiting his old roommate to see what he was up to. He needed to talk to someone, someone like Scott who could confirm what Trevor thought that Green Future was up to with this chemical.

Trevor hurriedly biked across the Harvard Bridge, remembering with a strange feeling in his stomach that day that he found Loren there. That day seemed like a long time ago since so much had happened, but it had only been a few weeks. He carried with him the burden of Loren's heavy gaze as she said to him with an elevated voice, which was extraordinarily rare for her, "It's not okay. Not with me".

The realization of what he was involved in weighed on

him—he had just passed off information that could potentially cause the destruction of wild areas, eliminating virgin forests in a giddy sleep-deprived delirium, compelled by the thrill of scientific discovery. He needed a different perspective on this and he wasn't keen on filling Loren in on what had transpired last night. He pedaled with decisiveness as he steered his bike toward his old dorm room. He hoped that they hadn't replaced his vacancy with a new student.

Trevor stormed into his old dorm room without thinking to knock. He shoulders slumped with relief when he saw Scott in his usual position, propped up in bed and hovering over a textbook.

"Don't you knock?" Scott asked Trevor over his dark-rimmed glasses. "You don't live here anymore, remember?"

"Hey, I need your help," Trevor said to him, ignoring his question and still out of breath from the ride over.

"Get fired already?"

"No—worse than that. Well, maybe worse than that. I'm not sure. See, I'm not supposed to talk about it—it's all top secret and all. I don't even know what I think I know. I mean, they only tell me as much as I need to know, which isn't much. But I think there's something going on, I mean, I think I've figured out what they hired me for, but I'm only guessing. I just need to talk to someone to figure it out."

"Okay, shoot."

"Well, what would happen if the entire earth no longer had forests, you know, like the population on the planet grew so large that we had to use all the forest land for crop production just to sustain the population? What would happen? I mean, I'm no ecologist—can the planet survive like that?"

"Maybe. I mean, whatever technical problem there is to solve in order to enable our survival, we might be able to figure it out. We can almost sustain life on a space station—certainly we can figure out how to create a new balance on earth with a reduced level of biological diversity." Scott said this matter of factly, as if it would make no difference at all to him if he lived in a space bubble as long as he had something to sustain his vitals. Trevor gave him a skeptical look.

"Look at it this way," Scott continued, "before the big bang, time did not exist. Matter and energy warp time and cause the time dimension to mix with the space dimensions. Time is directional. As time proceeds, the universe is evolving from a simple universe with very low entropy to a more complex universe with larger entropy."

"Entropy is a measure of the chaos in the world, right?" Trevor asked.

"Well, not exactly. Think of it like a measure of low-quality energy like heat that can't be used any more. Like how once you crack open an egg and scramble it, you can't put it back in its shell and unscramble it. All of the reactions taking place in the world are using up high quality energy. This fuels evolution and creates more complex biological life forms, all while giving off heat—creating more entropy. As complexity increases in the world, so does the total entropy. At some point in time, there will be no more high quality energy available to perform work. This is what is referred to as the heat death. You see, there is a limit to the complexity in the universe. We only have so much high quality energy before we hit the heat death. Nothing lasts forever, even the universe as we know it."

"What does this have to do with destroying forests?" Trevor asked.

"Well what is the definition of complexity?" Scott posed the question to Trevor.

Trevor answered with a blank stare so Scott continued, "Is complexity defined by the number of components a system has, or the complexity of any one of those components?"

"I don't know. What do you mean?" Trevor asked.

"For example," Scott continued, "a system like a forest ecosystem can be considered complex because of the number of components it has—animals, soil, bugs, plants, the hydrological cycle. But what about the human brain? By our metrics, the human brain is the most singularly complex thing in the universe that we know of. So if you are going to champion complexity and evolution, you might have to take sides. Some things on this planet have already reached their maximum efficiency and therefore their maximum capacity for evolution. For example, the fang of a snake has not undergone any kind of evolution for 20 million years. Its form is perfect for its desired function. Even though humans physically may not evolve any more, what about the potential evolution of our technologies? Have we reached the limit of our evolution? The answer is a resounding 'no'—there is much room for advancement. To keep advancing our technology, we may need to strip the earth of its resources. Everything has a price—even evolution. Especially evolution."

Trevor took a moment to soak all of this in. "So are you saying it's okay to trash the planet so that we can reach our full technological potential?"

"I'm not saying it's right—I'm just saying that the whole universe seems hell-bent on evolving—creating complexity— whatever that really means. It takes energy to do this. It takes the resources around us. We are just like little ants obeying some universal law that we don't understand on a conscious level. We're madly scurrying about connecting with each other, evolving, creating more amazing technologies every day and every day depleting the limited resources we have. There is a trade off. If you don't like what we're doing, throw yourself off a goddamn cliff."

At this last comment of Scott's, Trevor shuddered and looked away.

"Here's something that will hit home for you. How much energy from the universe do you think it took for the concept of phi to reach you? You started as a little baby, grew up, started being an internet junky where you stumbled across some crackpot's ideas. The internet was available to you through cables, powered by fossil fuels, and how many people carried around the idea before it got to you? Think about it. Nothing is for free. Every time you breathe air, you're helping us spiral down the tunnel of heat death."

"Man, you're depressing," Trever finally mumbled.

"You really don't get it, do you?" Scott sat up in bed and it looked for a moment that he might spring up and grab Trevor to shake him. "You're just like every other kid in this world who has been spoon-fed technology. Everything is so goddamn easy. You know why it's so easy—food, clothing, shelter? So that you can actually do something with your life. We have the time and resources to make even more progress, but instead we would rather burn time watching mindless television programs and tweeting useless information. You are taking up space—that's all. You're going to take up space and burn up resources regardless of what you do with your life, so you might as well do something productive. No matter what, we are going to hit a ceiling when we run out of resources. Nothing is going to keep that from happening, but how far can we go before that happens? That is the great mystery."

"I'm trying to understand," Trevor responded. "I mean, I know I've wasted a lot of what I have been given, but I'm supposedly helping Green Future create a planet that's sustainable for the human race, right? Isn't that what it's all about? Is that what you're saying?"

Scott looked at Trevor quietly for a moment before responding, "I think we're really self important bastards. It's not up to us to decide how the universe is going to evolve—the universe can carry on with or without us. There are probably more evolved beings than us out there somewhere. We decide our fate. We decide how long we are going to sustain ourselves on the planet. We can wisely meter out our rations, while maximizing the progress of humanity, or we can burn through our resources while numbing our minds and fearing death. The question is what is better—simply surviving, or *evolving*? How much more can we evolve if we treat our resources wisely so that we can last longer in this place?

"I'll tell you right now that Green Future doesn't give a rat's ass about feeding the world. They want to increase their market share. They can tell you or themselves whatever kind of bullshit sounds good to their critics. Quantity is not quality, and what kind of life can one have in a space bubble? Just because we can live that way, does that mean that we should? Are we really that much better than every other species on earth that we deserve rampant procreation at the expense of the survival of everything else on earth? The fact that we have been given all of these resources is an incredibly unique opportunity. The chance of having complex life forms on an inhabitable planet like ours in the Milky Way Galaxy is something on the order of one in one hundred billion. How you use this opportunity is up to you."

"I suppose technology doesn't intrinsically mean progress and evolution," Trevor responded thoughtfully.

"Exactly," said Scott. "At the very least, the technologies that a company like Green Future is creating should be an open book to the citizens in any area of the world where they are going to affect massive areas of land and the food chain itself. We need to know what is in that crap they put on the soil. They hide behind their intellectual property rights to keep this kind of information secret. But even if we don't know what's in the stuff, there should be an independent, long-term test of how it affects the soil and the crops. That would be the only way to keep them from commercializing the stuff before we know whether it's safe or not."

"Hmm." Trevor thought for a while. "What if some independent lab were to obtain samples of a Green Future chemical from an anonymous source?"

"Now you're talking," Scott said with a smile.

Chapter 27

Stan leaned over the lab bench and peered into the glass beaker. "Remarkable," he said in a reverential tone. "And this has only been in there since yesterday?"

"Yes sir," the lab technician responded. "Based on the composition, I wouldn't have expected it to produce such a quick reaction. There are actually no aggressive chemicals involved—it's all biological—just very, very fast. It is remarkable indeed."

"I need to know the persistence of this stuff in the soil. We need to allocate a space in the outdoor test plots ASAP. As soon as you're done with this batch I want the testing to continue outside. We can run the outside tests in parallel with the chemical safety evaluation."

Stan waved his palm over the beaker, wafting the odor of the reaction toward his nose. "That smell is somehow familiar. What is it... almost like burnt sugar."

Stan was careful not to be overly enthusiastic about the first round of testing. It was unheard of to hit the nail on the head the first time around, but he supposed there was a first time for everything. This solution was at least ready to go on to the second phase of testing. He grabbed the files generated so far from the lab results and took them with him as he made his way back to his office. He made a side trip to his secretary's desk and asked her to scan the files he had taken and then return them to his office.

Stan took his lab coat off and hung it on the coat rack at the entrance of his office. He straightened his tie as he sat down at his desk. He took a moment to gather himself at then picked up the phone receiver and dialed Jack Sims' extension.

"Mr. Sims, I have good news for you."

"Go on," Jack said quickly on the other end of the line.

"We have something that rapidly degrades cellulose. We're going to start both the chemical safety evaluation as well as the environmental persistence determination right away. It's time to start on the new crops, much sooner than anticipated. I just wanted to let you know the good news—I think we may have aced the first phase already."

"Just make sure nothing gets in the way. What about that new legislation?"

"It is already drafted. We put it in the Forestry bill. It is going to sound like it addresses slow-release fertilizers."

"Very good. Keep me informed of any new developments. The sooner we can make a press release the better."

"You know I will, sir."

The click in Stan's ear let him know that the conversation was   over.

Chapter 28

Our common sense does not represent reality. We are the odd balls of the universe.

Michio Kaku

Sarah was beside herself with the drive to intercept any back door approach that Green Future had in mind to introduce a new chemical to the market. She alerted her superior, Greg Walen, that she had come down with a flu bug. She packed up a few supplies and an overnight bag for a trip to Cincinnati. She knew that her job could be in jeopardy with a move like this. First of all, individuals who lie to their superiors aren't exactly welcomed by the CIA. She supposed she should have obtained a fake identity to purchase her airline tickets, but that was going one step too far down the road of criminality that she just wasn't willing to take. If it were to come to it, she could say she was embarrassed by some kind of personal business that she had to take care of in Cincinnati and so she made up the white lie about being under the weather.

When Sarah arrived in Cincinnati, the first thing she did after picking up her rental car was to head straight to the county building permit office. Since Green Future was planning for an expansion of their facility within the next year, she knew that building plans would be on file with the building permit office. Both existing and proposed construction would be shown on the plans.

After waiting in a short line, a young lady with glasses and the look of a librarian asked if she could help her.

"Oh yes," Sarah replied, using a broad smile to cover up her nervousness. "I am a concerned citizen and I live next door to a proposed building site. I heard that they have to file a proposed building plan set with you folks. Is that true?"

"Yes it is, ma'am, and the public is welcome to review it," the young lady replied. "What building is it?"

"The proposed Green Future building."

The young lady studied her skeptically for a moment and then replied, "One moment—I'll bring the plans right out."

When the plan set was delivered, it was a thick stack of large-size drawings bound along one edge.

"Is there somewhere I can spread these out and look at them?" Sarah asked.

"Sure—there's a table in that room just down the hall."

Sarah made her way down the hall and spread the plans out on the table. She went directly to the "EXISTING CONDITIONS" sheet and scanned it until spotting the location of the research and development laboratory. On the side of the laboratory building was an area labeled "hazardous waste disposal", which could be accessed by an outside service entrance.

"Perfect," she whispered to herself. She snapped a photo of the plan discretely with her iphone and closed the plan set before returning it to the young lady behind the counter.

Armed with the knowledge of the hazardous waste bin location, Sarah drove the rental car past the main entrance of Green Future, around to a side street that led to the hazardous waste bin access road. It was a dead end side street that probably never saw traffic except for the waste pickup. Performing surveillance on Green Future was completely outside of Sarah's personal skill set, in spite of her place of employment. If this worked, it would be a small miracle. Luckily the side street was located on the far opposite side of the main entrance and employee parking lot and was flanked with large trees. The side access road lacked the guard booths present at the main entrance. From the street, she could see the disposal bin with the assistance of a pair of binoculars. There was a back door to the laboratory— the only access to the building from this side. The results of whatever product testing they were doing at the moment would end up in that bin and then be carted away by a hazardous waste disposal company via the access road.

With her binoculars, she could see a pad lock on the disposal bin. She had brought along some coffee, water and a sandwich, since she had decided to make a day of watching the bin before making a move. It was late afternoon before she caught any movement on the side of the building. She watched through the binoculars as a man in a lab coat exited the building and then headed toward the hazardous waste bin. He drew a key out of his pocket and unlocked the padlock on the disposal bin before dropping a plastic bag into the bin.

The man in a lab coat replaced the padlock and then returned to the building, disappearing into the same door he had come out of. Sarah waited there for a few more moments and then pulled away from the curb with resolution.

Sarah made her way to the nearest thrift store. She grabbed the first pair of dark pants that would fit her and then found a dark turtleneck, a pair of gloves, and a dark blue baseball cap. In order to keep the cashier from being suspicious, she also grabbed a few brightly colored tee-shirts from the discount rack. After fishing a few dollars out of her pocket to pay for the mound of clothes, she made her way back to her hotel to wait for the sun to go down.

The moon was three quarters full—no need for a flashlight. She pulled her car up to the curb on the familiar side street leading to the side entrance and immediately turned off the headlights. The side street was about three hundred yards from the side of the building with the bin. There were no trees for cover once she left the side road. She scanned the building for signs of movement in the dark. She could see a few lights on inside the building.

Here goes nothing.

Sarah forced her limbs to life and got out of the rental car. She was moving quickly and with purpose. A pair of bolt cutters was tucked into the back of her pants, the handles hidden in the back of her shirt. An observer wouldn't notice them, but she could feel the handles poking awkwardly into the back of her should blades as she walked. Her heart was pounding as she made it to the bin. She kept to the side of the building, where a deep shadow was cast by the moonlight. She sat there for a few seconds with her back against the side of the building, scanning the walls for security cameras. She spotted one directly opposite the hazardous waste bin. It was attached to the building inconspicuously just under the overhang. She kept her chin tucked close to her chest, with the shadow of the baseball cap falling over her face. She moved to the side of the hazardous waste bin, opposite the door leading into the building.

She reached behind her with both hands to lift the bolt cutters out of the back of her pants. A part of the bolt cutters was caught on her pants and she struggled with them before they came loose. As soon as she held the bolt cutters in both hands in front of her, she heard the door latch sliding open from the other side of the bin. Her stomach tightened and her hands went numb as they clutched the bolt cutters in front of her, glinting in the moonlight just outside of the shadow cast by the building's overhang.

Chapter 29

At the end of the work day Stan made his way to the lab to check on testing progress. Various types of wood and plant matter had been exposed to the chemical in a row of beakers along the lab bench earlier that morning. What had started out as a collection of sticks and leaves was no longer recognizable. It was as if the items had spontaneously rotted in a span of hours rather than years, yielding a sticky gray substance.

It would take much longer to test the chemical for any negative health or environmental effects once it had done its job. In the meantime, Green Future staff was obliged to assume the worst and treat the chemical like it was a hazardous substance.

Stan put on a pair of latex gloves and put his hand into one of the beakers, which had contained an oak branch earlier in the day. He scooped up a small handful of the substance with his left hand and pinched it with his right hand. The few remaining pieces of the oak branch disintegrated under the pressure of his fingertips. A smile played on his face as he scanned the results sitting in heaps in the other beakers as well. The substance lost its cohesion sitting in the palm of his hand and it started to roll in drops through his fingers, splashing to a rest on the bench top.

"Darn it," Stan said to himself as he tried to contain the substance in his palm while reaching for some paper towels. He wiped the bench top clean with the paper towels and then found a plastic bag to dispose of the contents of the spill. When he had finished cleaning up the spill, he put his gloves in the bag along with the paper towels that had been used to clean up the substance.

It was time to wrap up after a long but exceptionally successful day. Stan made sure the counter top was clean before heading out to the hazardous waste bin to dispose of the plastic bag.

Chapter 30

Sarah leapt into the shadows as soon as she heard the metallic sliding of the door latch, forcing her small frame into the dark corner the bin and overhang created against the wall of the building. She guessed she was visible to a person standing in front of the bin if they were to scrutinize the shadow. She instinctively closed her eyes as if the person approaching the bin might feel the weight of her gaze. Heavy footsteps came closer and she could hear the rustle of a plastic bag, then a handful of keys. The lock made a clicking sound as it was opened, and then the metal bin let out a metallic yawn as it was opened. She could hear something without much weight being thrown into the bin and then the lid slamming down as it was let go. She remained as still as possible, knowing that any motion would attract attention—her heart beating in her ears as her arms still held up the bolt cutters in front of her. She could feel her knuckles go white inside of the cheap pair of used gloves.

It seemed like an eternity before she finally heard the footsteps retreat and then the door to the building opened and closed again. Her body was flooded with relief at the sound of the closing door, but it took her a good while of frozen disbelief before she dared to open her eyes and move. Her hands clutching the bolt cutters finally relaxed as the pounding of her heart slowed.

When the sound of movement inside of the building

stopped, she realized that she needed to work fast and then get the hell out of there. She got up on her haunches, took a deep breath, and quickly sprung forward. She fumbled with the large bolt cutters as she opened their jaws and positioned them around the lock. She pulled the lever arms together with all of her strength. She could feel the steel yielding slowly at first, and then faster, until the bolt cutter handles came together with a click. The lock fell at her feet and produced a dull thud on the asphalt. She tucked the bolt cutters back into her pants and then lifted the lid of the bin until the moonlight revealed its contents.

She could identify the bag that was just thrown in since it was right on top. She scanned the bin, not sure what she should be looking for. She scrutinized two bags—the most recent one and hopefully another recent one that was also near the top of the pile, both rather small compared to the other bags and containers. The second bag was quite a bit heavier, but still small enough to carry. She grabbed both bags with one hand and struggled to support the weight of the lid to keep it from slamming shut.

Once the bin was shut, she walked briskly back to her car, forcing herself not to look behind her so as to arouse suspicion if anyone should see her. Once she got inside the car, she scanned the grounds of the complex for any movement. She didn't see any. She started the car, turned on the lights, and slowly pulled away from the curb. Her right foot itched to crank down on the gas pedal as she drove back past the main entrance. The lights were on in the guard shacks, revealing the figures of the current watch. One guard looked up as her car drove past. She kept her eyes straight ahead and forced her foot to remain steady. She watched her rear view mirror until she was a few miles away, and then she took a deep breath. *Did I really just do that? I just hope it wasn't for nothing because I certainly don't want to do it again.*

When she reached her hotel room, she carefully opened the bags she had taken, keeping the contents inside of the bags to avoid touching them directly. The smaller plastic bag contained some disposable gloves and some paper towels with a gelatinous gray substance on them. They looked like items that had been used to clean up a spill. The larger bag had a few sealed plastic containers in it. They were labeled "0.5%", "1.0%" and "1.5%". The substance in the plastic containers could have been water; they were all perfectly clear liquid.

She had purchased a small ice chest and a roll of duct tape earlier that day. She placed the contents of the two bags carefully inside of the ice chest, holding them in place with crumpled up newspaper, and then sealed the ice chest with duct tape. She would mail the ice chest to her home in Virginia from a random local address before catching her flight home the next day. Once home, she would send samples to some old friends of hers from college who worked in an environmental testing lab and could be trusted to not ask questions.

Chapter 31

Stan got the call mid morning the following day. One of the lab techs called his office as he was working on the schedule for the second phase of testing.

"Mr. Cobald," the nervous voice said. "I went out to the hazardous waste bin just now and the lock was cut. I was out there yesterday afternoon and it was fine."

"Cut?" Stan nearly yelled into the phone in confusion. "I was just out there last night. That can't be. I'll be right over."

As soon as Stan hung up the phone, he stormed out of his office and headed to the lab. He went straight to the back door that he had used the evening before. When he opened the back door, he found two lab technicians standing at the hazardous waste bin, staring dumbly at the lock on the ground.

"Was anyone out here earlier today?" Stan asked the two.

"No. This is the first time we've been out here today," one of the lab technicians responded.

"Don't touch anything. I'll alert security," Stan retorted and turned on his heels.

One of Stan's biggest fears was his product getting into the hands of a competitor. Especially at this stage of the research, before any patents were secured, something like that could be devastating for a new product. Stan was sure that he could get to the bottom of this and criminally prosecute anyone who had trespassed in order to steal trade secrets. But time was of the essence—he needed to get any samples back that they might have taken immediately.

He stormed into the security office. It was a small room with several black and white monitors displaying real-time footage of each Green Future entrance. When Stan arrived, the look on his face caused the officer on duty to get up out of his chair immediately.

"We have had a security breech. At the hazardous waste bins. I need to see video footage since last night at about 7 pm from the camera across from the bins." Stan's breathing was haggard and the officer could tell that Stan had pushed the limits of his cardio to get there as quickly as possible.

"No problem, Dr. Cobald."

It took the officer a few minutes to bring up the video from the evening before. He started the footage at 6pm and then fast forwarded the video until movement was seen.

"There—stop right there," Stan said. "No, rewind a little." A small shape could be seen along the back wall of the building, quickly disappearing into the shadow cast by the bin. A few moments later, the back door of the building opened and Stan saw himself exit the building, unlock the bin and deposit a bag into it. There was no further movement for quite a while, until a shadow emerged from beside the bin. The shadow was tiny in comparison to Stan's body which had stood in the same spot a moment before. The person's back was to the camera as the person set to work on the lock. Even though the figure wore a baseball cap and baggy clothing, it was evident by the way the shadow moved that it was a woman. The woman took something from the bin before closing the lid and disappearing off the grainy black and white screen.

Stan had the officer replay the scene over and over again as his agitation grew. When he was satisfied that he had learned everything he could from the video, he left the surveillance room and walked back to the lab, exiting the door to the hazardous waste bin. He opened the familiar lid of the bin and scanned its contents. The plastic bag he had just deposited in there the night before was gone. He couldn't tell what else might be gone, but he knew that whoever had been here had at least a small sample of the new chemical.

Without bothering to call ahead of time, Stan made his way directly to Jack Sims' office. Jack Sims' secretary gave him a disapproving look.

"I'm sorry to come unannounced but I have an urgent matter that I need to discuss with Mr. Sims," Stan said to her.

Maintaining the scowl on her face, Simone picked up the phone to alert Mr. Sims of his presence. Stan paced back and forth in the reception room, unable to sit still. His hands were clenched inside the pockets of his slacks.

"Go ahead," the secretary said to him, grateful to get him and his nervous pacing out of the reception area.

When Stan entered Jack Sims' office, Jack looked up from his desk with an obvious look of irritation.

"So what is this urgent matter?" Jack started as Stan closed the door behind him.

"Someone came onto the property last night and took some samples of the new product that we're working on. They cut the lock on the hazardous waste bins to get at them. I have no idea how they knew we were working on a new product. You know, those bins have to be accessible for pickup—there's only one padlock..."

Stan was cut short by Mr. Sims, "Did you review the footage?"

"Yes, of course. It looks like it was a woman. She was wearing a baseball cap—I couldn't see her face."

Stan deliberately left out the detail that he had been at the bin disposing of samples only moments before the woman had cut the lock. He felt that missing piece of information weighing on him under the penetrating gaze of Mr. Sims.

"Check the perimeter footage. If she parked on the side street near the haz waste access we might be able to make out the license plate number." Jack paused for a minute and looked reflective. He opened the bottom right drawer on his desk and rifled through it for a little while before pulling out a business card. He handed the card to Stan and waited for him to read it before continuing. "Call this man if you get the license plate number. He can help you."

Stan turned the card over in his hands, then looked again at the face of the card as if looking for something. The card was not a typical business card. It had a single name on it, "Pete" and a phone number.

"Who is this guy?" Stan asked.

"Just think of him as a private investigator. He will know who you are."

Stan stood there for a moment longer until he noticed Mr. Sims' expectant glare and he realized that this conversation was over.

"Okay—thank you. I will let you know if I can get an identity."

"I expect so," Mr. Sims answered coldly. "Good day Mr. Cobald."

As Stan exited his office, Jack Sims had second thoughts. He wasn't sure he could trust a man like Stan with this task. This was something he should be handling—he just didn't want to be bothered with it just now. This could be a case of simple vandalism, which he didn't have time for. But he also wanted to feel out Stan to find out just what kind of a man he was—to see if he might be worthy of becoming part of the inner circle of Green Future. Jack would give him a taste to see how it suited him.

Chapter 32

Stan returned to the security office and asked briskly to review footage from perimeter camera 12 during the same time period that the woman could be seen at the bins. The guard clicked through a few screens, then located the feed from camera 12 and set it to play at the same time that the woman could be seen on the other camera. There was indeed a car parked on the side street. The street was fairly dark but a street light illuminated the back half of the car.

The guards centered the license plate in the frame on the screen, zoomed in and adjusted the contrast so that the grainy numbers and letters came into focus. Stan scribbled the numbers and letters on a piece of paper, thanked the guard, and went back to his office.

He closed his office door and sat with deliberation at his desk before pulling the business card and the license plate number out of his shirt pocket. He picked up the phone and dialed the number.

"Pete here," said a man on the other end.

"Hi, this is Stan Cobald of Green Future."

"Uh-huh," said the voice without sounding surprised.

Stan continued, "I have a license plate number. I am told you can find out the identity of the person who owns this car."

"I can. Go ahead with the number."

"It's an Ohio plate, number FDJ 539."

"No problem—just give me a little while. I'll call you back." The man called Pete hung up before Stan could tell him his phone number, leaving Stan holding the phone as the dial tone started up in his ear.

After hanging up the phone, Stan's mind churned over the details of the security breach. He hoped that this was nothing— simple vandalism—but he had a knot in his stomach that gnawed at his optimism. The hazardous waste bin was the perfect target and the timing was too perfect to be a coincidence. This person knew what she was doing. He couldn't imagine how an outside person could have found out about the new product. He mentally went down the list of people who knew about it and his mind rested on Trevor. Trevor was the wild card. He was brand new to Green Future and Stan didn't know where his loyalties might lie. He hadn't given Trevor any information on what the chemical might be for, but perhaps he had figured it out, or perhaps he was just curious. Either way, Stan needed to bring this kid in a little closer. It could have been a friend of his on the security footage—a girlfriend perhaps. Stan was just about to pick up the phone to call Trevor when the phone rang.

"This is Stan," he answered.

"This is Pete. The car is a rental, but I can tell you who rented the car."

Stan fumbled around his desk for the closest pen and started writing.

"Her name is Sarah Addison," Pete said, "and she works for the CIA."

Stan's mouth suddenly felt dry as Pete paused on the other end.

"What else do you need to know?"

"Uh... I guess whatever else you have on her," Stan answered.

"I can get anything you need to know," Pete answered.

Stan thought for a moment. "I guess employment history, home address, her position at the CIA, education, where she's from, what her interests are. I need to know what makes this person tick—why she is interested in what we are doing. Can you dig up anything that might help me understand that?"

"No problem. I will email you a report as soon as possible. Just call if you need anything else."

Stan was baffled. *Is it possible that Trevor contacted the CIA?* He considered as he tried to make sense of it. Stan picked up the phone and dialed Trevor's number.

"Hello?"

"Trevor, it's Stan."

"Oh, hi Dr. Cobald."

Stan searched Trevor's voice for any sign of nervousness, but he couldn't detect any.

"Trevor, I was wondering if you would like to take more of an active role in the lab trials here in Cincinnati. You would have to come out here and spend a couple of weeks with us."

"Sure. I mean, that would be neat. It would be great to see how the chemical is behaving in person."

"Great. I'll have my secretary arrange flights and accommodation. We'd like to have you here as soon as possible."

"Sure—no problem."

Stan hung up the phone and clasped his hands together under his chin. Having Trevor within arm's reach would make it easy to keep tabs on him. In the meantime, he had to find out who this Sarah Addison person was.

Chapter 33

Trevor hung up the phone with Stan and then immediately called Scott. He realized as Scott answered the phone that he was already considering breaking the terms of the non-disclosure agreement that he had signed a few weeks before. *Typical Trevor,* he thought to himself, *I was never cut out for abiding by rules.*

"Hey Scott, you free right now? I need to talk."

"Yeah, for a couple of hours anyway. Is this about…" Trevor quickly hung up before Scott could get out another word.

Trevor hopped on his bike and got to Scott's dorm room in record time. This time when Trevor barged in Scott was waiting for him expectantly, a textbook with a pencil shoved in it as a placeholder sitting on his desk.

"I'm going to Cincinnati to observe the lab testing. I'll probably be there for a few weeks. This is a perfect opportunity to find out what's going on and maybe even get a sample of the stuff."

"Awesome," Scott responded. "We're going to have to get some cool spy gear for you to take. I have a friend who can help us out. He's a computer science major but I think he wants to be some kind of international hacker when he grows up. He'll love this."

A nervous excitement formed in the pit of Trevor's stomach. He wanted to tell Loren about this plan but he didn't want to endanger her. Someday he would be able to tell her about it and he knew she would be proud of him.

"Hey, thanks," Trevor said to Scott. "I mean, I know we were never really great friends or anything, but thanks for doing this for me."

"Oh, don't worry. I'm not doing it for you."

Trevor smiled and nodded. "Well we don't have long to get ready. I'm supposed to fly there as soon as possible. I figure as soon as tomorrow if we can get all this together in time."

"Well there's no time to waste then. Go home and pack and I'll be over at your place tonight."

"No—Loren will be home then."

"Don't worry. I'm not going to bust in and say, 'here's all the gear that will put you in jail someday'. It will be packaged appropriately."

Trevor realized that he should never underestimate Scott's razor sharp logic.

"Okay—see you tonight."

Chapter 34

The results that came back from the lab confused Sarah. She had sent in the samples of the clear liquid with the percentage labels on them and also a sample of the grayish goo. She expected them to be two different substances, only one of which might be of interest to her, but the lab results seemed to be saying otherwise. They appeared to be the same substance, but the gray goo was a kind of biodegraded form of the clear substance. The other thing that confused her was that there was nothing remotely toxic about any of the samples, at least as far as the lab could tell. It had none of the constituents of concern that one would expect to find from a product coming out of Green Future. *So why were they in the hazardous waste bin?*

She eyed the three plastic containers sitting on her lab bench with suspicion. She had not dared to open them without gloves, a mask, and the whole gamut of personal protective gear when she had carefully poured a small amount into a vial to send to her lab friends for a rush analysis. This time, she put on a pair of latex gloves and took the top off of the one labeled "1.5%". She set out four glass dishes across her basement lab bench and poured a small amount of the solution in each of the dishes before replacing the plastic lid. She opened her sample storage cabinet and took out a soil sample from one of her jars labeled "organic plot" and sprinkled it in one of the solution-filled dishes. She then took a soil sample from one of her jars labeled "GF plot 10A" and sprinkled some in the second dish. She watched as a grayish cloud started to slowly leach out of the soil, most noticeably from the dish with the soil sample from her organic garden plot.

Sarah then got up from the lab bench and headed upstairs. She wanted to get a fresh sample of plant matter to see how they were affected by this stuff. As she made her way up from the basement and through the house, she grabbed her buck knife that she kept by the side door leading to the garden and two large ziploc bags. As she opened the door to let herself outside, she felt a weird stomach cramp. It was the same cramp that she had started to feel lately, but this one was even stronger and forced her to stop in her tracks. It wasn't exactly a cramp—that was just the only thing that she could think to equate it to. At first she had assumed that it was her period coming on, but she didn't keep track of her periods so she couldn't be sure. She had no need to track them—at least not until recently. Sarah let go of the door with her hand and instead brought it to her belly. She had such a high metabolism that she kept very lean, but her stomach felt soft now—much softer than normal. The softness of her belly in her right hand felt wrong with the contrast of her left hand still clutching the buck knife. She thought about Darin and that night that now seemed like a far away fantasy. He had been trying to keep in touch by phone since that night. She had undeniable feelings for him, but she couldn't allow it to happen. She had much bigger things going on—things that would endanger him.

She shook off thoughts of Darin as the cramping subsided and went out to the garden. She wanted to sample the same type of material from each plot—her organic garden and the Green Future crop plot. Only the remnants of last year's crops were available, but they would have to do. She grabbed leaves, stems, and anything she could find that looked remotely green. She put the material in one zip loc bag and made her way to the Green Future plot to do the same to fill a separate bag. When she had gathered enough material, she returned to the basement.

She cut the leaves into small pieces and put the organic and Green Future leaves into their respective solution-filled dishes. To her surprise, the leaves instantly dissolved, changing the clear liquid to a gray gel where the leaves had been. She kept adding more and more leaf matter, but it just kept transforming into gray globules like something out of a science fiction movie. The solution with the soil samples hadn't been as spectacular—there was just a hint of gray emanating from the soil, particularly from the organic soil. She wrote the date and time on four scraps of paper, and put each piece of paper underneath each of the glass dishes.

She then opened the smaller of the two bags that she had nabbed from the hazardous waste bin and took out one of the goo-laden gloves. She held the glove over the dishes that had just dissolved the leaves. The shade of gray that was slowly deepening in the dishes of leaves was an unmistakable match for the gray goo on the gloves.

Sarah thought she should be more excited about this discovery, but she was tired—really tired—more than she should be at this time of day. She had to admit to herself what the fear was that had struck her just before walking out to the garden. She put the glove back into the plastic bag and then put her forehead into her hands as she slumped over her lab bench.

"I can't be pregnant," she said aloud. "I just *can't* be."

Then her thoughts started into a downward spiral. *I'm so stupid. What was I thinking?*

She recalled the night she spent with Darin.

I wasn't thinking—that was the problem.

She had to get this resolved—not knowing was just making things worse.

She got up from the lab bench and went upstairs to grab her purse. There was a drug store not far from her suburban home. She didn't want to waste one more moment wondering.

Chapter 35

Sarah used up every pregnancy test that had come in the box—as if repeating the test were going to give her a different result—as if that second line would just disappear. She read the instructions over and over and finally threw the box and all the opened wrappers and used plastic indicators into the garbage in disgust.

She had tried most of her life to do the right thing and she did not believe in bringing a child into this mess of a world. Her life was exactly as it was supposed to be. It was a rather monastic existence but she had a purpose and she would do more good in the world on her current path than in being a procreator. But she couldn't just make this thing go away.

No killing. No stealing. No lying. No intoxicants. No sexual misconduct. These were the fundamental moral building blocks of her current existence. She had built her life brick by brick of non-harmful actions. Placing even one faulty brick would affect all of those above it. If she were to get an abortion there would be no telling how it might affect her. *First one wrong action, then the others become easier to make.* She could rationalize it to herself if she wanted—that she would be doing more good by not having it, but it still felt wrong.

No killing.

The ideals she held dear were built upon ethical conduct. It was the lack of ethical conduct in others that created all the problems in the world. She had dedicated her personal and professional life to combat unethical actions. People could rationalize their actions no matter what kind of crimes they committed, but that didn't change the consequences of their actions and the harm they incurred.

How can I condemn a new life to death before it even has a chance to make any mistakes? She thought to herself and frantically searched for other options.

There was always adoption. She could take an extended leave from work as soon as it started to show. Perhaps she could work out something with her boss where she could still work remotely somehow. None of her options were good ones so she resigned, mentally exhausted, to putting off any decisions until another time. This was a decision that she realized she shouldn't make alone, to the chagrin of her deeply independent nature.

Sarah picked up the phone and dialed.

"Hi Darin, It's Sarah," she began.

"Hey beautiful! I thought you might try to disappear on me. I'm glad you called." It was a voice that traveled through her body like an electric shock. His voice lifted her mood, but she still felt the weight of her dilemma straining her vocal chords like a tightrope.

"I'm on a leave of absence from work right now," she told him. The thought of seeing him again put a smile on her lips in spite of her predicament. "What are you doing this weekend?"

"Hanging out with you, I hope. The snow's gone right now and it's actually starting to look green again around here. Vermont is trying to tempt you back here—I'm sure of it."

"Well it sure did a good job of trying to get me stuck there the last time I visited."

"Not good enough, I'm afraid."

Sarah smiled and all of the emotions in her that only this man seemed to be able to invoke came flooding back.

"It's a date, then. I'll spend Friday driving and I'll see you Friday night."

"Sounds perfect. Get here by six o'clock and I'll even make you dinner. I'll make your favorite—bunny and butterfly stew with a side of spotted owl."

"You know me so well—sounds delicious. I'll bring your favorite—a bucket of kale from the garden for dessert."

"Now you're talking! I can't remember the last time I had a whole bucket of kale. Maybe it was when I had dinner with the neighbor's horse."

"Sounds romantic. Should I be jealous?"

"You should—she was mighty pretty. I do have to warn you about one thing though—it's mud season up here, so bring your muck boots."

"My favorite kind of footwear—and I'm not kidding about that."

"That doesn't surprise me in the least."

Sarah hung up the phone with mixed emotions—eager to see him again but dreading having to tell him. The feeling of losing control over her life struck a fear in her that was uncomfortably akin to the feeling of loss—she had had enough of that feeling for one lifetime. *The way that the universe can make people appear and disappear without any warning—the sudden actions that change life irrevocably.*

Chapter 36

Sarah returned to the basement the next day and studied the four glass containers on the lab bench. The gray goo looked slightly darker and thicker than it had the day before. She added more corn leaves to the two dishes that had swallowed a whole handful of leaves yesterday. They just stuck into the gray matter like candles in a birthday cake. She then put some leaves in the two samples with the soil, whose liquid had turned a homogenous cloudy light gray color. Although the consistency of the samples with the soil was still more like water the pudding-like gray goo of the other samples, the leaves just floated on the surface rather than instantly dissolving as they had the day before. The substance seemed to have lost its reactivity within the span of less than twenty four hours. It was as if the reaction that targeted plant matter had a time limit. Once the plant matter hit the substance, the reaction was triggered, and once the reaction was complete it was no longer reactive.

"Very interesting," she said to herself, and then became thoughtful.

After a long pause, she went over to her seed starting rack where she would start the seeds for her garden starts in the dead of winter. At this time of year, most of the shelves were full of starts to be transferred to the garden, but there were a few extra shelves not being used. She took some seed starting soil mix and put it into a large bowl where she typically mixed in water before packing the seed starting trays full of moist soil. She then put on a pair of latex gloves and took the glass containers that had dissolved the plant matter and dumped a portion of their sticky contents into the bowl of soil. She added some water and then thoroughly mixed the soil and gray goo with her gloved fingers until she had a sticky, wet mass. She packed a whole seed starter tray full of the mixture and then took off the sticky gloves. She washed and dried her hands and then selected seeds from various jars. She populated the tray with half organic seeds of all kinds and half Green Future GMO seeds of all kinds. She put the sticky gloves back on before covering the seeds gently with more soil. After disposing of the soiled gloves, she prepared a growing tray with potting soil and water, without the gray goo, with the same mix of seeds. If she watered the trays on Friday morning before leaving for Vermont she could be out of town for probably four days before they would need to be watered again.

She opened her laptop and wrote some notes on the past two days of work. Once that was done, she opened her modeling software. The program she was running would project the Green Future farming practices into the future in terms of how it would affect the health of the soil, which in turn would start affecting the health of the crops. With this new bit of information about a chemical that breaks down plant matter and anticipating what this substance could be used for by Green Future, she realized that she needed to start looking at not only the quality of the arable land on earth, but also the quantity. Removing forests to plant agricultural land would make a significant difference in atmospheric levels of carbon dioxide. It would also disrupt the hydrological cycle and water quality in a major way. Sarah had studied the ancient Middle East, the cradle of civilization, where large-scale agriculture had been born. Deforestation and agriculture had ultimately led to the desertification of that entire region, resulting in a plague of unrest and war that still lingered on that soil. On the other hand, replanting forests could bring back rainfall and recreate ecosystems. But there would be a tipping point—a point when there would be too much deforestation for replanting—when the whole earth would be on an irreversible path toward desertification.

She started to set up the input files and worked until late in the evening—until her stomach reminded her that it was time to call it a day. She reluctantly shut down her computer and took it upstairs. She brought it to her home office and set the laptop down on her desk as she took a seat. She opened the top drawer of her desk and took out a small key. She then opened the bottom right drawer of her desk and took out a fire-proof security box. She opened the box with the key and took out an external hard drive. She plugged the hard drive into the wall outlet and connected the USB to the laptop to start her backup. She would make dinner while it finished and then pack for her trip up North.

Chapter 37

Scott brought a package to Trevor's house the night before he left for Cincinnati.

"Hey man, you left this stuff at the dorm. I was just trying to clean out the room a little and came across it," Scott said casually as Loren was sketching in a notebook within earshot.

"You cleaned the dorm room? I don't believe it," Trevor replied throwing Scott a mischievous grin.

Later that evening, Trevor slipped the package into his suitcase when Loren was in the bathroom and covered it quickly with some dress shirts that had been freshly sprung from their packaging.

Trevor unwrapped the package in his hotel room as soon as he got to Cincinnati. There were instructions printed out and taped to various electronic items. He went through each one, reading the instructions taped to each of them and putting them neatly in the drawer of his hotel room. There was a prepaid cell phone included with a note on it from Scott that said, "Call me if you need help". He placed neatly folded clothes over the items in case any maids got nosey.

He decided to scope out the office and lab before bringing any of the items with him to make sure he would get them past security. When he met Stan in the lobby of the biotechnology building the first day of working at Green Future's headquarters,

Trevor shook his hand with a twinge of guilt. He didn't have anything against Stan personally—but he also couldn't trust him.

There were cameras but no metal detectors or individual searches to get past the lobby of the building. Before gaining admittance, Trevor was photographed and provided with a badge in a small office adjacent to the lobby. Once he was graced with an official Green Future employee badge, Stan proudly directed him to the lab where the initial trials were taking place.

"You will soon learn about what all of this can do, but let's first get you situated in your office space," Stan said, and indicated for Trevor to follow him.

Trevor was given a small office located a few doors down from Stan's own office.

"You can keep your laptop and any personal items in here. You don't have to worry about security—your belongings will be safer in here than anywhere else in St. Luis. Even trusted employees are only allowed access to the areas they need to be in," Stan said to Trevor. "You will have access to this office wing and the lab we just saw where the initial trials are taking place."

"Sounds good," said Trevor.

The next morning before heading into the office for the day, Trevor carefully placed a small USB stick, a tiny microphone and a phone tap tucked inside of the sock on his left foot. He would bring these items with him every day that he came in to work, patiently waiting for the right opportunity to use them.

Chapter 38

The report on Sarah Addison arrived in Stan's inbox three days after Stan had spoken with "Pete". Stan had asked Pete if he could also try to dig up any ties that Sarah Addison might have with Trevor. This last minute request was what had taken the report longer than expected to arrive. Pete was not able to find any connections between the two and he had made an exhaustive effort.

The amount of personal information that Pete was able to dig up on the woman was uncanny. He had even produced recently taken photos. Her environmental extremism and her position in the CIA led Stan to believe that this situation could be even worse than a competing company stealing trade secrets. The CIA could have sent her to Green Future to collect intelligence that could potentially shut down the development of the new product. They could have stolen that sample in order to do independent testing. Part of Stan was confident that the chemical was benign and that allowing another lab to analyze it wouldn't matter. But those environmentalists had their own agenda. Perhaps she meant to tamper with the sample in order to bias the test results and report false results of the testing to the CIA. You couldn't put anything past the environmental extremists.

Stan was hunched over his computer with a grimace rubbing his forehead as he read the report from Pete when Trevor walked into his office. He jumped as soon as Trevor entered the room. He immediately closed his email and addressed Trevor.

"Oh sorry—I was deep in thought and you startled me a bit."

"Are you okay? You look a little stressed out," Trevor said, concerned.

"Oh no, I'm fine. It's just that I just got some disturbing news from one of our distributors—nothing to do with what you and I are working on. I'm going to have to run over to Mr. Sims .and talk to him for a couple of minutes."

"Hey, no problem—I just really wanted to talk to you about the next phase of testing. I'll just wait here until you get back."

A confused look passed over Stan's face for a second, but the urgency of telling Sims what he had found out overpowered any suspicion he might have of Trevor.

As soon as Stan left the room, Trevor took a seat in one of the chairs in front of Stan's desk. He crossed his legs and then felt for the USB chip in his sock. He looked around the office, looking for cameras, and then he noticed something that looked like it could be a camera, embedded in the base of a little potted plant, pointed right at the chair he was sitting in. Trevor got up and exited the office, going to the break room where he poured himself a cup of coffee. He brought the cup of coffee back into Stan's office and sat back down in the chair. He took a sip of the coffee and then innocently set it down on Stan's desk, right in front of the little lens that had been staring at him blankly.

He immediately got up and went behind Stan's desk, glancing at the doorway nervously. He took the USB drive and inserted it into Stan's computer. All he had to do was run an executable file from the USB drive per Scott's instructions. He double-clicked on the icon on the USB drive that popped up and then saw a window open up. The window contained a task bar for the program installation progress.

He then took the tiny microphone out of his shoe and looked around Stan's office. He walked over to the bookshelf and reached up to the top shelf and ran his finger across the top of it. He examined his finger, which was coated with a healthy layer of dust. He then took the microphone and set it as far back on the top shelf as he could reach, almost touching the back wall. He then walked over to the phone sitting on Stan's desk. He picked up the receiver and examined the plastic mouthpiece. He would have to put the phone tap inside the phone, but the cheap plastic mouthpiece looked like it might break apart if he tried to open it up. He grabbed the mouthpiece and tugged on it to see if it would come loose. *Nothing.* It was a cheap plastic mouthpiece that was destined to be replaced rather than repaired. He was afraid that even if he was able to get it off, he wouldn't be able to get it back on again.

He put the phone down and looked back at Stan's computer. *60% complete.* He glanced nervously at the door again. He lifted up the base of the phone and examined the underside of the phone. He still couldn't see how he was going to open this thing in order to insert the phone tap. He pulled out his key chain from his pocket and slid one of his keys in the seam of the phone mouth piece. He pressed the key into the seam and slowly moved it back and forth to see if the plastic piece might pop off with some leverage. He then heard the shuffling of feet approaching the office door.

Chapter 39

Stan didn't like leaving Trevor in his office, but it was for exactly these occasions that he had installed a little wireless camera in the base of the potted plant in his office. The camera had the door to his office in view, as well as the front of his desk. Stan's life work was too important not to have safeguards like this in place.

When Stan arrived at Jack Sims' office, his secretary acted like her tolerance to him had grown since the last time he had arrived unannounced. She picked up the phone without a word to him and informed Mr. Sims that Mr. Cobald was here to see him. This time, he was ushered in immediately.

"I think we may have a problem," Stan told Mr. Sims, without standing on ceremony.

"Continue," Jack said, bringing his hands thoughtfully together as he leaned back in his oversized executive chair.

"That woman—her name is Sarah Addison. She works for the CIA."

Jack's eyebrows raised and Stan continued. "She may or may not be working with the CIA to spy on us. She's apparently a pretty extreme environmentalist, or at least she used to be when she was younger. Since she has been working for the CIA she has been keeping under the radar, but she was formerly a member of Greenpeace. She seems to fit the profile of a typical protestor type—the kind of person who would want to shut us down. She has a sample of our new product that we are currently testing. She is not someone who would be trying to sell trade secrets, but this could be even worse than that for us. If anyone in Washington catches wind of what we are doing, they are going to shoot down that bill that Bly is working on if they manage to connect the dots."

Jack Sims' face grew dark and he quietly soaked in what Stan was telling him. There was a long pause before Jack responded to Stan. "The first thing we have to do is figure out if she is working alone or if she is just following orders from the CIA. Then we have to find out what she knows. We also need those samples back. How did she find out about what we are doing? Have you looked at our people on the inside? Could someone be feeding her information?" Jack fired the questions at Stan.

Stan thought for a moment before responding. "I don't know yet but I am going to try to find that out."

"This breach came from your lab. She has a sample of the new product, for Christ's sake." Jack's voice started to rise in anger as he realized the gravity of the situation. "You need to fix this problem. Find her. Follow her. Get those samples back. Find out what the hell she is up to. This new product line is your job right now. If there's no new product for you to work on, you might as well start looking for another line of work."

This last comment from Mr. Sims took Stan completely off guard. "You can't be serious, Mr. Sims."

"Oh I am *very* serious. This is your job. You allowed your lab to leak a top secret new product—the product that would potentially have kept you occupied with product development and support for the next decade at least before you reached retirement age."

"But Mr. Sims..."

"This conversation is over. I don't want to hear from you until you have cleaned up this mess. Find her. Find out what she knows. Find out whom she is working for or if she is alone and for Christ's sake bring back that sample."

Stan's face flushed red with emotion. He felt belittled that his whole life's work could be threatened by one apparent blunder. He resented that his entire future rested in the palm of this man, who was obviously not a man of God. He knew it was no use to argue with this man, who had the authoritative last word in every conversation. He nodded sharply and turned around to leave. He hesitated before opening the door and then turned back to Mr. Sims. "I will be out of the office for a few days. I *will* get that sample back," he said with determination before exiting the room.

When Stan left Jack Sim's office, Jack immediately opened one of his desk drawers and took out a pre-paid cell phone. He dialed and a familiar voice answered on the other end.

"I have a job for you," Jack said. "Tail Stan Cobald and wait for further instructions."

He hung up the phone and then promptly resumed what he had been working on before Stan had interrupted him.

Chapter 40

Trevor quickly put down Stan's office phone and looked at the screen of Stan's computer in a panic as the footsteps approached. The open window read "100% complete. Click to Finish." He grabbed Stan's mouse and clicked "Finish", then yanked the USB stick out of the side of the computer. The shuffling footsteps stopped at Stan's closed office door. Trevor had no time to return to the seat in front of Stan's desk. Instead, he quickly put the USB stick and phone tap in his pocket and moved over the window next to Stan's desk.

Stan entered the office with his head bowed and when he looked up and saw Trevor next to the window by his desk with his back toward him, he looked surprised to see him. He suddenly remembered that Trevor had wanted to talk to him about the second phase of testing. He was deflated. The second phase of testing was meaningless until he could get this situation with the woman under control.

"Nice, uh... view," Trevor stammered awkwardly, realizing as he said it that the only thing in view of Stan's window was some overly manicured shrubs and the corner of a lawn. He kept his hands rigidly in his pockets, clutching at the small electronic pieces.

Stan paused in front of his desk, and Trevor took the cue to move away from the window and take the seat where he had been in one of the chairs in front of Stan's desk. Stan moved around his desk and then took the spot where Trevor had just been standing at the window. He stared vacantly out the window as Trevor watched him expectantly from the chair. Trevor picked up the coffee cup that he had set down in front of the small potted plant and sipped it nervously.

"So what were you going to say about the second phase of testing?" Stan asked Trevor, still with his back to him and his eyes trained on something far away outside the window.

"Well you haven't shared the final goal with me for this product that I've been helping you develop, so I'm kind of at a loss with trying to help with what's next. I mean, it seems to me like the product is ready—it does exactly what you requested. I think we're done with preliminary testing, don't you? I would like to see what's next, and hopefully help out with it."

Stan turned around and studied Trevor, his eyes narrowing.

"You're right, Trevor," Stan said before taking a seat at his desk. He leaned forward and gave Trevor a half smile. "You have amazed me. It appears that you hit it right on the nose the first time. What can I say—I'm impressed."

Stan paused in thought before continuing. "You know, we don't usually let new employees in on much intel, especially on new products, but you are in a unique situation. We need you to help to develop this new product. However, corporate protocol requires that we keep essential bits of information from you until you have been here for a while.

"That being said, I will need your help for the next phase of testing, but we aren't ready yet. I have some things to take care of in Washington. When I get back, we can get started. If you can hang out here for a couple of days and finish up the final reports on the preliminary testing, we will be set to start the next phase when I get back. Sound good?"

"Yeah—sounds great. No problem," Trevor said with some surprise.

"Good," said Stan. "Well I have some things to wrap up before I leave. If you will excuse me, I will see you when I return."

Trevor looked around and then quickly stood up, clutching at his pockets lest the little gadgets had a mind to slip out of his pockets. "Great. Okay, then. See you when you get back, Dr. Cobald. Have a safe trip."

Trevor awkwardly made his way out of Stan's office and with a sigh of relief, closed the door behind him, feeling the small plastic articles safely tucked away in his pocket.

Chapter 41

The address from the report that Pete had emailed him led Stan to a residential neighborhood on the outskirts of Washington D.C. It was Thursday evening. It had taken him the better part of the day to get here from Cincinnati. He first drove slowly past the house. There was a light blue hybrid sedan parked in the driveway and the lights inside the house let him know that someone was home. He drove down the street, then turned around and returned to a property that was across the street from the house. There were perhaps a half dozen cars parked along the street. He chose a spot right between two driveways so that his car could belong to either of the houses. From the inside of his rental car, he had a view of the sedan and one of the front windows that shed the house's interior light onto the driveway.

It was going to be a long night. Stan had bought some bottles of caffeinated soda and some snacks. He would use empty soda bottles to urinate in. He scanned the adjacent houses. He saw the flicker of television sets in a few of them, a couple of lights, and an occasional shadow passing across a curtained window, but no one seemed to have noticed him. Stan picked up a newspaper that he had purchased at the airport and read it with only partial interest until he noticed the light go off in the house. He looked at his watch. It was half past nine. He tugged at the lever at the side of his seat until it reclined. He set his phone alarm to wake him up before dawn the next morning.

His plan was to be awake before anyone might leave the house in the morning. Then, he would follow the woman if she left the house. Hopefully she would be going in to the CIA headquarters. Once he was sure that she was heading to work for the day, he could come back to her house, comfortable with the knowledge that he would have at least a full day before she would be back from work. Ideally, he would be back on a plane to Cincinnati that same evening. He just needed to get through this night. At least sleeping in a car was far more comfortable than sleeping on a plane, which he had done dozens of times for international business trips.

The physical discomfort wasn't what kept him from sleeping—it was the thoughts rattling around in his head. He dreaded the morning, when he would be committing the first crime of his life—breaking and entering. He didn't even know if that was a felony or misdemeanor—he just planned on not getting caught so that he would never have to find out. As far as he was concerned, he was only there to get what rightfully belonged to him. This woman had stolen from him, so he was there to recuperate it. He would take back the samples and try to figure out why she would have stolen them. Hopefully the samples were at her house. If they were not, that probably meant that she had brought them to the CIA headquarters. If that were the case, things were about to get a lot worse for both him and Green Future.

He doubted that the CIA would have used such covert tactics to steal samples. If the CIA were endorsing what this woman was up to, they would have come through the front door of

Green Future with a warrant in their hands. But that just wouldn't make any sense—Green Future had committed no crime. The only thing that made sense was that she was working on her own. After all, she used to work for Green Peace. She was a terrorist at heart who hid behind environmental ideals. He had no problem with breaking into a terrorist's house in order to keep her from impeding on Green Future's momentum. Perhaps she would even sell the information to one of Green Future's competitors, just to remove the financial incentive of completing the research and development of the product.

Stan's eyelids started to burn from lack of sleep and he looked at his watch. It was already past midnight. The time was speeding by as the anxiety for the next day kept building. He knew he had to sleep, if only for a few hours, or else he would jeopardize the mission. He forced his mind to stop revolving around nervous thoughts and instead he thought of the sound of a jet plane engine, which usually lulled him to sleep on long intercontinental flights. The dull white noise of the engine vibrating through the seat and the disorientating feeling of slight turbulence made him feel like he was slowly drifting as a speck floating in space, unconnected to ground.

His mind felt semi conscious as the sound of the alarm suddenly filled the rental car. He must have slept because he had no memory of the last hours of the night, but he also felt like his brain had been slightly alert all night long, on watch until the sound of the alarm told him it was time to open his eyes. Sunlight had barely started to light up the morning sky.

The lights were already on in the house, but thankfully the

hybrid sedan was still there. He didn't need to wait long before he saw the familiar slight frame of the woman walk out of the house with a small suitcase and open the trunk of the car. She put the suitcase in the trunk and then went back into the house. Stan sat up in the rental car and adjusted the seat back to its upright position.

The woman came back out of the house with another small bag and got into the driver's seat. Within a few moments, she turned the car's headlights on and pulled out of the driveway. Stan waited until her tail lights were out of view and then started up his own car. There was only one main road leading out of this residential area, so he was sure that he could catch up with her without making himself too obvious.

Once the sun came up it was easier to follow the sedan, but the car was definitely not going the direction he knew to be the way to the CIA headquarters. The car had entered the freeway and started heading north. Stan recalled the suitcase that he had seen her place in the trunk. He stayed as far behind the car as possible, burning its shape into his memory—ragged from lack of sleep.

He kept expecting the car to pull off the highway, but it wasn't until a few hours had gone by that it finally stopped at a gas station. Stan stopped at the gas station on the other side of the street. The woman went into the gas station store, which gave him time to fuel up and then position his car so that it would be ready to pull out when she exited the gas station. He did this several times as he followed the car across several state borders. He watched her carefully each time for any signs that she noticed him, but she hadn't seemed to. He would have to watch, wait, and follow closely behind—just not too close.

Chapter 42

Sarah was intending to wait until the weekend with Darin was over before telling him her predicament. She supposed this might be the last time she would ever see him, and she wanted to enjoy the light-hearted happiness that only he could spark in her. The feeling that had blossomed in her since she had first met him seemed to grow more intense the more time they spent together. She didn't know him well enough to know what his reaction would be, so she tried to completely forget about it until just before it was time for her to leave for the weekend, as one enjoys something for the last time—with a consuming recklessness.

When she arrived at his house the sun was just setting. Lights were on inside his house and the smell of wood smoke greeted her as she stepped out of her car. It had rained recently— the smell of the earth and the woods around the house grabbed her like a seductive perfume. It was impossible to sneak up on the house, since Adah had already sounded the alert that a car had pulled up in the driveway. Darin opened the door as Adah sprung out to greet Sarah.

"She's happy to see you again!" Darin called from the doorway. Sarah felt girlish butterflies in her stomach as she smiled and hurried to the front door.

"And I am happy to see you as well," Darin said as soon as she made it to the entryway, and he bent down and picked her small frame up as he brought her in for a kiss. Sarah felt her feet come off of the ground, as she was held up tenderly by a muscular set of arms. She was transported, as she was every time she was with him, from the woman holding the worries of the world on her shoulders, to a happy young woman with the promise of new love in her heart. The cares of her normal life melted away and she welcomed more heartily than ever this brief transportation into Darin's life.

He had made dinner for them and had even forgone his typical carnivorous diet in honor of having her there. The inside of the stone house was warmed by the wood stove, which emanated from the center of the living room. Sarah took a seat at a large wooden table that looked like it could have come from a hundred year old farmhouse.

"It's nothing fancy," Darin said as he placed a large tray on the table. "Vegetarian lasagna. I found the recipe online. I have never tried it before, so if it's awful, well, you'll just have to pretend that you like it."

"It's very sweet of you, and it looks delicious. I'm starving," Sarah responded.

"I'm glad you came," Darin said to Sarah across the table. His direct gaze unnerved her, and she blushed and looked down at her plate before looking up at him again.

"I am too," she said simply, returning his lingering gaze.

"Spring is here, finally," Darin said, breaking the silence. "I think that cold snap while you were here last time was the last of winter. That means that the moose should be out. I was thinking we could take Adah and go for a hike. There's a lake not far from here with a bunch of surrounding wetlands—it's the easiest place to spot them. You ever seen a moose before?"

"No but I would absolutely love to."

"You won't believe how big they are in person. It's one thing to see them on a postcard, but in person they are awesome."

"I bet they are. Do you know how lucky you are to live here?"

"Well, I don't know where I would rather live, but I've been here so long that I guess I don't think about it much."

"Take it from me; you're lucky. For my work I have to study natural resources all over the country." Sarah's face suddenly because serious. "I focus on the U.S., but we also look at other countries to see how they are managing their water resources. It actually feels untouched up here. You are water rich— there are streams and lakes everywhere you look. You haven't had any major industries contaminating your groundwater, and there is rainfall year-round. You have forests and real wildlife. The ecosystem is still healthy up here. I guess there just haven't been enough people up here to mess it up."

"And hopefully there never will be," Darin said.

Sarah continued, "You know, the problem is that once it's gone, it's gone. Once groundwater is contaminated, it can be cost-prohibitive to clean up. A company will just declare bankruptcy, and there are only so much federal funds to go around to clean up the mess that they made while they were enjoying record earnings.

And the clean-up is only so effective—it will never be the same. We are going to get to a point where we are drinking poisoned water because there is no more clean water left. It's no coincidence that cancer is rampant. Carcinogens are everywhere—the air, the soil, the water, the food."

Sarah stopped abruptly as she realized that her voice had gotten louder and louder and even Adah had snapped out of her slumber to see what the woman was getting so excited about.

"I'm sorry," she said. "It's really hard to leave my work at the office."

"Don't be sorry. Say it like it is. It needs to be said. I want to know about this stuff." Darin leaned closer to her, his elbows on the table and his eyes focused completely on her.

"You know, I used to be a pretty militant environmentalist. I have since become less idealistic and more active in ways that I think have more impact, but I am a typical American. I have a house that is way bigger than I actually need. I drive a car to work. I live in a concrete jungle, as you call it. I'm really not that much better than everyone else, so I often ask myself why I think that I deserve those things, while more than half of the world's population doesn't even have clean water to drink."

"Luck," Darin said.

"But I'm unwilling to give up those things," Sarah said, then grew silent for a moment. She looked up at Darin after a long pause and continued, "I've never been able to talk to anyone like this before, but for some reason I feel like it's okay to tell you—that you won't judge me or disapprove."

"Me, disapprove? Of a beautiful woman who wants to save the world?" he responded. "You're kidding, right?"

"Most people seek out things that make them feel good. They don't want to hear the gloom and doom, but I can't ignore it. There are so many beautiful things and beautiful places worth preserving, but the truth is, the earth is drastically out of balance. The droughts, the floods—it's no coincidence. And there is no place to hide from it. We're all connected by an ocean and the air we breathe. The pollution coming out of factories in China will eventually make its way here. The radioactive material coming out of Fukushima has already hit California. We are trashing this planet, but this is the only home we've got. And what for? Comfort? Luxury? Profit? We simply aren't going to live long enough to enjoy those things. *None of that really matters.*"

Sarah watched Darin's face as he soaked in her words. She grew quiet and then calmly looked around her. "When I come up here, none of that exists. It's like a wonderful dream. It makes me feel like not all is lost. I see a future. I see life, *real* life."

"Well that's because not all is lost. We can turn it around," he finally answered.

"Who is going do to that?" she asked him rhetorically. "Me? China? Some governor somewhere? The problem is so big."

"It sounds to me like we just need to get together and give a damn," Darin said.

Sarah was quiet before she asked him, "Do you think people give a damn?"

Darin took a moment before responding. "People don't know what you know, Sarah. I think that if they knew, they would give a damn."

Sarah smiled and reached across the table, pressing her hand into the rough skin of his palm. "You're really hopeful. I like that."

"I have to be—I put kids into this world and I love them more than anything. I want my grandkids and their grandkids to keep enjoying a healthy life."

Sarah suddenly remembered her predicament and she grew ashen. "I never wanted to have kids. I mean, I guess I was never that much of an optimist to think that the human race could get its act together."

"And what do you think now?" he asked her.

Sarah felt a weight spread over her and the reality of the decision that she didn't want to make seemed to fill her lungs with water as she tried to take in air. She took a few deep, involuntary breaths and then put her head in her hands as two tears slid between her fingers and hit the wood of the rustic table.

"What's wrong? Was it something I said?" Darin asked her as he moved to her side of the table and put his arms around her. He waited until she could control her breathing and the tears subsided.

"Darin, we're not young people. There's something I need to tell you. I wanted to wait until Sunday, but apparently I can't seem to keep it inside for that long."

"Go ahead."

"I don't have boyfriends. I mean, I haven't in a really, really long time. I've been completely focused on my work. You really took me by surprise. I had no idea. I wasn't prepared."

Darin's face looked grief-stricken, trying to guess at what she was trying to get at.

"Darin, I'm sorry but I don't take birth control pills and I didn't know where I was in my cycle. I figured the chance was so remote. What I'm trying to say is... I'm pregnant."

Darin was surprised, but a look a relief came over his face that she didn't expect. "You're pregnant? Here I was thinking you were trying to tell me to go take a hike because you're too busy trying to save the world. You're pregnant?"

"Yes. I realize that neither of us want me to be pregnant, but here I am, a knocked up old spinster. I haven't made a decision yet—I just thought you should know. I be honest, I didn't really want to make the decision on my own."

"Sarah, whatever you want to do I'm okay with. I know we haven't known each other for that long, but it doesn't take time to know what you want when you see it. I want to be with you. I mean I would like to be with you, if you'd allow it. And I could be a dad again, as long as he or she doesn't mind pushing me around in a wheelchair."

Sarah smiled and looked up at Darin. *The best things in life seem to come at you from nowhere. You can't plan for them or even hope for them, and sometimes they come disguised as the things you fear the most.* She marveled to herself.

Sarah didn't answer—she knew her vocal chords would fail her. She just let him hold her as the tears dried on her face and she realized that everything was going to be okay, just very different than her previous definition of okay. She closed her eyes and a vivid future opened up to her that she never thought could belong to her.

"Move up here and live with me," Darin finally said in the tender quietness. "Kid or no kid—this is where you belong."

Part II

Chapter 43

After the accident, Stan was deeply shaken. His heart was pounding with the fear that someone might have seen him leaving the scene. He glanced in the rearview mirror compulsively for any sign of a police car. This whole plan had gotten out of control the moment he had agreed to go to Virginia to get the sample back from Sarah Addison. It was one thing after another, taking him down this path that seemed to go more and more wrong. As soon as he got to Sarah's house, he would look for what he needed and then get on the first plane back to Cincinnati. He couldn't wait for this to be over. He struggled not to speed as he made the long trip back to Virginia. He would dispose of the samples and he would never do something like this again. If he got caught, it would ruin both his life and his career, but he was too deep to pull back now. Without the recuperation of those samples, he wouldn't have a job to go back to.

I just need to not get caught and everything will be fine. His mind burned as he clutched the steering wheel with his large, sweaty palms.

When Stan arrived at Sarah Addison's house it was past sunset. He put gloves on and grabbed a flashlight before getting out of the car. He gratefully used the cover of night as he walked up her driveway and then walked around the side of her house. He glanced around him at the neighborhood—silent, dormant. He spotted a side gate and then opened it with the help of his flashlight, which he kept shielded from the street view in case anyone happened to be looking his way from across the street. A thick row of trees and bushes filled the perimeter of the woman's property. Apparently she valued her privacy, which made this task much easier for Stan. He closed the gate behind him and walked around to the back side of the house. He scanned the house and noticed that a small window leading to the basement seemed to be unlatched. He shined his flashlight on it, sizing it up and thinking of his oversized frame. He pulled on the window incredulously and it opened.

There was a table just below the window inside of the basement. He clenched the flashlight between his teeth and sat on the ground, putting both legs into the open window, then shimmying his body until up to his waist. He turned around, sliding his belly painfully against the lower edge of the window, then lowered himself onto the table. He felt the flimsy table start to yield under his weight, so he quickly shifted his weight and then clumsily fell to the floor trying to keep the table from collapsing. He shined the flashlight around the basement and noticed a fairly complete lab set up, as well as gardening tools and a wall of plant growing racks. There were also numerous file cabinets and shelves full of textbooks, notebooks and reference manuals. He walked over to what was obviously a lab bench, stocked with glass dishes and vials. He immediately recognized the containers with familiar labels that had come from his lab with enormous relief. The samples being here suggested that she was working alone. They were lined up on the back of the work bench behind four glass dishes, each filled about halfway with the familiar gray substance. She had evidently been testing the new product with various types of organic matter.

He scanned the basement until he saw a box of garbage bags sitting on a bottom shelf. He took a garbage bag and filled it will the containers she had stolen as well as the glass dishes. He went over to the growing racks, which were mostly full of bright green vegetable starts. He scanned each shelf carefully until he came upon a shelf with moist soil filling the start tray but no vegetation. He took off one of his gloves and put his finger into the soil. It looked freshly packed, newly watered, and felt too sticky to be just soil and water.

"Clever woman," he whispered to himself in the near darkness. He took both trays full of the freshly prepared soil and dumped them in the garbage bag as well. He then started looking through her file cabinets. There were stacks of literature on Green Future crops and agricultural methods. He then found a stack of spiral notebooks. The top one had "Green Future Plot Year 12" written on the front. The notebook underneath it was labeled "year 11", and so on, to "year 1". He opened "Year 1" and the first page showed a diagram of her property, with the location of her house and a square called "Green Future Plot –year 1" in the back corner of her property. It suddenly clicked. This was the long-term testing that was required by no one, and so was done by no one. Or so he had thought.

Stan scooped up the pile of notebooks and put them in a separate garbage bag. He scoured her file cabinets for anything further but found nothing else. She must have entered most of the data into her laptop, which was in the trunk of his car. He located the stairway up to the house and navigated his way up the dark passageway with a shaky flashlight.

Stan went through every room of the woman's house opening drawers and cabinets, finding nothing until he got to the study. There were two large book cases and a desk in the center of the room. He went straight for the desk drawers. In the bottom drawer on the right he found a small safe. He took the safe out of the drawer and set it on the desk. He could just take the safe, in case there was anything regarding her testing in there, but the thought of seeing himself arrested for grand theft caused him to look around for common hiding spots for keys instead. He opened the top desk drawer and he couldn't believe what he saw. A small silver key was in plain view in the front of the drawer—it was a place so obvious that it couldn't possibly be right. He took the small silver key and slid it into the keyhole of the safe. It slid in deftly and he turned the knob. The door of the safe swung open.

Inside the safe was a hard drive. He put the hard drive in the garbage bag with the notebooks before returning the safe and key to where he had found them. He made his way back down to the basement and made sure that nothing looked disheveled. He would get out of the house, close it up as if no one had entered, and make his way to the airport to catch the redeye back to Cincinnati.

"Thank God," he whispered to himself in the otherwise silent house.

Chapter 44

It was a state trooper who had noticed that the guardrail on a particularly nasty curve of the interstate was missing. He parked alongside the road and got out of his patrol car. As soon as he walked over to where the guardrail had been, he picked up his radio and called for ambulance assistance. A car had gone through the guardrail and then flipped over before settling on the steep embankment almost a hundred feet or so from the road.

He quickly scaled down the embankment and approached the driver's side window. There was a woman in the car and she appeared unconscious, hanging upside down limply from her seatbelt. Dried blood covered her face and the front of her shirt. A pool of blood, dried around the edges, lay underneath her body, on the roof of the car. Blood was clumped in a gelatinous mass on her forehead. The windshield was gone and glass filled the roof of the car. The woman's skin was sickeningly pale. The state trooper took a hold of her small wrist and checked for a pulse. It was weak, but it was there.

The ambulance arrived shortly after the call was placed. The EMTs carefully extracted the woman's body from the car and gently conveyed her up the slope with two medics on either side of a stretcher. As soon as they got her into the ambulance, they started a blood transfusion and checked her vital signs.

"Stay with us." One of the EMTs gently coached her lifeless

body.

The woman remained unconscious and her body was in shock. Her vital signs were weak. She could be in a coma with this kind of head trauma. The EMTs made every effort to stabilize her while they transported her to Albany Medical Center.

Chapter 45

Stan went to the office the next morning. He first put the woman's hard drive in one of his desk drawers and her notebooks in one of his filing cabinets and then headed to Jack Sims' office with her laptop. He had already checked once he had arrived home the night before that all of her research was both on the laptop and the hard drive that he had taken from her office. He breezed past Mr. Sims' secretary as she glared at him disapprovingly. He knocked sharply on Mr. Sims' door before letting himself in. Mr. Sims looked up from his desk crossly, then his features softened when he saw the look of triumph on Stan's face. Stan placed the laptop bag on Mr. Sims desk.

"This is her laptop. It has all of her research on it. She's been trying to bring us down for over a decade. She has a small test plot at her house where she has been planting our seeds, applying our herbicides and fertilizers, and monitoring the soil year after year. I found the samples of the new product, *all* of them. She was trying to figure out what it was, but I don't think she had gotten very far. I took all of her test samples. I disposed of all remnants of the new product. They should all be sitting in the county dump by now. I have all of her lab notebooks and her backup hard drive in my office," Stan said boldly.

Mr. Sims raised his eyebrows. "Are you sure you got everything."

"As far as I could tell. I searched the whole house."

"Was she working alone?"

"It looks like it, but she visited someone in Vermont while I was there. I actually followed her all the way up there." Stan grew pale and then slowed down and lowered his voice. "There was an accident on the way back. She lost control of her car and slid down an embankment."

Mr. Sims leaned forward in his chair. "Well, what happened?"

"I don't know. She was unconscious. I took the laptop out of her car. The windows were broken and the car had flipped upside down. The laptop was just sitting there on the roof of the car. Then I left."

"Did anyone see you?" Mr. Sims voice was elevating with agitation.

"No—no one was on the highway at the time. I just... I just drove away."

Mr. Sims seemed to relax a little. "Who was this person she was visiting?"

"I don't know. A friend I guess—maybe her boyfriend. I didn't get too close to the house. I had to keep an eye on his driveway from down the road. All I know is that she went there on Friday and stayed until Sunday morning. They went out during the day on Saturday in his truck for most of the day. I tried to approach the house after they had gone, but a dog inside the house was barking and I was afraid it would alert the neighbors."

Jack Sims quietly processed the information before responding. "Good. Good Job, Stan. Your work is done. I will keep tabs on the situation, but it sounds like it is under control for now."

Stan paused for a minute, trying to grasp his meaning before he responded. "Now that that issue is resolved, we should be ready to launch the second phase of testing this week."

"Good. Proceed." Mr. Sims responded absently, as his mind was clearly elsewhere now.

Stan looked relieved at Mr. Sims' acquiescence. He left his office without another word and closed the door behind him.

Jack Sims waited for a few moments after Stan closed the door. He heard his lumbering footsteps getting further and further away until they could no longer be heard. He then picked up the cell phone he kept in his desk and dialed a familiar number.

"Where are you?" asked Jack into the phone.

"In Virginia. I followed Stan here last night. He followed the woman to Vermont and then came back to Virginia last night," said the familiar voice on the other end.

"Did you see the accident?"

"Accident? What accident?"

"Apparently the woman got in an accident on the way back."

"I stayed about fifteen minutes behind Dr. Cobald. I used a tracking device so I wouldn't lose him. I didn't see anything. That would explain why I never saw the woman return to Virginia."

"The woman knows too much. I don't know how bad the accident was, but make sure that it will take care of any concerns we might have."

"No problem."

"There's one more thing. The person she went to visit in Vermont. This person may know too much as well."

"I will take care of it. I will let you know when it is finished."

"Good," Jack Sims said as he hung up the phone.

Chapter 46

Trevor spent the weekend in his hotel room, checking in on Dr. Cobald's computer with the spyware that he had been able to install on it. Whenever Dr. Cobald turned his computer on and was hooked up to some kind of network, Trevor was able to watch him work and even copy files from his computer if he wanted to. The first thing he copied over was his email files. He started reviewing the most recent ones, and then started to go back in time. Whenever an email stuck him as strange, he would go back and find earlier emails from the same person to figure out what the email string was about. There was one strange email immediately before Dr. Cobald had suddenly picked up and gone to Washington D.C. It was an email from a person named Pete and it contained information on a woman named Sarah Addison. He couldn't figure out what the importance of this email was, except that her home address was near Washington D.C.

He was getting bleary-eyed reading though email strings that seemed to lead him nowhere until Trevor was able to copy over some of Dr. Cobald's lab files. He found outlines for the multi-tiered testing that Dr. Cobald was planning for the new product. First there was a phase to make sure that the product could break down cellulose before itself being rapidly degraded. Then during the second phase it was tested for its toxicity. The third phase was where its persistence in the environment would be tested. But there was something that Dr. Cobald was calling phase

3B. Apparently there was going to be a "partner" chemical, applied immediately after the first product, or in tandem with it. New seeds were to be developed, which were immune to the partner chemical. The seeds were to be the staple crops that Green Future typically produced, but they would have to be genetically modified so that they were immune to the partner chemical, which would have long-term persistence in the soil. Trevor read about a testing protocol to develop application rates for the new product on various types of terrain, including virgin forests.

Trevor forwarded all the key bits of information he found to Scott. When he thought he was sure what was going on, he picked up the prepaid cell phone and called Scott.

"Hey," Scott answered.

"Hey, are you thinking what I'm thinking?" Trevor asked.

"Yeah I think so. What are you thinking?"

"It looks to me like Green Future wants to be able to quickly and cheaply take out massive tracts of vegetation, forests included, and then put some kind of chemical in the soil that would only allow their engineered crops to grow there."

"Yeah, I think so too."

"Even if the farmer decides a few years down the line that he doesn't want the Green Future crops anymore, he can't go back. Hell, the forest wouldn't even be able to grow back—not with a persistent chemical that inhibits all other plant growth."

"What are you going to do?"

"I don't know yet. I think I might hang around long enough

to collect more evidence. I certainly won't help them with that second chemical."

"Okay, be careful. Come home right away if you think they're on to you."

"Thanks. See you when I get back."

Trevor hung up the prepaid cell and then picked up his personal cell phone and called Loren.

"When are you coming home?" he heard her voice say, and he felt a pang of homesickness.

"Soon, I hope. Maybe real soon. I'm not sure how much my boss needs me for this second phase of testing. Hopefully I can just help set it up and come home. How are you doing?"

"Good. I've been drawing a lot. Not much to do without you here. Work is fine. I'm thinking of looking for a different job. Maybe I can be a museum guard or something at the MFA. It would be great to stand around getting paid to look at paintings all day."

"That's great. Yeah, I think you could do better than the job at the fake food factory." Trevor wanted to tell her to go ahead and quit her job, but he wasn't sure how long he was going to remain on the payroll of Green Future, so he held back.

"Hey, I've been thinking about what you said and I've been staring at your board," Loren said.

"My board?"

"Yeah, the phi board, you know, the one with all those

diagrams."

"Oh yeah. Have you? What have you been thinking about?"

"Well I just got curious so I started doing some research of my own. Did you know that the leaves of plant stems grow in Fibonacci spirals?"

"Yeah, I did."

"But do you know why?"

"No, not really, not any more than I know why the golden ratio pops up in so many other places."

"Well it turns out that some botanist came up with this theory in the 1990's. They think that plants grow that way because it's a maximum efficiency thing. They said it minimizes the entropy or something like that. What's entropy?"

"That's weird," Trevor mused, "Scott was just talking about entropy the other day. He was talking about heat death, or the point at which there's no more useable energy in the universe. Entropy is created in the process of using up high quality energy. Entropy is basically like the waste produced in the process of using energy. As high quality energy is used to create complex life forms, entropy increases. Eventually there will be no more high quality energy in the universe and complex life forms will cease to be. Complex life forms need high quality energy. At that point, entropy will be at a maximum."

"So in a way, the faster entropy is created, the faster we are reaching the death of the universe?"

"Yeah, something like that."

"Well, this article I read made it seem like an evolutionary thing. The more efficient the plants get, the more likely they are to survive. Anyway, I just thought it was interesting. I miss you. I miss talking to you about stuff like this."

"I miss you too. I'll come back as soon as I can. I'm going to bed. I gotta go into work in the morning. Hopefully my boss will be in so I can find out when I'll be able to come home."

"Okay. Let me know. I love you."

"I love you too, Loren. Good night."

"Good night."

Chapter 47

There's something I need to tell you. Darin listened to the message that Sarah had left on his voicemail several times. *I need your help.* He had been trying to call her cell phone as soon as he had listened to it the first time, cursing himself for missing the call. He didn't want to worry, but it was getting late and he still hadn't heard from her. *If something were to happen to me...*

He finally decided to wait until the morning and if he still couldn't get a hold of her, he would make the call to her boss. He could tell by the tone of her voice that he shouldn't take this lightly. He could sense that the call to her boss was a last resort only if something was terribly wrong, but he was starting to feel like something was terribly wrong.

He tried his best to sleep that night, but mostly just stared into the dark, wondering what it was that Sarah was involved in that she hadn't been able to tell him about. He slept for a few fitful hours just before dawn. As soon as it was 8:00 am, he started to dial one possible number for Greg Walen's department that he had located. It took a few different numbers he had dug up before he got a receptionist who was able to transfer him to Greg Walen.

"This is Greg Walen," the voice in the phone said to Darin.

"Hi, my name is Darin Hemming. I'm a friend of Sarah Addison. She was visiting me over the weekend and I can't get a hold of her now."

"Her friend? Yes, I got a call from Albany Medical Center. I am her emergency contact person. There was an accident."

Darin felt his stomach grow tight and Greg's words suddenly felt very far away.

"I'm sorry—what? What did you say? Is Sarah okay? What kind of accident?"

"I don't know yet. I'm actually going to leave for Albany as soon as I wrap up a few things here."

Darin felt like the ground was starting to move under his feet and he sat down hard on a nearby chair. He took a moment to gather his thoughts before responding. "I'll head to the hospital as soon as I hang up the phone. There is one thing, though. Sarah left a message for me before the accident. She was saying something about something on her laptop."

"Did she have her laptop with her?" asked Greg with some agitation.

"Yeah; she always keeps that thing with her. She said to make sure you look at a specific folder on her laptop if something were to happen to her."

"Yes, of course. Her laptop has classified information on it. I will make sure we secure the laptop from the accident site to make sure it doesn't fall into the wrong hands."

As soon as Darin hung up the phone, he rushed to the front door and grabbed his jacket. He stopped suddenly and turned around. Adah was sitting stiffly, sensing that something was wrong and looking at him with her full attention. She had been reading his body language and was wound tight, waiting for instructions. He took his phone back out of his pocket and dialed the neighbor.

"Hi Glen, it's Darin. Hey, I have to visit a friend at the hospital in Albany. I really don't know how long I'm gonna be. Can you let Adah out while I'm gone at about noon? I'll leave her dinner on the counter—all you have to do is put it on the floor."

He waited for the voice on the other end to agree before thanking him.

He put the phone back in his pocket and rushed to the pantry to put some dog food in Adah's bowl.

"Adah, you're going to have to watch the house. I'll be back in a little while."

Adah relaxed a little at his words. She watched him attentively as he hurried out the front door.

Chapter 48

The man who called himself Pete saw Darin's truck pull out of his driveway and quickly maneuver down the dirt road toward town. He felt his pulse speed up slightly in anticipation of his work. There was a true art to assassination. It was the art of crafting "accidents"—an art form with only the most privileged of practitioners and an audience of one. His skill was indispensible for a high profile client like Green Future, who could not afford for the authorities to suspect foul play. He thoroughly enjoyed the challenge and his own seemingly endless ingenuity in response to the call of duty, as well as the compensation that came with it.

Pete checked the coordinates of the tracking device on Darin's truck and made sure that he was heading to Albany before pulling into the driveway. The house was hidden from all neighboring views by thick stands of forest. As soon as Pete neared the front of the house, he heard the sound of a canine inside. He quickly stopped the car and got out, closing the door softly behind him. He lost no time making his way to the front door and took a NightHawk Custom AAC 1911 .45 out of his inside coat pocket. He deftly threaded on the suppressor before slowly cracking open the front door. He would need to take care of this little problem before designing his hit.

Adah smelled him through the slowly widening crack of the front door. She lunged at him through the opening with such force that the door slammed back shut and Pete nearly lost his grip on the weapon. The easy part about hits with canines is that they always leave the front door open. The hard part was getting an easy shot on such an aggressive target. These kinds of dogs never bought the hot dog ruse. He scanned the front of the house and then moved away from the front door. His feet were silent as they moved through the moist soil—honed by years of practice.

Pete walked around the side of the house slowly, eyeing a propane tank as he made his way to the back of the house. The open-concept first floor allowed him a view of the front door from one of the back windows. He held up his hand gun, aiming at the muscular, lurching form of the canine as it faced the front door. He chose a spot just behind the shoulder blades. A green laser dot appeared on the thick fur of the canine. Pete waited for the canine to pause briefly to listen for further movement on the other side of the door. The window pane made a musical popping noise as the bullet traveled through it. Instantaneously the canine dropped to the floor and the silence of the forest filled the air in place of the agitated barking.

He made his way back around to the front door and slowly opened it, keeping an eye on the canine's body. There was no sign of breathing—the shot had been a clean one. He pulled the lifeless body away from the doorway and dragged it out of the way of the front entry. He left the body just out of eyeshot of anyone entering the front door. He scanned the room from floor to ceiling, sizing up the tools he had to work with as a plot slowly formed in his mind. He knelt down and touched the large stone that formed the rustic entryway to the house. He put one hand under the front door made of hand-crafted hardwood. Pete stood up and returned to his car and quietly opened the trunk. In it was a large black tool case. He opened the case and revealed an arsenal of various objects—his artist's palette. There was the obvious array of poisons, razor blades, piano wire, and flammable liquids, but there were also the tools and common household items that had helped him set up some of the work that he was most proud of. He pulled open the third tray from the top and opened the compartment where he kept his collection of flint. He also grabbed a hammer, a chisel, a tape measure and a small tube of epoxy.

When Pete returned to the entryway of the house, he knelt down and moved the flint across the face of the stone. He smiled to himself as he saw the sparks that were set off. He measured the gap between the bottom of the door and the entryway stone and then tapped the pins out of the hinges of the front door. He set the door down on a flat area of the floor. He then chiseled out a notch in the bottom of the door just inside of the outer edge, where the velocity of the door opening over the entryway would be the greatest. He set the flint inside the bottom of the edge of the door and secured it with epoxy once he had a snug fit. He checked the length of the flint protruding from the bottom of the door and then smiled with satisfaction.

Pete replaced the front door and secured the pins. As he slowly opened and closed the front door, sparks were given off where the flint was dragged across the entryway stone. He then went over to the kitchen area and turned on one of the burners on the stove. It came to life with a whooshing sound and a large flame. Pete took a large lid from a pot rack and covered the burner with it. When he lifted up the lid, the hissing sound of the gas remained but the fire was out. He took one last look around the room, and then made his way to the front door, closing it behind him ever so slowly.

Chapter 49

The local police were unable to locate Sarah's laptop, even after they had scoured the scene of the accident. Greg Walen grimaced in consternation as he went to the scene of the accident in person, unconvinced of the competence of the local police. Glass and blood were scattered throughout the hillside where the remains of Sarah's familiar sedan lay. The luggage in the trunk had been taken out and laid out on the hillside. The objects taken out of her luggage were carefully laid out on a white sheet, but there was no laptop, and nothing else inside of the car.

The situation was going from bad to worse and Greg didn't have a good feeling about it. He had visited Sarah in the hospital but there was nothing for him to do there—not until she came to. The doctors were hopeful. It was not a coma, but she had not yet regained consciousness. Greg made sure that he would be notified immediately if she came to, then headed to the accident site. He recalled his conversation with Sarah's friend, Darin. She had made a phone call to him before the accident, as if she knew something was going to happen. She had expressly told him to relay the message to Greg to procure her laptop. She must have seen something that spooked her. The whole thing stank of foul play.

Every moment that the laptop was missing could be working against them. Part of Sarah's job had been to identify key water resources, which might be the target of terrorist attack.

There were detailed methods that could be used to either poison or otherwise destroy significant sources of potable water.

It was time to make a decision. He might be wrong about this, but he would rather be wrong and play it safe than to risk the lives of U.S. citizens.

He called a press conference as soon as he arrived back in Albany. Flanked by local police, he spoke slowly and deliberately as he looked into a sea of news cameras and a continuous stream of flashing bulbs.

"We have reason to believe that terrorists may be targeting some significant sources of potable water within the United States. I urge all public and private employees of water treatment facilities and any and all potable water reservoirs to consult your hazard management plans and identify any potential methods of terrorism. I cannot be any more specific than this due to the sensitive nature of this information. You know who you are and what you need to do. Please work with your local law enforcement to step up security at key points. Report any suspicious activities or persons immediately.

"In addition, we are looking for any and all information about a car accident that occurred Southbound on I-87 fifteen miles south of Albany at approximately ten thirty am yesterday. The accident involved a member of the CIA named Sarah Addison. I have asked local news agencies to post her photo in tandem with this press conference. If you saw this woman or have any information that will help us to assess the cause of the accident, please call the eight hundred number we have set up."

Chapter 50

Darin spent the remainder of his morning by Sarah's side watching her slow, shallow breathing. The doctors were hopeful, but he couldn't stand to see her like this. Her normally thoughtful face was like a pale sculpture. The hours went by in slow motion as he constantly scanned her for signs of movement.

Darin met Greg Walen of the CIA but to Darin, the guy seemed more interested in Sarah's laptop than in Sarah's prognosis. Sarah had made Greg her emergency contact. He supposed that made sense, since he was her boss and she was an important employee, but she was also a wonderful woman. He wondered who she was to other people. She had been loath to talk about her family. She said that her extended family had drifted apart after some kind of accident that killed her immediate family. Darin hoped that someday she would open up to him about that. He faced a challenge in trying to get her to give up her work with the CIA to move to Vermont—it was starting to look like her work was all she really had.

His thoughts drifted back to Vermont and the weekend they had shared together. She fit into his life perfectly. He felt like he had been waiting for this woman to come into his life since he was a boy, and now here he was on the verge of losing her. Even Adah took to her immediately, which rarely happened. He felt bad for leaving Adah at home for so long, but it was about time that

Glen should be coming over to let her out. He would call Glen this afternoon—he should be returning this evening regardless. He would come back the next morning, and every morning thereafter for as long as it took for her to regain consciousness. It was important for him to be there for Sarah when she woke up. He wanted her to know that there was something more to her life than work now. He wanted to be her new family.

Φ

As Glen walked up Darin's driveway it was too quiet. Adah always barked once she heard someone coming up the driveway. When he got to the front door, he peered in the front window to look for signs of Adah but saw none. Perhaps she wasn't feeling well or she was deep in slumber somewhere. He went ahead and let himself in as usual.

The explosion happened so fast that he didn't even have time to register it. The door he had just opened flew outward in a rush of fire, throwing his body back onto the driveway as the entire house burst into flames.

Chapter 51

The man who called himself Pete stopped at a specialty store near the hospital to purchase some janitorial clothing. He would need to get close to Sarah Addison. He knew the hospital routine. Especially at a large one like Albany Medical Center, there were so many nurses, interns and part-time employees in and out that it would not be a challenge to go unnoticed for a short while as long as he dressed the part.

He spent some time outside the hospital observing the routine of the hospital personnel and the public going in and out of the building. He packed the newly purchased clothes into a small handbag and headed for the emergency room entrance. The waiting room was filled with worried faces in various states of distraction. The reception desk was in a separate area for privacy. The elevators were adjacent to the waiting room, near the front entrance. He looked past the reception area and saw that a stairwell was located at the end of the hallway, accessible out of sight of the main entrance. He went up to the reception desk and addressed the older woman behind the counter.

Pete tried to soften his severe features as he addressed the woman. "Hi. I'm looking for a friend of mine. We were on a jobsite and he fell from a scaffold. It was a pretty bad head injury. I'm not sure if he was taken here, but can you tell me what room they might have put him in if he was?"

"What is your friend's name?"

"Tony Avery."

The woman at the reception desk typed into her computer and scanned down a list of names. "No. No one of that name has been admitted today. Where was the jobsite?"

"Are you sure? Can you ask one of the nurses who has been on duty since this morning if a man in his mid forties came in with a bad head injury? Maybe no one rode in the ambulance with him and he didn't have his I.D. on him."

The receptionist gave him a hard look and then stood up slowly. "I'm not supposed to leave the reception area, but it'll just take a minute. If anyone else comes by tell them I'll be right back."

"I will—thank you so much. You are so kind."

When the woman disappeared through the doorway behind the reception area, Pete immediately reached over the reception counter and turned her computer screen toward him, scanning down the list of names. "Sarah Addison" was right on top. He pushed the down arrow key until her name was highlighted and hit return. A page of information came up and he scanned it until he saw a column entitled "ROOM ASSIGNMENT". Under the column heading, the screen displayed the words "Second Floor, Room 15".

He quickly turned the computer screen back and headed directly for the stairwell at the end of the hallway.

Chapter 52

Darin was sitting beside Sarah's hospital bed when he felt his phone vibrating in his pocket. He stood up to take the phone out of his back pocket and looked at the caller. It was his neighbor Glen. He wondered if there was a problem with Adah. He answered the call as he quietly made his way out of Sarah's hospital room.

"Hello?"

"Darin." The voice on the other end was not Glen. It was Glen's wife, Pam, but Darin could barely hear her.

"Hello, Pam? Is that you? I can barely hear you."

Pam's voice was weak and trembling. "Darin, there has been an accident," she finally managed to get out, and then her voice broke up with a sob.

"What happened? Where's Glen? Is Adah okay?"

"I...I don't think so. The whole house—the whole house exploded. The fire department is there. Glen was...", her voice cut out for a second and then came back. "They found his body halfway up the driveway. The explosion threw him a few dozen feet. He's dead, Darin."

Darin was dumbfounded as he listened to her quiet sobbing. "What happened? How could there have been an explosion?"

"They say propane. There must have been a leak."

"That just doesn't make any sense." Darin's legs seemed to go numb as the shock spread through his body. His legs started to slowly walk on their own, lumbering down the hall away from Sarah's door.

"I'm so sorry Pam. It just doesn't make any sense; I was there only this morning. There was no leak. I didn't cook anything or turn the heat on. I'm coming home right away. Just hold tight. I'll be there as soon as I can."

He ended the call and put the phone back in his pocket as he slowly walked down the hallway. Time seemed to slow down and the faces he passed in the hallway took on a surreal quality. He tried to consciously make his legs speed up but felt like he had lost control of them. Every detail around him grew crystal clear—the expressionless faces of the nurses as they scurried about with clipboards, the sterile whiteness of the tile floor.

He was passing the nurse's station on his way to the elevator when a middle-aged janitor passed him. A baseball cap hid his eyes from view as he pushed along a cart filled with clean bedding. Darin scooted out of his way and he let his eyes fall to the floor to make sure that his legs were still cooperating underneath him. The janitor's shoes had a familiar coating of mud on them—a piece of real life. This was too vivid to be a dream.

Darin got on the elevator and forced himself to take deep breaths, scanning around him desperately for signs that he might be dreaming. He hit the button that would take him back down to the main entrance on the ground floor. Before the elevator doors closed a half dozen people filed in. They were silently absorbed in their own cares—loved ones whose futures were uncertain. Darin looked down at the floor of the elevator, averting his eyes and feeling a cloak of grief threatening to envelope him. He recalled the mud on the shoes of the janitor while his eyes were trained at the shoes of the people on the elevator. They were all either perfectly clean or slightly dusty. Something didn't feel right to Darin. Nothing felt right, to be exact.

Darin exited the elevator and then made his way out of the main entrance, the large double doors closing autonomously behind him. He looked around the parking lot of the medical center. The parking lot was coated with the dusting of salt from the long winter. *Something isn't right.* He stopped in mid stride and stood there in the parking lot looking around him, trying to find some standing water or patch of dirt. There were only the manicured beds of mulch around hedges and an occasional ornamental tree. An image of the mud on the janitor's shoes flashed in his mind. Darin recalled Sarah's phone call that he had listened to at least a dozen times. There had been fear in her voice. She had seen something, or *someone.* Darin was not one to leave his house with an active gas leak. *Two accidents in the space of twenty four hours.*

That was Vermont mud.

Turning around abruptly, Darin ran back into the emergency room. He went straight to the elevator and slammed the elevator call button.

"Come on, come on," he said impatiently to himself. He

looked around frantically for a stairwell, but the elevator door opened with the sound of a bell before he spotted one. Once in the elevator, he pushed the number 2 and then immediately pushed the button to close the doors repeatedly. The elevator felt like it took a lifetime to reach the second floor. As soon as the doors opened, he sprinted out and headed directly for Sarah's room, nearly knocking over a nurse in the hallway.

Darin threw open Sarah's door as a group of nurses gathered in the hallway around the nurse he nearly collided with. He could hear shouts of "Sir, please slow down" behind him.

From the doorway, he saw the janitor next to Sarah's bed. He had a syringe directed at the IV bag hanging on a stand next to Sarah.

"Hey!" Darin yelled, as he sprung forward at the man.

A look of surprise and anger came across the man's face, distracting him from the IV bag. His hand remained steady, with his thumb on the back of the plunger of the syringe, as he looked at the man in the doorway, coming at him quickly. Darin wasted no time and went directly for the man's arm poised with the syringe. In exactly the same instant that Darin grabbed the man's arm, he saw the man's fist clench, forcing the plunger down and the contents of the syringe into Sarah's IV bag.

"No!" Darin shouted as he grabbed the man around the shoulders. The nurses from the hallway scurried into the room as the two men fell to the ground. "The IV bag!" he yelled as he wrapped his massive arms around the man to hold him down. "Please help! There's poison in the IV bag!"

The nurses stared blankly from the doorway, cemented by shock and confusion. The man was working hard to struggle free of Darin's grip. The nurses weren't moving. Darin let go of the man in disgust and lunged at the IV stand, throwing it to the ground as the IV needle ripped out of Sarah's arm, leaving a bright red streak on the white linen. Darin fell to the ground as the IV stand clattered to the floor on top of him. Once free from Darin's grip, the man scrambled to his feet and shoved the nurses out of the doorway as he fled the room.

"Help her!" Darin yelled to the nurses as he untangled himself from the IV bag and got up off the floor. The man ran past the elevator and to the stairwell down the hall. Darin was a dozen yards behind him, but shortening the distance. When the man hit the door to enter the stairwell, it slowed him down by a few fractions of a second. Darin came flying through the door before it started to close itself behind the man. The man had just made a right turn to descend the stairwell when Darin's full mass hit him. The man's body hit the stairwell leading to the third floor as Darin's body landed on top of him. The right angle of the concrete stairs hit the man in the ribs and he let out a grunt as several bones audibly cracked. Darin pinned him against the stairs.

"Don't move, asshole," Darin said to the man.

In a few moments, one of the nurses appeared in the doorway leading to the stairwell.

"Call the cops," Darin said to her and he kept the injured man pinned to the stairwell. "This guy is a murderer."

Chapter 53

Trevor's heart felt like it stopped for a moment, then started pounding furiously, drowning out the last few words of the newscaster. He was lying in bed in his hotel room winding down after a day at work until the national news made him sit upright.

"Be vigilant and report any suspicious activities to local authorities. If you saw this woman at all yesterday or know anything about the accident on I-87 please call this hotline."

The photo that was shown on the screen was unmistakably a photo of the woman from the report in Stan's email. Sarah Addison. *Yes, this was the woman.* Dr. Cobald went to Washington D.C. after receiving a file of information about this woman, then returned right after she was in an accident. The likelihood that it was a coincidence was remote in Trevor's mind. He sat up in his bed in the hotel room, feeling nauseous. *Who was this woman? Why would she be of interest to Green Future? Was Dr. Cobald responsible for this?*

Trevor had spoken with Dr. Cobald at work during the day after his return from Washington. He noticed that Stan was lacking his usual easy manner. He seemed distracted, even on edge at times. *Something was eating at him.*

Trevor got out of bed and walked over to the little desk in the hotel room where his laptop sat. He opened his laptop and started it up. Once he opened the spyware program, he scanned for any new additions to Dr. Cobald's computer. A new folder had been created called "M10". When he clicked on one of the excel spreadsheets inside of the folder, he looked at the file information at the bottom of the window. His eyes glossed over the "Date modified" and "Size" and went straight to "Author: saddison". Trevor's mind started spinning—he could hardly believe it. He paused for a second and wondered if this was a bad dream. He clenched his hands, driving his fingernails into the fleshy part of his palms. He was awake.

Trevor shook off his inertia and then set up his laptop to copy all of the contents of the folder "M10" onto his computer. He picked up his prepaid cell phone, considered it for a few moments, and then decided against calling Scott. Instead, he turned back to his computer and starting shopping for an airline ticket back to Boston first thing in the morning. He would leave without saying anything to anyone from Green Future. Once he arrived in Boston, he would contact Dr. Cobald and claim a family emergency. He would attach the protocol for the second phase of testing that he had been asked to work on to the email so that Dr. Cobald wouldn't get suspicious.

Trevor didn't know how long he would be able to keep up this façade, but he intended to try to maintain it at least until he could figure out why Green Future was interested in that woman. He hoped the answer was in that folder.

Chapter 54

After holding the man until the arrival of the police, Darin's first phone call was to Greg Walen. Greg immediately returned to the hospital, where Darin played him the voicemail that Sarah had left him.

"I'm sorry I kept it from you earlier—I just didn't want her to get into any trouble with her work," Darin said to him. "Do you think this message has anything to do with all of this?"

"I don't know but we are certainly going to find out. I will have our team search her house in Virginia right away to look for that hard drive. We still don't know where her laptop is. We will have to search this guy's car and find out who he is, who he works for, and if there is anywhere around here where he might have taken the laptop. We have a lot of work ahead of us."

"There is something else," Darin said, as he felt his chest go empty with sadness. "There was an explosion at my house earlier today. I don't think it was an accident. It killed my neighbor who had come over to feed my dog. I think it was meant for me or Sarah."

The stern expression on Greg Walen's face deepened. "I'm sorry, Darin. I will make sure our team goes to your house as well to investigate. We will get to the bottom of this."

Darin put his head in his hands as he thought about the life he had only twenty four hours earlier—the hopeful promise that this woman had brought to his existence. He had nowhere to go back to, but he didn't want to give up hope of finding Adah.

"I need to get home," Darin said.

"Yes," Greg Walen said, "go home. Stay with friends if you can. I'll let you know as soon as I know anything. I'm sending a team up there to investigate the explosion right away. The doctor will call you as soon as Sarah wakes up."

Greg's calculating face softened a bit before he continued, reading the desperation on Darin's face. "You know, she's lucky to have you. That guy would certainly have killed her. Nice work."

Darin was silent for a moment, as if he didn't want to accept Greg's words. "Hopefully it will make a difference and she will wake up."

Greg Walen shook Darin's hand and patted his shoulder with his other hand reassuringly as Darin turned to leave.

Φ

The man who called himself Pete lay in a hospital bed, crippled with pain. His breathing was ragged and shallow. Every breathe he took felt like several knives in the side of his ribcage. His half-closed eyes stared out at the two detectives who were questioning him. Despite his incapacitated state, the detectives felt like those two mean slits were taunting them.

"We're going to ask you again and this time we want an

answer. We have concrete evidence that links you to one murder and one attempted murder. Who are you working for?"

Pete's face contorted into a half smile and said nothing.

The detectives exchanged glances and then began again. "We can make you a real nice deal if you agree to cooperate. We're going to find out anyway. We are offering you a chance to make it easier on us so that we can make it easier on you. Why were you targeting Sarah Addison?"

The look of complacent smugness remained on the man's otherwise stony face and he remained unresponsive. The two detectives knew they were getting nowhere with this guy—he was a professional—and were relieved when there was a sharp knock on the door. This was their cue to wrap it up. They left the room and shut the door behind them as Pete followed them with his eyes. As soon as they left the room, an officer entered the room to keep an eye on the suspect.

"We have a lead," Greg Walen said to them in a quiet voice as the three of them huddled in the busy hallway of the hospital. "This guy had a pre-paid cell phone on him. Only a couple of calls have been made on it. Every call was traced to a company in Cincinnati called Green Future. I presume you have heard of them."

"Yeah," said one of the detectives as the other one nodded in agreement, "it's a controversial company. They have a history of being protested by environmental activists."

"I wouldn't put it past Sarah to be involved in something against Green Future. This could be what the voicemail was referring to, about being involved in something outside of work. The problem is, the team hasn't recovered anything from Sarah's house. No hard drive and nothing to suggest that she might be a part of some anti-Green Future group."

"Is this enough for a search warrant?" asked one of the detectives.

"I don't think so," Greg answered. "We need something concrete to connect Sarah to Green Future".

Chapter 55

When Darin returned to what had been his home, it was surrounded by fire department vehicles. Hoses were strung about the property dousing the smoking remains of the conflagration. He parked along the road and then jogged up his driveway. The feeling he usually had when approaching his house, a happy eagerness to see his dog, was replaced by an awful feeling of dread. The place where his home had been was a wreck of rubble, ashes, and wisps of smoke.

"Darin." A young firefighter that he knew approached him. "I'm terribly sorry."

"My dog Adah—have you seen her?"

The young man lowered his eyes before responding. "Yeah we did. Well, we found parts of her. The explosion was bad. Looks like a gas leak that had been a pretty good one."

Darin sobbed loudly and the young man put an arm around his shoulders. "I'm sorry. She's gone. She was a good dog."

Darin stumbled forward toward the house. "Where is she?"

"You can't go in there Darin. Don't worry—we'll get her for you. Do you need somewhere to stay tonight?"

"I have to go talk to Pam," Darin answered, "but first, I need to see what's left."

Darin walked around the perimeter of the remnants of his

house as the firefighters continued to spray water on the smoking rubble. The explosion had taken the roof and all of the windows but the stone walls that he had shaped with his own hands still stood. They were black with soot on the top and on the insides, but looked structurally sound.

The thought of rebuilding at this point was a thought that he didn't even want to entertain. Every time he thought of his house the way it had stood earlier that day, he could see the expectant, loving eyes of Adah as she watched him silently. He wanted this house to remain how he felt right now—empty and devoid of hope—struck down incomprehensively. He wanted to be angry—to feel something other than this emptiness, but even his rage felt defeated as he yearned for the soft ears and the wagging tail that he would never see again. He knew that man had done this—it was only a matter of time before the cops were able to prove it. He only hoped that Adah had not seen that man—that in the second before she expired she never caught a glimpse of the ugliness that can reside in man's soul.

Chapter 56

Darin returned to Albany after visiting with Pam that night. There was nothing for him in Wilmington and he needed to get away from that sad reminder. What remained for him lay in a hospital bed at Albany Medical Center. He felt like he and Sarah were two orphans—destined to find one another—made perfectly for each other.

He spent the night in a hotel near the hospital and when he returned to the hospital the next day, the nurses greeted him with good news.

"She's awake," one of the nurses said to him as soon as he came out of the second floor elevator. He felt a weight lift from his chest and his pace suddenly picked up as he headed to her room.

The nurse followed him. "She just woke up about a half an hour ago," she said. "The doctor is in there now. When he gives us the go ahead, we can call Greg Walen. You'll have to wait until the doctor comes out."

Darin looked at the nurse disappointedly. "Okay; I'll wait right here."

He paced the hallway for a few minutes before a doctor emerged from her room, closing the door behind him and noticing Darin in the hallway.

"You must be Darin," the doctor said to him.

"Yes. How is she?"

"She's not well, but she is doing okay. She was very lucky, actually. There was no permanent damage and she seems to have retained her memory. The head trauma will require a few weeks of convalescence, but she should recover fully."

Darin eyes filled with tears of relief.

"She was asking about you," the doctor told him.

"Can I go in to see her?" Darin asked.

"Yes, but if she falls asleep, let her sleep. She needs it."

Darin quietly opened the door and looked at Sarah as she lay there. Her eyes were closed, but her face looked more composed than it had previously looked. He sat down in the chair next to her and took her hand gently in his. He felt her squeeze his hand lightly as she opened her eyes. She looked at him as if she expected him to be there and it took her a while to speak.

"Darin," she said in a faint voice, "I have to tell you something."

"Don't worry—it can wait. Take your time. You need to rest."

"I have to tell you or I won't be able to rest. Green Future did this—I'm sure of it. I can't prove it, but I stole something of theirs. I think they're trying to get it back."

A shadow spread across Darin's face but he listened quietly as she continued.

"I have spent over ten years trying to prove that their

products are going to destroy the environment. I think they finally found me out. I trespassed onto their property last week and stole samples. The samples are in my basement at my house. I don't know exactly what they're up to, but whatever it is they're trying to keep me or anyone else from finding out. I feel like the pieces of the puzzle are all there—I just don't know how to assemble them. I think those samples I stole were important pieces. There was a guy following me... I..."

"I played the voicemail you left me to your boss. Is this what you were talking about?" Darin asked her.

"Yes. Greg Walen needs to know. Tell him to search my house."

"He's already there—don't worry. He'll find the samples."

Sarah's face lost its look of urgency and she closed her eyes again.

"You've done enough—now it's time to rest," Darin said to her. "I can't tell you how happy I am to hear your voice again. I'll be right here. I'm staying with you, no matter what."

"I put you in danger," Sarah said to him.

"There's no danger any more, Sarah. Greg is going to pin those guys to the wall. Don't worry. We already have one of them—the guy who did this to you."

A look of confusion crossed Sarah's face, replaced immediately by a look of exhaustion. Her eyes closed and her breathing slowed down as she fell asleep.

Φ

When Greg Walen arrived at the hospital, Sarah was sleeping deeply. Darin relayed what she had said to him.

"This should be enough for a warrant," Greg said, "we didn't find anything at Sarah's house but there an open window in the basement and some evidence of a break in. It looks like whatever it was that Sarah wanted us to find, Green Future did not want us to find it. We are sending a team to Cincinnati immediately and as soon as we get the warrant we will go in."

Chapter 57

It was Wednesday before the paperwork was approved and a search warrant was generated. A stream of black vehicles and squad cars flowed into the parking lot of Green Future, like a snake silently approaching its prey. The vehicles fanned out in front of the building's main entrance and the vehicle doors opened as several dozen officers filed out.

Phone calls to and from the phone carried by the perpetrator at Albany Medical Center were traced to the direct line of Dr. Stan Cobald and a cell phone linked to CEO Jack Sims of Green Future. The Green Future test plot was found at Sarah Addison's house, forming a potential motive, which was enough to secure the warrant. The search would begin in the two men's offices simultaneously. Greg Walen approached the front desk of Green Future, flanked by a team of FBI agents. The receptionist picked up the phone to alert Jack Sims.

"Please put the phone down, ma'am," Greg said to her.

The secretary stared at him blankly.

Greg continued, "We are going to need to be directed to the offices of Jack Sims and Dr. Stan Cobald."

"I'm sorry, but I can't let you go in unannounced," she responded, snapping out of her confusion.

"Actually you can, according to this piece of paper," Greg

said as he flashed the warrant at her. "If you don't give us your assistance, you will be charged with obstruction of justice."

"I see. Well seeing as how getting arrested is not part of my job description, let me show you a map of the building."

She pulled out a map and showed them the route to Jack Sims' office in the corporate building and Dr. Cobald's office in the biotechnology building. The group of darkly dressed agents split roughly in two. Greg went with the group that headed for Dr. Cobald's office.

Stan's secretary Nancy sat at the front desk with a look of utter confusion as the group of darkly clad officers filled the lobby.

"Dr. Cobald's office please," Greg Walen barked at her curtly.

"Oh my," she stuttered, gathering her wits about her. "I will let him know you are coming."

"No need. Just point the way to his office," he responded shortly.

The woman pointed down an aisle to the right and spoke softly as she picked up the phone. "It's at the end of the building."

She picked up the phone and looked guiltily over her shoulder as the group walked briskly past her.

Stan was intently typing when the buzzing of the secretary's page through his phone speaker snapped him out of his train of thought. He ignored the buzzing and continued to type. The buzzing stopped for a few moments, and then began again. He looked at the phone with annoyance, then conceded to answer. As he reached for the phone, his door opened abruptly and a group of officers quickly filled the room, making the office suddenly seem very small. Stan pushed his overstuffed chair away from his computer and stood up. The phone continued to buzz insistently and he picked up the receiver.

"Yes I know—they're here," he said into the phone and then placed it back down on its cradle.

"Dr. Stan Cobald," said Greg Walen authoritatively, "we have reason to believe that are responsible for the attempted murder of Sarah Addison. We have a warrant to search both your home and your place of work. You can cooperate and make this easy on yourself, or you can make it difficult for all of us, especially yourself. It's up to you."

"Attempted murder?" said Stan, incredulously, "No, no, you have it all wrong. It was an accident. She had an accident. She drove her car off the road."

"How do you know she drove off the road?" Greg quipped.

Stan sat back down in his chair, slumping over his desk and putting his head in his hands. "Oh dear God," he said, his voice straining with emotion. He stayed there without moving for several moments and then finally gathered himself together and replied "I will need the company's attorney present before I can talk to you."

"Very well." Greg Walen motioned to one of the men in the group and two officers came behind Stan's desk. One of them took out a pair of handcuffs and started to read Stan his rights.

The room went out of focus for Stan but all of the events leading up to this moment came clearly into view, step after regretful step. *Breaking and Entering. Leaving the scene of an accident.* He was not a murderer, but he knew that he was guilty. And it was over. He somehow felt some relief at being caught. The guilt he had been carrying since he had started tailing the woman took flight the moment the handcuffs clicked around his wrists. He didn't know what the consequences would be for him—he supposed jail. But perhaps that repentance and time behind bars would cleanse him of the sins he had committed.

Chapter 58

Stan Cobald sat in the interrogation room in disbelief. Ever since he had gotten on the plane to Washington D.C., his life seemed like it had been turned over to someone else. *This wasn't me. I wouldn't do those things. I am a man of God.*

He had been on God's mission. His actions were destined to save the human race from extinction. *Is it possible that I have been lead astray?* He wondered painfully to himself.

His bulky frame slumped over the table in front of him, a large kidney-shaped pool of sweat on his upper back.

"I swear—I had nothing to do with any kind of murder," he restated to the two police officers across the table from him.

"Who was this guy that you keep referring to as Pete?" they asked him sharply.

"I don't know. He just supplied me with information on Sarah Addison—that's all. I was supposed to take back the items she had stolen from us."

"As well as her laptop with sensitive information on it?"

"Well, no. I mean, I didn't know. I...," his hands flailed in the space between him and the officers. "Look, I broke into a woman's house and took some items that aren't worth much. How serious can the charges really be?"

"That man called Pete, who you communicated with,

attempted to kill Sarah Addison in the hospital and was caught in the act. We are also working on tying him to an explosion that occurred at a house in Vermont where Sarah Addison had spent the weekend, which killed a neighbor."

"Dear God. I didn't know anything about that—I *swear*," Stan said as he gripped his temples with both hands.

Stan looked over at Green Future's lawyer, who was sitting beside him stiffly in an impeccable suit that no doubt had cost a small fortune. He then looked back at the two FBI agents who were interrogating him, their unyielding stares expecting answers.

I am turning my fate over to you, Dear God. It is time to expunge myself. Stan's expression transformed from helplessness to resolve as he addressed the police officers.

"I am going to need a new lawyer," Stan said. "I think I know who is behind this. I will let you know whatever you want to know, but please know that I never intended anyone to get hurt."

The demeanor of the FBI agent softened. "We can make you a deal. You help us and we'll help you. If you need time to find another lawyer then you can have a public defender in the meantime."

"Just wait a minute," said Green Future's lawyer. "I would like a word with my client in private."

Stan cut him off angrily, "No. I'm done with you. Jack Sims is going to need your help more than I will."

Chapter 59

Beauty in the mathematics has often been a guide to reality.

Frank Close

Trevor pored through Sarah's files from the moment he returned to his apartment in Boston. When he heard the news story on the search of Green Future headquarters and the taking into custody of Dr. Stan Cobald and CEO Jack Sims, he realized that he would probably not have a job there for much longer—nor did he want one. He had saved enough of his initial pay from Green Future to return to school as soon as possible, but in the meantime he had more important things to do.

The picture of what Sarah Addison had been doing for over a decade was slowly shaping in his mind. He imagined her test plot of Green Future crops, replanted each year as the soil biology was slowly altered. He could feel her persistent frustration at not being able to point a decisive finger at the flaw of the system. Even though the ecology of the soil grew simpler and the soil structure more compact, it still sustained life year after year. The crop yields decreased as rogue weeds resistant to the crop's partner herbicide began to appear, but nothing catastrophic had happened yet. Her last hope was to take the data collected during that decade and extrapolate it out for a few more decades in order to estimate the potential effects over an even longer term. But the model she was using wasn't quite right. It was too linear—the parallel reactions were not allowed to interact with each other. She had also neglected the effects of the changing climate and also the bioaccumulation of the herbicide in the local insects and bees.

Sarah's approach was correct and the variables she accounted for exhaustive, but the equations were too simple. The computer program itself would have to be recoded. This was right up Trevor's alley. He had a new project to obsess over. Trevor was an artist with equations.

It took him about four days to rewrite the equations. The moment he was waiting for arrived and he could barely contain himself. He hit "RUN" on the model, and then he waited. The familiar results screens were not popping up. He waited a little longer and then hit the keyboard's "esc" key.

"Dammit," he said aloud when the computer remained frozen.

Trevor did a hard reboot and then ran the program again.

"Not enough processing power," he said to himself, and then killed the computer with a hard shut down. He picked up his cell phone and dialed.

"Hey Trevor," a familiar voice answered. "You got that thing figured out yet or what?"

"I'm so close, Scott." Trevor said. "I think the equations are correct but now the program won't run. My computer keeps freezing. I don't think it has enough processing power."

"Aha," said Scott. "Are you thinking what I'm thinking?"

"Is it something that might get you kicked out of school?"

"Yup."

"Then yes, I am. Are you game?"

"Are you kidding? Of course! I'll meet you at the lab in half an hour."

Scott had access to one of the largest computers on the MIT campus. It was off limits to most students, but Scott was a teaching assistant and had a key to the lab.

"Did you know that we can analyze data from CERN with this thing?" Scott asked Trevor as he inserted his key into the lock.

"That's that particle accelerator in Switzerland, right?"

"Yup."

"What is that thing for, anyway?" Trevor asked, following Scott into the lab as he turned on lights and pulled two seats up in front of a large monitor.

"The short answer is: to discover what the universe is made of and how it works. The particle accelerator can simulate conditions directly after the big bang. It looks at how the particles behave so that we can try to figure out how we got from that to here and now."

"Wow, I didn't realize that," Trevor said as Scott booted up the computer. "So what have they found out?"

"Well, they have validated the standard model of particle physics. They also have explained why there is matter in the universe as opposed to everything being swallowed by antimatter."

"Antimatter? What is that?"

"Antimatter is exactly what it sounds like—it's the complete opposite of matter. If one particle of matter meets its evil twin of anti-matter, the meeting results in mutual oblivion. At the big bang, there was complete balance—equal parts of matter were created alongside anti-matter. This was one of the great mysteries before the trials at CERN—how the universe started in complete balance with equal parts matter and anti-matter and ended up as a matter-filled universe."

"Maybe there is anti-matter hanging around in clumps somewhere in the universe, like a mirror universe of anti-matter alongside our universe of matter," Trevor offered.

"Nope. If that were the case, there would be gamma ray bursts at the boundary of where the matter universe meets the anti-matter universe. We have telescopes powerful enough that we would be able to see that."

"So what happened to the anti-matter?"

"Well, it turns out that the universe is, I guess you could say, lopsided. Physicists found a particle called a 'kaon'. For each kaon that is created, there is an antikaon that is created in tandem. This matter/anti-matter pair is unique in that it is unbalanced with respect to time—antikaons turn into kaons faster than kaons turn into antikaons. If you start with equal parts kaon and antikaon, eventually you will end up with more kaons—more matter. They think that the creation of mass was what led to the eventual imbalance."

"Can that little of a difference in one particle actually create a whole universe of matter?"

"Eventually. Just think about our planet. It took more than four billion years of energy input from the sun for human intelligence to emerge. It's all just tiny photons, one after another, slowly building up year after year. If the universe had remained perfectly symmetrical, we would never be having this conversation."

"I always thought that the universe was in balance."

"Complete balance is too stable for growth. It's a dynamic balance—a building, always forward, toward complexity, or enlightenment, or to whatever you want to believe. Just look at nature. DNA forms in a chiral asymmetry—one direction dominates the twisting structure. This asymmetrical structure is more efficient for reproduction. Life itself depends on asymmetry."

"But there must be an end to the growth."

"Isn't that what we're here to find out?" Scott winked at him, and then said, "All right, give me that USB. We need to load up the program and the input files—she's ready to rock."

"The lopsidedness of the universe—it's kind of like the phi proportion," Trevor said as he handed Scott the USB drive. "You know, DNA has phi proportions."

"There you go again with that phi nonsense," Scott laughed as he slid the USB stick into the lab computer.

"Some people call it the divine proportion," Trevor mused as Scott navigated through the contents of the USB. "Scott, do you believe in God?"

"Well, it depends on what you want to call God. If you mean some bloke who meddles in peoples' lives, then no. But there are some interpretations of quantum theory that make some compelling suggestions."

"Like?"

"Well, you have heard about the collapse of the wave function, right?"

"Yeah—supposedly there are infinite states of being until the wave function collapses, which is caused by observation. So some people think that our consciousness actually creates our reality. Super creepy."

"Yeah, so if the universe started in a big bang and then experienced inflation and eventually formed galaxies, planets, and finally inhabitants, what created the existence of everything before we got here? There had to have been an observer to collapse the wave function and create the reality the whole time, even before us, right?"

A lightbulb went off in Trevor's face. "Aha. The scientific theory that can prove the existence of a divine creator. Is that what you think?"

"No—that's too simple. Who says that the 'observer' has to be like us? Who says that only consciousness on our level or above can collapse the wave function? What if there are varying levels of consciousness and even something as simple as a collection of gas particles can have an emergent consciousness of sorts?"

"Whoa—you think that gas particles have consciousness?"

"Maybe, I mean there are some experiments that show that plants exhibit some form of consciousness—just not as complex as ours. Where is the cut-off? Mold? Bacteria? Ever hear of that experiment by that Japanese guy that suggested that water could have a sort of consciousness? It was in that 'What the Bleep' documentary."

"Is that what you think?"

"It's possible. But I tend to think that the thing that most resembles 'God'—a creator—is something even more fundamental. It's the structure itself behind the organization from which consciousness can emerge. *Mathematics*. I wouldn't be surprised if it is an equation that is short enough to write on a napkin—the 'Theory of Everything' that mankind has been searching for since Ancient Greece. I imagine that the mathematics propagate the formation of matter, which propagates biological life, which propagates consciousness—it's like the mathematical structure forms a string, which resonates tones that can be arranged to create harmonies. That is basically string theory."

"String theory? I've heard of it, but what is it exactly?"

"Well you know how the universe is made up of tiny particles? According to string theory, those tiny particles are actually strings. So, if you looked very closely at something like an electron, you would see a string. The strings vibrate at different frequencies. The various subatomic particles like quarks and neutrinos are manifested by plucking the strings to resonate at different frequencies. Basically, the subatomic particles are like musical notes. Physics is a description of the laws of harmony.

Chemistry is an infinite combination of melodies and the universe is creating a symphony."

"Then who is the composer?"

"I suppose it can be us, or anything with a consciousness and the ability to manipulate matter. Isn't manipulating matter, after all, being God? Once humans completely understand the laws of physics, there is nearly nothing that is impossible. We may be able to create baby universes, time travel, create a warp drive by bending space in order to make space travel feasible through vast distances—the possibilities are endless."

"But who wrote the equations for the laws of physics?"

"Our physical laws are an iteration of infinite universes that played out every possible equation with every possible value of the universal constants. One in one hundred billion, man—those are the odds of getting to the point where we are at in our evolution. There would be no 'us' sitting here with even slightly different equations or constants."

"So basically luck? That seems too unlikely to be a coincidence."

"Not luck. We are sitting here *because* the conditions were just right in our universe. An infinite number of universes with slightly different laws of physics and fundamental constants collapsed in on themselves or failed to form galaxies—there are an infinite number of scenarios, which would have failed to sustain complex life forms.

"Speaking of luck, check this out."

Scott pointed to the screen of the computer, which had successfully ran the program installed from the USB stick. Trevor leaned in closer to the computer screen, reading the numbers that were displayed in the output file.

"Holy Crap," Trevor said. "No wonder Green Future didn't want anyone to know about this stuff."

Chapter 60

A person starts to live when he can live outside of himself.

Albert Einstein

Sarah lay in the hospital bed with her right hand on her abdomen. She had been in and out of consciousness, but mostly out. She had no way of telling how long she had been there. She had a few foggy memories of Darin being there next to her, but this time when she awoke she was starting to feel aware of her complete surroundings. Darin was not there now.

There had been no signs of a miscarriage since the accident, at least not that she was aware of. That would have been too easy. She would just have to wait and see if her period returned as normal, or if she continued to feel some of that morning sickness. Her head was so foggy and her system still so traumatized that she couldn't tell.

She didn't want to bring a person into this world. She felt that it was hugely irresponsible. Humans had not yet figured out how to live on this planet with respect for all the various forms of life, including each other. But it wasn't a simple decision of whether or not she should have this child—it was a moral dilemma that she wasn't sure she had the answer to. There was something inside of her, which seemed to grow steadier as she aged, as she nurtured the wisdom she gleaned and applied it to all of her life decisions. It was her moral compass. It was wrong to bring a child into an already overpopulated world, but also wrong to take a life. She had to decide which action was the least wrong. *Do the ends justify the means when the means create the end? Won't the ends be forever defined by the means?*

This was the same kind of debate she had with herself even when it came to taking the lives of vegetables from her garden. She knew plants—she felt that they were alive and may even have consciousness in some subtle way that humans are not capable of sensing. She had to take their lives in order for her to survive. That was the distasteful price of life. She accepted this, but chose not to eat meat, since the emotional lives and intelligence of animals were more developed than those of carrots.

But I don't know what this child will become. She thought to herself as she closed her eyes and remembered. The memories that she had fought to suppress for years came rising to the surface with disturbing clarity. Reluctantly, she felt she had to welcome them—this once.

Φ

It was the middle of the week and she had just come out of geology class. Her dorm room was located a short walk across campus. She loved attending university. She had always been an excellent student and at the top of her class—college was like being in heaven. Her young mind thirsted for knowledge and all of her home life distractions had been left behind in West Virginia. She eschewed the college partying life and instead spent her weekends reading more deeply on the topics that piqued her interest from her course work.

She remembered still ruminating on something that had been discussed in class as she approached her dormitory. She walked in the large building and made her way up to the floor where her room was located. As soon as she entered her floor, she saw two police officers standing in the hallway near her room. She wondered if her quiet roommate had turned out to be a nut job, or maybe they were waiting for the girl across the hall. She approached her room and stopped in front of the door. The officers turned to look at her—they were waiting directly in front of her room.

"Sarah Addison?" the female police officer addressed her. The male officer stood awkwardly next to her, watching Sarah expectantly.

"Yes?" Sarah responded, her voice with a question in it.

"I am Officer Kendall and this is Officer Stone. I'm afraid we have some bad news for you. I think it would be best for us to go inside and for you to sit down first."

"Oh, okay." Sarah felt her heart flutter nervously—she couldn't imagine what this could be about. She fumbled with her room key for a moment before managing to unlock the door.

She opened the door and once inside, pulled out the chairs from both her and her roommate's desks and positioned them in the middle of the room for the police officers. She then threw her backpack down on her desk and took a seat on the bed facing them.

"Thank you," the officers said as they each took a seat.

"What is this about?" she asked them, feeling panic rising in her throat.

"We're afraid there has been an incident at your home in West Virginia," the female officer said. Apparently they had decided ahead of time that the woman would do all the talking.

"What happened?" Sarah said impatiently, now feeling adrenaline flow through her limbs, cramping her throat and making her voice squeak.

"Your parents were shot and killed last night. I am so very sorry."

The words that came out of the police officer's mouth felt like they had shot through Sarah's chest, leaving a ringing silence in the room, blasting all feeling from Sarah's body. Everything immediately came into focus visually, but she could no longer hear the words coming out of the female police officer's mouth. She noticed the spotless and stiff uniforms, in contrast to the dorm room in disarray. She watched the female officer's mouth as it continued to form words, but the words were unintelligible.

"It was my brother, wasn't it?" Sarah spat out the words like an accusation, choking back sobs.

The police officers looked at each other with a strange look and then turned back to Sarah. "We have your brother in custody. Yes, it looks like he was the shooter. Of course, he will have to be tried before being declared guilty."

"It was my brother," Sarah said, more to herself than to the two officers in front of her.

"Does he have a history?" the police officers asked her.

"Yes. He is a paranoid schizophrenic. My parents were trying to keep him out of the system. They thought that with enough love and care..." Sarah suddenly gasped and put her head in her hands.

Φ

Sarah opened her eyes to stop the old images from flooding her as she lay there in the hospital bed. Just like that, with two small bullets, her family had become undone. She had never been able to face her brother again after that. She knew that he didn't totally understand what he had done, but he had done it. Sarah didn't know whether or not she had forgiven him—she just tried very hard to forget, and mostly she had.

That kind of blood was growing in her belly.

She remembered how determined her parents had been— how they had loved their son in spite of everything. They would have done anything for him. They did do just about everything for him. After all, her mother had once had held him in her arms as a baby, vowing to love and protect him for as long as she lived. Both of her parents had been committed to being responsible for the monster they had unwittingly created. They still saw the face of their son in that monster. In the end, they ended up literally giving him their very lives. She hated him for that for a long, long time until she grew weary of hating. She was so weary of hating.

The door of the hospital room slowly opened and Darin walked in, carrying a large cup of coffee and a small bag. When he noticed that Sarah's eyes were open, his face lighted up. Sarah felt like her future had just walked in the door, breaking up the painful fragments of her past.

"Hey beautiful," he said to her, "I thought you were gonna sleep there forever, lazy bones. I got some pastries to counteract the mush they feed you around here if you feel up to it."

"Maybe in a little while," she said to him groggily. "What happened, Darin?"

"Well first of all, things look good for you. The doctor says you should make a full recovery. It looks like this company, Green Future, was after your data. Your laptop is missing and there are things missing from your house. This guy who was up here to hurt you—he was probably someone hired by Green Future. They had enough evidence for a search warrant for Green Future's headquarters and so that's where they are now. I guess it will take some time to sort it all out unless they fess up." Darin paused and watched her face, glad that she was coherent enough to understand. "There is one more thing. That guy who was hired to hurt you, well I guess he had been following you for a while and he knew where I lived. They haven't been able to prove it yet because everything is such a mess, but my house conveniently exploded the same day you had your accident."

"My god," Sarah responded. "I'm so sorry Darin. That's horrible. I'm so sorry to have dragged you into this."

"I dragged myself into it. Your problems are my problems, and I wouldn't have it any other way," he replied sternly. "Besides," he said tenderly as he placed her hand on her abdomen, "that house is too small for us anyway. Insurance had it covered. I'll build another one for us."

"What about Adah?"

"She didn't make it," Darin said with pain in his voice.

"I'm so sorry."

"My neighbor was killed in the explosion, too."

"*What?* That's awful. Those people are animals. And for what? Trade secrets? Profits? They are ruthless. They have to be stopped."

"Well that's not your concern any more. They committed murder. They won't get away with it. No one will look at their company name the same again."

"I need to call my boss." Sarah suddenly sat up, but then winced. "Where's my phone?"

"'Don't move. It's right here. I kept it charging for you." Darin handed her the cell phone that had been sitting in the corner of the room near the outlet.

Sarah took the phone, tapped the screen a few times and put it to her ear.

"Sarah," the voice started on the other end, "I'm glad you finally felt up to call."

"Greg, what's going on with Green Future?"

"We need to talk," Greg said, with a serious tone. "You are going to need to submit a statement about what you were doing on the Green Future property. Charges are likely going to get filed, but I think that I can take care of that for you. You know, I understand why you were doing what you were doing, but I can't have that reflective upon the CIA. We can't operate like that. I'm sure I can get the criminal charges dropped, but only if you do something for me."

"What's that?"

"I need you to resign from your position at the CIA," Greg paused before continuing. "If you won't resign, I'm going to have to fire you. It's the only way to get you out of this situation and to preserve the reputation of the agency. It's nothing personal Sarah—you have been an exemplary member of our staff, but you know that you stepped over the line when you cut the lock on that hazardous waste bin. I have been talking to senior staff and trying to figure out another way, but we have no choice."

"I see," Sarah said, and then she fell silent, waiting for Greg to continue.

"I'm sorry Sarah—I know how dedicated you are and how devastating this must be for you," Greg finally said. "As soon as you feel up to it, come into the office. We have some paperwork to address before we can put this all to bed."

"I see," Sarah repeated, dazed. "I'll come in as soon as I can. Thank you, Greg."

Sarah put her phone down on the bedside table and looked up to meet Darin's expectant gaze. He could tell it was not good news by the downcast look on Sarah's face.

"I'm fired," Sarah said flatly.

"No kidding?" Darin didn't try to disguise his happiness. "That's great news!"

Sarah scowled at him. "Great news?"

"Yeah! It's a new beginning. For both of us. You'll see."

Sarah looked at the eagerness on Darin's face and couldn't help but smile. Somehow, she thought he might just be right.

Chapter 61

The properties of the world around us stem not from properties of its ultimate building blocks, but from the relations between these building blocks.

Max Tegmark

Once he had access to a working model, Trevor ran the program with every most likely variable and every range of possible input parameters until he found the balance number with a high level of confidence. He left the program with Scott in case he or anyone else needed to run it again and bundled up all of his output files and brought them home.

He sat down at the computer and typed in the personal email address that he had found in Sarah's file—lifted from his old boss. He then composed the following:

Dear Sarah,

I feel like I know you, though we have never met. I used to work for Green Future and I found your work on Stan Cobald's computer. I have to say, not bad work for a start, but there was something that your program was lacking. I took the liberty of rewriting some of the equations and allowing the increase in global warming to influence the other reactions. In essence, I got your model to work. What you refer to as the "balance number" is 2 billion, give or take a half billion depending on per capita energy usage. Apparently a few intellectuals have known that the number is somewhere around 2 billion for a while, but once the "Green Revolution" hit, with engineered crops, we thought that we could overcome that boundary with technology. Today, our population is already over three times greater than the true carrying capacity of the earth. Apparently, there is too much interest in economical growth to take on the problem of overpopulation. Perhaps now that your model shows the specific mechanism for the imminent collapse, which is supported by ten years of field data, people will finally listen.

In the model, the agricultural practices of Green Future slowly sterilize the soil. The beneficial microbes that create a dynamic, balanced ecosystem in organic soil are slowly poisoned through years of herbicide and pesticide applications. Fungal populations in the soil slowly start to take over. Eventually, there is a fungal outbreak and crop production crashes. With the dependence on these vast crop monocultures, mass starvation ensues. With the land then barren and infertile from the crash, the forest cannot repopulate fast enough. This further exacerbates climate change, destroying other types of crops around the world and causing widespread desertification. Only regions of the world that are not dependent on outside trade and that have perfected sustainable lifestyles using organic agriculture will survive. The environmental containment facilities, which are currently closely monitored and controlled in order to keep radioactive and other hazardous wastes from the environment, will slowly degrade without the funds or means of continued containment. The ensuing contamination plumes will further poison life in their vicinity. This further reduces human survival to remote areas still containing natural resources and local agricultural economies.

The way I was able to resolve some of the equations was by using an irrational number that perhaps you have heard of before. It is referred to as phi—the golden ratio. It turns out that this mysterious number, which governs the way that plants grow and even guides the formation of our DNA, is an inescapable fact of nature. We fit into nature only in dynamic balance—without the correct proportion we are doomed for extinction.

In order to keep from exhausting the remaining resources, the 2 billion humans on earth must grow all sustenance from the sun rather than using fossil fuels. I like to call this number the golden proportion. It is not sustainable to artificially boost the population—organic farming practices are necessary to naturally limit it. Once we need to grow food where or how it can't be grown naturally—dependent on fuels that cannot regenerate themselves quickly enough—our human footprint steps beyond where it can tread lightly.

Just as plants are formed in harmony with the golden ratio because this formation limits the amount of entropy produced, we must limit the amount of entropy and waste that we produce, and limit the consumption of high quality energy, or else we will become extinct as surely many strains of plants did before the arrival of the species we know today.

Your job is done. I will get this information to the folks who need to know.

Your Friend,

Phi_guy

Trevor hit "Send" and Loren walked up behind him and put her hands tenderly on his shoulders.

"Did you email her yet?" Loren asked eagerly.

"Yup—just sent it." He replied.

"What are you going to do with the model?" she asked.

"Oh, I figure I will send the results in anonymous packages

to the President, the CIA, and anyone else who might give a damn. I'll send a copy to my old boss as well, just for the hell of it."

"Do you think it will help?"

"I hope so. The thing is, you can't talk about population control without offending nearly every culture on earth. There are areas of the world where the only way people feel they can compete with their adversaries is to have more children than them. To some people, it comes off as threatening their very survival. Population control cannot be forced on people. It just wouldn't be accepted in this day and age."

"Yeah—it can't be forced. It has to be a personal decision. It has to be deeper than that." Loren said thoughtfully. "We need to look at other races and cultures not as 'the other', but as members of our own species. Our environmental problems are not going to be solved until everyone on earth comes together and makes a common decision with a common goal. We have to work together—working as separate entities only creates disparity. If we can realize that we are all members of the same species and we all inhabit the same earth and we all have similar needs and desires, and that our perceived enemy is actually just someone like us, then we can solve our problems together. This would take self-realization on the part of everyone. Is it even realistic to think that the majority of people on earth can come to this realization?"

"Probably not," Trevor frowned.

"Well if we don't, I don't think we deserve this planet," Loren said with disgust.

"You're probably right. We are going to decide for

ourselves. The thing is, we're all in this together. If our population doesn't contract soon enough, there will surely be a collapse, just like so many civilizations before ours that have exhausted their resources. The collapse will mean all of us, not just the bad decision makers."

"The decision makers will never encourage something that counteracts the economy," Loren said dubiously. "It was greed itself that has gotten us to where we are today. It's all about money. But then again, for some people it's just about survival. Sometimes it's all poor farmers can do to sell their land to loggers because not to sell it would be to go hungry. Maybe you sometimes have to step on individuals for the greater good because there are just too many people now—there's not enough to go around. And who is going to draw the line between sustenance and greed? How in the world are we going to contract our population to something that is sustainable, especially when world leaders are still encouraging population growth for political or economical reasons?"

"Yeah, and it's not just leaders—it's individuals as well. Everyone wants to make their situation better in life. It's human nature. If it's there for the taking, we take it. We always have."

"There are just too many of us to act like we can abuse the earth as much as we want and it will just keep taking it. I don't know, Trevor. When I look at it realistically, I think we are already beyond the tipping point."

"I agree that we are as a whole, but when I look at where we live, I can hardly believe that it would be the case for this country. We do still have so many wide open spaces and forests. This was the New World at one point. Not one square foot of Europe hasn't been manipulated by generation after generation. That's why the Europeans originally came here. It wasn't just gold. They were out of old growth forests—they had overfished the rivers and coastlines, and there were just plain too many people for their remaining resources. We are a relatively new country and there are still people here who live off the land. We did it before—we can do it again. There probably are enough resources left to provide for us at least. We are the bread basket of the world, after all. And we do have environmental regulation that at least tries to minimize our impacts."

"Yeah, but most of our bread basket is genetically modified and dependent on chemical fertilizers and herbicides. The reason why we still have forests is because we use fossil fuels so we don't have to keep taking down trees to heat our homes."

"Things have to change. They just *have* to," replied Trevor, turning toward her.

"I suppose we just have to hope that there is a favorable imbalance in the world of good and evil, and that in the end good will outweigh the bad."

Loren looked at Trevor and he took both of her hands in his. The world's problems weighed on them too heavy for words. They simply looked at each other tenderly, like an old couple who just realized that the ship they were on would shortly sink, and that all they had time for was to hold each other and remember what life was all about. Simply loving each other, in spite of everything.

Chapter 62

Medicine cures ailments of the body; wisdom removes negative emotions from the mind.

Leucippus

"Thank you for coming," Stan Cobald said through the telephone receiver. A thick pane of glass separated him from his visitor.

"No problem," said Trevor. "When I got your letter I have to admit I was a little surprised that you wrote to me."

"Well, I appreciate your coming—I wasn't sure you would. First of all, I want to let you know that I had no idea that Jack Sims was using those tactics. Hiring hits on farmers and environmentalists? I never would have supported something like that."

"Yeah, you don't seem like the type who would. At least they put him away for a long time."

"That is what I wanted to talk to you about. Have you seen the Green Future press releases from the new CEO?"

"Yes I have. It looks like they are going to recover from the bad press that Jack Sims created for them."

"Yes it does look that way. This isn't going to end with Jack Sims behind bars."

"No. It looks like it's back to business as usual with the new CEO."

"I started this, and I have to stop it."

"Stop it? I don't work for them anymore, in case you didn't know. But you, I mean, I thought you believed in what they're trying to do."

"Yes, I know. I mean, I *did*. I have had some time to think in here, Trevor. When I found out about my boss, I started to doubt everything in my life. The reason I asked you to come here today is that I need to know something." Stan paused for a moment before continuing. "Do you know what their intention is with the project that I hired you for?"

"Yeah, I think so. They want to clear forests and then put a chemical in the soil that only allows their crops to grow."

"Yes, that is precisely what they intend to do. I know you don't work for them anymore and I'm glad, but I need to know if you have figured out how to do it."

"Well, to tell you the truth, it was an irresistible puzzle to try to solve. Once I figured out that that was what they were up to, I got to work formulating the chemical, just to see if I could do it, you know?"

Stan's face paled and took on a rigidity that Trevor had never seen before.

"So yeah," Trevor said sheepishly, "I figured it out, but I haven't told anyone about it. I figured it out after I had already resigned."

"Please do me a favor," Stan said urgently, leaning closer to the glass that separated them, "and destroy anything you have with the chemical formula on it and don't tell anyone that you have figured it out. Just forget about it, as best you can. Please."

"Yeah, but I'm sure someone is going to figure it out eventually."

"It's possible," Stan said pensively, "but I don't want to be personally responsible for making any part of it happen."

"I see. Okay, I can do that."

"Thank you," Stan said, looking directly into Trevor's eyes.

"No problem. So what are you going to do now?"

"Well I only have to be in here for a few months, since I helped them get the information they needed to put Jack Sims and the hit man away, but I don't actually know right now what I'm going to do when I get out. I know what I'm not going to do. I'm not going back to Green Future."

"That's good to hear."

"One thing that I have come to realize in here is that the only thing that we will leave behind us when we are called back by our maker is the effect we have had on the world and the people around us. I haven't done such a great job of it in the past, but I'd like to do better from here on out. I set some things in motion that should be stopped. The new legislation—God forbid—it passed. It flew right under the radar."

"What legislation?"

"Never mind. I'm not sure it can be undone at this point." Stan lowered his head and shook it as if to cast off a distasteful thought.

"Stan," Trevor said earnestly, "it's never too late to be the man that you want to be. If life doesn't provide you with the ideal circumstances, you can start to change them from the inside."

"And I thought I would be the one to mentor you," Stan said with a wry smile.

"Sometimes the best advice comes from the most unlikely sources and sometimes something happens that seems disastrous but it turns out to be the best thing that could have happened. It just sometimes takes time to figure it out." Trevor's voice trailed off and he became lost in private thoughts for a moment—those words had a strange familiarity that gave him goose bumps.

Stan looked at Trevor like he knew exactly what he meant. Trevor suddenly looked embarrassed and his eyes started to scan the visiting room restlessly.

"Well I guess you have better things to do than chat with an inmate." Stan broke the awkward silence.

"I guess so, but I'm glad I came."

"Remember what I said about that chemical and any of your data. Not a trace. And be careful. I don't know this new CEO personally but I already don't trust him."

"Will do. Thanks, Dr Cobald."

Stan's words replayed themselves to Trevor as he made his way out of the visiting room and navigated to the exit of the massive concrete structure.

Be Careful.

Epilogue

Nothing occurs at random, but everything happens for a reason and because it has to.

Leucippus

Sarah hadn't been prepared for her first Vermont winter. She had been counting the days until the last frost and eagerly scanning the sky in anticipation of the return of the Canadian geese. The piles of snow that had been shoveled to the sides of the driveway and walkways started trickling into small streams on the south side of the house, softening the surface of the soil and revealing the sickly looking vegetation that had been smothered all winter.

The new house was finished just before the hard frost started to set in the previous Fall. The insurance company had fully covered the construction of the new house, since they funded the full assessed value of the house that Darin had built. He had pushed aside all of his other work that summer and he and Sarah had built the entire structure themselves. The house was designed to be completely energy independent. A geothermal system was installed under the basement floor, which could heat and cool the structure with the touch of a button. It was powered by an array of solar panels, which also supplied the house's electrical needs. The house was oriented with a large bay of windows to the south, heating up the soapstone floor of the sun room for passive solar gain. A massive chimney at the center of the house provided thermal mass as well as a hearth for the woodstove. Darin preferred to heat with the wood he had felled from the property rather than succumb to the unnatural ease of heat from the push of a button. The stove was where they gathered every winter evening, feeling the intense heat of an oversized stove as the flames licked the glass before retiring upstairs to where the heat from the embers slowly migrated during the night.

The explosion at Darin's previous house and the ensuing fire had cleared out a large area for a vegetable garden near the house. Sarah had started her seeds in the solarium in February and was eagerly waiting for the winter to subside in order to break ground in the new garden space.

The garden located on a south-facing hill had been soaking up the Spring sun. Sarah eagerly let herself into the garden gate carrying a spade-tipped shovel. She leaned her weight into the shovel, directing it straight into the earth, and felt it give way immediately. It was like scratching a winter-long itch as she lifted the first shovel-full of dark soil. There would be plenty of work trenching and working in compost before the planting could begin.

Sarah missed nothing of her old life. Green Future had not been stopped, but she realized that the only thing she truly had control of was her own life. She could either let the pursuit of Green Future run her life, or she could forge ahead and find a better way for herself. The information was in the hands of the people who could change the course of history, thanks to Phi_guy. Now was her time to change the course of her own life.

She was able to sell her house in Virginia for enough to be comfortable for a while before having to look for other work. But with the new house built and paid for, the electric bills non-existent, and the prospect of being able to grow most of what they ate, she could afford to simply get a modest part-time job. She could work for an organic farm in the summer, or maybe even start one herself on a small part of their land. *Their land.*

After the accident, Darin's life and Sarah's life suddenly became Darin and Sarah's life. They were not immune to the bickering common to all couples, but there was something unyielding about their bond that no amount of disagreement could shake. They knew without having to say it that they just fit together and that life together just worked. Whatever else life dealt them, they knew they could take whatever it was head-on, as long as they were together. Whatever it was that each of them had been lacking, they had found it in each other.

Φ

At the corner of their property there was a knoll dotted by birch trees, with an old stone wall running along the ridge. The stones at one time had been carefully placed by the pioneers of the New World to clear land for agriculture and grazing cattle. Now, the wall was loose rubble, the faces of its stones dotted by lichen and smothered by moss. Standing just inside of the stone wall, one could make out the view of a small valley below through the trees in the Spring, when the leaves were not yet thick enough to obscure the view. The gentle outlines of the mountains softened by rain, layered through thicker and thicker depths of atmosphere, receded into the sky in the distance.

Just before the ridge descended to the valley, there was a little outcropping of earth with two small granite slabs poking out of the surface of the soil. One of them had the word "Adah" lovingly carved on the face, and the other one was blank.

Epilogue 1.618

The great book of nature is written in mathematical symbols.

Galileo

"What are you thinking about?" Loren asked Trevor. She looked up from the drafting table where a small table lamp was shedding a Chardinesque glow across neatly arranged objects.

Trevor jumped at her sudden words. He looked down to find a piece of paper folded in tight little triangles in his hands, a fidgeting habit he had while working out mental problems. His hands had been deftly creasing the paper over and over again while he had been staring blankly at a long-dead computer screen. He smiled self-consciously at her and paused a moment to organize his thoughts.

"Something Scott was telling me. It didn't make sense at the time. Apparently Einstein said that the passing of time is an illusion—there is no such thing as past, present and future. It is all one space-time continuum. That doesn't seem right. It seems to me that if the future already exists, then free will can't exist—our fate is already written somewhere in the cosmos."

He looked at her to check that she was following him. She was tapping her pencil thoughtfully on the table while the corners of her mouth tightened in thought.

Trevor continued, "But then he also talked about some

theory that says that there are infinitely many universes, as in every possible thing that can happen does happen in some universe somewhere. For example, every decision we make creates a fork in our path, but it's not that only one path is actualized. All possible paths are actualized somewhere. Apparently in infinitely many parallel universes or something."

"Sounds pretty sci-fi if you ask me," she responded.

"Yeah it does—imagine an infinite number of you and I. In some of the universes we never meet—we just passed each other by."

"That seems impossible—we belong together. But if that's true then I'm glad I live in this universe," she smiled at him.

"Well that's just the thing I'm thinking about. If we accept the notion that there are infinitely many universes, then free will becomes possible. We are choosing which branch of reality we are following. That retains the validity of Einstein's mathematics. The space-time continuum branches out into the future with ever more complexity, like the branches of a tree that grows infinitely. We are constantly choosing which path to take, at least this version of us."

"It seems to me that physicists put a little too much faith in the mathematics." Loren looked at him dubiously.

"But the whole universe is mathematics—everything can be described mathematically, from the atoms we are made up of to the chemical reactions happening in our body to the neurons firing in our brains. We are some kind of emergent intelligence—somehow greater than the sum of its parts."

"So I am basically a very fancy computer?"

"In a sense, yes."

"So what is so unique about now? Why am I not conscious of the past and the future right now? The only thing that seems to exist to me is the present."

"Well, we are a product of evolution. Evolutionarily, that is what is useful for us to be aware of. Are you controlling the beating of your heart right now? Are you even aware of all of the chemical reactions taking place in your body right now?"

"I guess not. But if there's nothing unique about now, what is unique about me?"

"It may even be evolutionarily useful for use to see ourselves as individuals. We may just be small computers—part of a larger network inside of a super computer. We believe so strongly in our individuality that we are willing to do whatever it takes to survive. Ultimately, this is useful for the larger super computer because it can't survive without its parts."

"But what of feelings—of inspiration—of awe—of love? Are all of these just evolutionarily useful so that we don't off ourselves?"

"To tell you the truth, I was lost before I met you, and I didn't really even know it. I didn't have a place somehow. But perhaps this feeling we call love is just our way of finding our place within the network. We are forming a new branch of the tree together—something that could not have been formed had we not found each other. Just like the trend of increasing complexity in the universe over time, the forming of galaxies from individual pieces of matter, we gravitate toward each other to form new complexity—we are greater than the sum of our parts."

"That isn't very romantic," she smiled at him wryly.

"It depends on what you consider romantic," he smiled back. "We are like merging galaxies, our spiral arms entangling as our star matter flies past one another in a series of near misses and spectacular collisions, destined ultimately for unity. Is that romantic enough for you?"

"Yeah—that's better. But what comes next, after the galaxies merge?"

"The more mass is collected, the more complex elements can be formed at the heart of the largest stars, which eventually become supernova, which can spew out all 92 elements into the surrounding universe. Every element found on earth is the result of the fusion inside these massive stars, which provide a pressure and temperature so great that it can create new elements."

"Hmm, all that from the gravitational attraction of mass?"

"Yup. That's what makes everything that we're made of. That, and billions of years of evolution spurred by cosmic rays randomly disrupting our DNA."

Loren squinted her eyes dubiously before responding. "There's something missing in your world view. It's what drove Van Gogh, Dostoyevsky, Mozart. It's a real thing that causes action—action that often changes the course of history and inspires millions of people. It's an overwhelming desire, but not desire so much as need. What am I doing right now, trying to recreate some banal objects on paper for hours on end? What is the logical point? There is none, but nonetheless, the way the light touches this vase and comes to a crescendo at a point—the shape of the shell as the shadow wraps around it—I can feel the vibration of this arrangement through my entire being. I feel like the only way to realize myself is to connect with this arrangement of objects in this way. It's like I need to do this with the same urgency that I need to eat or sleep. Just what the hell am I doing here?"

Trevor's eyes softened as he looked at this precious girl, his mate, the perfect complement to his dissection knife of a mind, the resting place of his restless soul. He recollected the conversation he had with Scott about God just before they had successfully run Sarah Addison's program to find the balance number. *Mathematics—reason—logic—harmony—morality—beauty—evolution.*

Trevor's answer to Loren's inquiry was simple.

"You're finding phi."

Author's End Note

For the first time in human history, we possess both the means for destroying all life on earth or realizing a paradise on the planet.

Michio Kaku

Although the characters and events in this novel are purely fictional, the environmental problems the characters face are very real. They are key problems that we need to solve in our lifetime if we hope to pass an inhabitable planet on to our children. In order to appreciate the magnitude of the problem of overpopulation, I encourage the reading of Alan Weisman's "Countdown", which forms the basis of the factually based "balance number" calculated in this novel.

The human race has reached a pivotal juncture in its history. We must as individuals choose between immediate gratification and the greater good—between a life of mere diversion and one of evolution of the spirit. I am an optimist by nature and do believe that it is not too late for us to make the right decisions, but not without a formidable amount of work, sacrifice, cooperation and wisdom. In the absence of religious dogma, it is pure morality that needs to form the foundation of our technological goals.

British cosmologist and astrophysicist Sir Martin Rees gives the human race a mere fifty-fifty chance of successfully navigating the challenges of terrorism, bioengineered germs, and other technological nightmares. That is a *fifty-fifty* chance of our species either destroying itself or continuing its evolution.

It is up to each one of us to decide which path to take, but the path can only be carved out together.

I would sincerely appreciate your honest review of this novel via Amazon. I look forward to hearing your feedback. Thank you in advance for your time.

ABOUT THE AUTHOR

Happiness resides not in cattle nor in gold; the soul is the dwelling-place of happiness.

Democritus, the father of the Atomic Theory

Abigail Beck holds a Bachelor's Degree in Fine Arts with an emphasis in painting and a Master's Degree in Civil/Environmental Engineering. As a young artist, she lived in Prague and Paris while painting, writing and teaching English. She now travels world-wide as an environmental consultant using geophysical methods to prevent contamination to ground water. She has published numerous technical papers and taught educational seminars world-wide on environmental containment facility design, construction and testing. When she is not traveling and consulting, Abigail lives with her husband on a solar-powered farmstead in Southern Vermont.